MIKE MACKAY

SCAM AT 7th STREET

Also by the Author

Scam at Old River - 2020

Scam at Five Mile Road - 2021

Scam at Mount Diablo - 2022

Scam at Higgins Canyon Road - 2024

Copyright © 2026 Mike Mackay

ISBN: 978-1-923601-10-9

Published by Vivid Publishing

A division of Fontaine Publishing Group

P.O. Box 948, Fremantle

Western Australia 6959

www.vividpublishing.com.au

A catalogue record for this book is available from the National Library of Australia

To Danise, my wife, the best and kindest doctor in the world, who has allowed me the time and space to write and keeps telling me to do this in my own voice and stop trying to be clever.

ACKNOWLEDGEMENTS

I have a great team that is an abiding source of motivation.

My five wonderful beta readers who kept me on track in the early stages of the journey: Jean Jenkins, Penelope Klopper, Maria Lonie, Jimmy and Grace Andrews, and Sean Sinclair.

Danielle Line, the superb copy editor, who keeps the Scam series charging along and keeping me in check.

Tracey Regan, the wonderful proof editor who, like a ninja, spots things we all missed.

CHAPTER ONE

It was Monday, 9 pm, but the hospital didn't care. It was too busy taking care of Ted in the hospital bed. The room had a single fluorescent light that hummed intermittently like a trapped mosquito. The heart monitor's steady beep cut through the hush, each pulse mapping his last stand. A nurse had hovered by the door, her face drawn tight around the truth she wouldn't voice, but she had left.

Ted's wife, Marie, sat on the chair beside him, one hand pressed to his chest where the bullet had been a few hours ago. Her gaze stayed fixed on the monitor, as if will alone would keep it from flatlining. Jack leaned back against the far wall, arms crossed, jaw clenched against the racket of his thoughts.

Moonlight cast straight shadows like bars, through the blinds and across the linoleum floor, turning the room into a cage of light and dark. The air smelled faintly of antiseptic and regret. Outside, distant sirens mingled with a wind that rattled the window.

Ted's breathing shallowed. An alarm went off, and the nurse arrived to check the IV drip, adjusting the tube with mechanical precision. Marie's hands made fists, knuckles whitening. Jack rubbed his forehead, his gaze darting to the heart monitor. Time bled between heartbeats as if night had nowhere else to go.

Ted took a long breath, and it escaped as the monitor flatlined.

"Ted, where have you gone?" Marie held her dead husband's head between her hands as it lay on the white hospital pillow. His final breath slipped away while his vacant eyes locked onto Marie as if they could see eternity.

Jack Rhodes knew Ted and Marie Clark were atheists, and at the last moment in Ted's life, Marie's question filled up the room like a fog. No one had an answer.

* * *

Ted had served alongside Sergeant Kenny Braithwaite in the San Francisco Police Department. Jack stood on the opposite side of the bed to Marie, giving her space, but she knew he was there. He would always be there for her. There was no one else at his passing.

Ted was in his late fifties and had served in the SFPD since he was eighteen. He had seen the worst that San Francisco had to offer. Jack didn't know the details but knew from his own PTSD that it was like trying to keep the dark genie in the bottle. Had Ted seen one too many horrific incidents, or was it one particular incident that tipped the scales? Did it matter? To the allocated psychiatrist, from whom Ted was receiving treatment, it did. Ted didn't take the prescribed medication, but every weekday, he attended Kenny's morning martial arts class at the San Francisco Police Department Training Academy on Amber Drive. He trained like someone thirty years his junior, knowing it would release endorphins to improve his mood and the exercise would help him sleep. However, lately, Ted had been expressing dark thoughts.

One guy in Kenny's class had committed suicide. It was a topic of conversation one morning.

"The trouble with suicide," said Ted, "is that the insurance companies won't pay out any of the policies. And it has a bigger impact on the family than just being run over by a bus."

Some nodded, like reflections of Ted's thoughts. Others, mostly the younger ones, chuckled at Ted's comments. And then it seemed to be forgotten as they hit the showers. This topic was like a prairie dog sticking its head out of its burrow, then vanishing. You couldn't see him, but everyone knew he was underground, waiting for another opportunity to show his face.

Jack relayed the conversation to Kenny, as he knew Kenny was worried about Ted.

* * *

That evening was to be a night out for Jack and Kenny to have a few drinks with Ted. Jack was not a fan of the bar Ted had chosen. It was a place where drowning souls clutched cheap whiskey and hid their sorrows in the shadows.

Rain-curdled neon bled across the cracked sidewalk as Jack pushed through the door. There was a bell on the door that made a tinny jangle, swallowed by the bar's low hum. The air hung heavy with stale malt and unspoken debts, each breath a promise of regret. A lone bulb swung overhead, casting long shadows that danced across the scarred mahogany counter. The barkeep's eyes were slate. He knew your secrets before you spilled them, and he measured your worth by the weight of your silence.

Booths lined the far wall like grave markers, their vinyl wounds oozing stories of last calls and broken hearts. In the corner, a crooked pool table groaned under the weight of crooked bets, its felt stained with desperation and chalk dust. The jukebox coughed out ragged blues, each note a lament that cut deeper than any blade. Regulars hunched over cards, faces etched in cigarette ash and hard years, trading glances that smelled of suspicion. In this part of South Market (SoMa) truth came cheap, and bitterness ran free. Outside, the city glittered in lies, blind to the souls hiding in its gutter-lit underbelly. Welcome to the heart of midnight, where hope checks its coat at the door.

Jack arrived five minutes early to find Ted already there, and in trouble. His bald head, with its broad forehead, was easily visible. His unbroken nose was straight and narrow. The square jaw sat below the thin-lipped mouth, which displayed a smirk as he stood with his back against the bar, surrounded by three mid-twenties steroid-looking types.

All three were hammering at Ted with a flurry of punches. Jack didn't question how Ted got himself into this dilemma. When there's a fight, be it in a ring, a street, or a bar, it's like poker. You play the cards the dealer gave you.

The Cards. Jack was six feet tall and one hundred and eighty pounds. Ted was ten pounds lighter and two inches shorter. The one in the middle was doing most of the shouting and swearing, and was thirty pounds and three inches taller. The other two were Jack's weight, but they only came up to Jack's shoulder. A lot of information to absorb in one second. All three had purchased their T-shirts in a size too small. They looked like a set of primary colors on display. The one closest to Jack wore yellow, the big guy in the middle wore red, and the guy on the far side wore blue. They each wore a pale blue denim jacket. Perhaps they were members of a club, making a statement, or had the same mother who dressed them. They looked alike, but that was a discussion for later.

All Ted could do was defend. Jack knew that if the big guy went down, the fight was over, but first, he had to remove the shorter guy closest to him. This would have been a basic barroom brawl until Jack saw the closest guy pull a knife. All rules now vanished like smoke out the window.

Jack's lizard brain kicked into the Krav Maga philosophy. Everything is a weapon. Jack grabbed a wooden barstool by the seat and swung it into the face of the closest guy. There was an eruption like lava as blood erupted from his nose and teeth, leaving a pattern on the yellow T-shirt like a child dabbling with paint for the first time. As he was falling, he grabbed the legs of the stool. Jack let go, and the wooden seat landed on the guy's crotch when he hit the floor, where he grunted and rolled into the fetal position.

With a roar, the big guy turned his attention to Jack. Jack was unsure whether he was shouting to instill fear. He came at Jack with a right roundhouse kick to Jack's knee, a straight left punch to the head, a left straight kick to Jack's stomach, and a right cross punch to the head. Jack stepped back, slipping the punches and kicks as he looked past him to see that Ted had almost finished dispatching his opponent. One-on-one, Ted was a good fighter.

The big guy was clumsy but powerful and propped to set himself up for another round. Jack realized the four-part combination was the big guy's practiced set piece, with the right cross being the knockout blow. Jack didn't wait for him to start again, but threw a reverse round-house kick, catching the big guy in the temple with his heel, which dropped him onto his back, but he was still conscious. Ted's opponent landed next to him. The big guy reached into the fallen man's jacket and came away with a revolver. Jack saw him pull the hammer back, take a two-handed grip, shouting and swearing as he pointed it at Jack, and squeezed the trigger. Ted stepped in front of Jack, taking the bullet in the middle of the chest and falling back into Jack's arms.

Kenny came in with a flying tackle onto the body of the yellow shirt, who grunted as Kenny reached past him and grabbed the revolver held by the big guy, twisting the gun from his grasp, stabbing him in the solar plexus with the butt, and rolling him over onto his stomach. Midway, the big guy put up a fight, which Kenny ended by bouncing the guy's head on the floor, the force of which made him submit to Kenny's strength.

In the gym during training, Kenny was all technique and discipline. In the field, like now, he was a thing of beauty. An angry, six-foot-three-inch, two hundred and ten-pound, red-haired ballerina with kicks, strikes, and throws, and a strength that he seemed to pull from his core.

Kenny glanced at the barman, shouted, and showed his badge. "SFPD. I'm SFPD. Bring me cable ties or a rope."

Kenny pulled Ted's opponent by his jacket over onto his back, frisked him for weapons, found another gun, and slid it in Jack's direction, who was sitting on the floor, back against the bar, cradling Ted in his arms. Jack had his palm on the entry point of the bullet, trying to stem the flow of blood. Ted's eyes closed, and his breathing rattled through his damaged lungs. Jack watched Ted's blood seeping through the fingers of his right hand.

As the ambulance guys arrived, Ted's eyes opened, and he made a thin-lipped smile as his lips moved. Jack had to lean forward to hear the words spoken with a one-second gap between each one. "You weren't meant to be involved."

The ambulance guys attended to Ted and rushed him away on a gurney. Eight SFPD cops were dealing with the three assailants, who were still on the floor. Jack could hear Kenny telling the cops that this must be handled by the book. Meaning he wanted the court to put them away for a long time, with no margin for a defense attorney to find a procedural gap.

* * *

The memory faded as the wardroom door opened. It was Freddie. He looked at Jack, indicating with his head for him to come outside. Marie didn't move, an indication she hadn't noticed Freddie had arrived or that Jack had stood.

Outside the room, they stopped in a corner, a complicated twosome bound through circumstance.

"He's gone," said Jack.

Freddie sighed, looked at the ceiling as if he were hoping to find an answer, and shook his head. "I'm going back to the office. Ted's burial ceremony will be with full honors, and the insurance company will pay out his insurance policies without question to Marie in full."

Jack knew Freddie had the authority and gravitas to make that happen. No one would object or stand in his way. "That's great."

"Kenny is busy processing Ted's assailants."

Sergeant Kenny Braithwaite reported to Freddie at the San Francisco Police Department Training Academy premises on Amber Drive. Jack could only guess at what Freddie's unit did, even though he helped them monthly as a sideline to his forensic data analysis consultancy. It had nothing to do with training. The extent of the unit's authority was a mystery to Jack.

Kenny had only recently returned from a sabbatical dealing with his own issues. A loved one lost. Jack knew Kenny was resonating with Marie, reliving his loss all over again. Freddie had done the paperwork to indicate that Kenny was on extended leave, whereas Kenny was MIA (Missing In Action) for over three months. There was no explanation of where he had been or what he had been doing when he walked onto the apartment's roof, where Jack and Freddie were having a BBQ, and sat down with them without a word.

There was no luggage, and Kenny's clothes were the same ones he'd worn when he'd left. When they asked him how he got to the apartment,

Kenny said he'd walked. A shave, a haircut, a shower, and new clothes were mandatory. They gave him a steak and beer. He ate the steak like a wolf and pushed the beer aside.

"You know I don't drink alcohol. May I please have a glass of water?" Kenny was back.

Freddie and Jack had grown up in the same house ever since a drunk driver had run a red traffic light and crashed into Jack's parents' car, killing them both. Jack was five years old, strapped to the back seat in a high-tech baby chair. He remembered the quiet, the cold, and calling for his parents. Freddie's father, Uncle Alan, took Jack out of the car and passed him to Aunt Louise, and they'd brought him home. Uncle Alan said Jack was family, and they would raise him as Jack's father was his brother.

Freddie was a year older than Jack and had always assumed the role of the wiser one, the steadying influence. His legal training had only reinforced this persona. They knew each other well. In the hospital corridor, Freddie tilted his head to one side, put his hand on Jack's shoulder, and turned him so he had to look Freddie in the eye. "What's bugging you, Jack?"

"I've never had anyone take a bullet for me before."

"Jack, Ted has been looking for that bullet for a while. This time, he found what he was looking for. My guys checked with the bartender. Ted intervened when three men became aggressive toward a college student and his girlfriend. Ted had his badge on him and never showed it or mentioned he was with the SFPD."

"It doesn't matter, Freddie," said Jack. "I looked down that barrel. Did I get religion? Did my life flash before my eyes? Did I recall regrets? No. I felt it was all over. There was nothing. Then Ted fell back into my arms."

Jack could still feel the weight of Ted's body as he caught him under the arms, lowered him to the floor, and tried to stop the bleeding. In the background, he had heard Kenny on the phone, calling for an ambulance.

"Jack," said Freddie, "it might be a good idea for you to visit one of our counselors who helps with PTSD."

"Thanks, but no thanks. I have other plans."

CHAPTER TWO

"Not your fault, Jack," said Stella. "You have no reason to feel guilty, but I guess Freddie or Kenny has told you that already."

Jack gazed out the floor-to-ceiling living room window in Stella's house on Vallejo Street, Pacific Heights, looking down onto The Bay, with the Golden Gate Bridge to the left and Alcatraz to the right. It was 11 pm, and not all of the city had gone to sleep. There was no moon, and the lights on The Bridge, Alcatraz, and the boats and ships shone through the fog, damp like they were sweating, creating a melancholy mood that did nothing to improve his disposition. Stella had poured him a single malt whiskey, which he held as if unaware of it being in his hand. He had not put it to his lips.

"Intellectually, yes, I know."

"But emotionally, you don't. Right?"

"Correct."

Stella picked up her glass of Napa Valley Merlot and stood barefoot beside Jack. At five feet, five inches tall, and one-twenty pounds, the top of her head was below Jack's shoulder. She was still wearing her black business suit and a white shirt, her attire as the owner and CEO of her company, which she had rebranded because of all the acquisitions. It was now Node Industries. She was at home, still working when Jack phoned. Lately, she was busy with yet another acquisition, and, as the final decision-maker, the inconsistent meetings played havoc with their relationship. Jack had just returned from an assignment at a Las Vegas casino, where he'd improved their data analytics on betting patterns to help identify suspicious activities.

Stella, being ten years older than Jack, kept their relationship a secret … because no one needed to know.

Stella loved her work, but it came with stress. She took this out in her private gym, the bedroom, and the gun range with her Glock, the smallest one, a 42 chambered in .38 Auto. Her permit said, 'concealed carry'.

"What are you going to do?"

"Tomorrow, I'm going to visit Marie Clark."

"At her house?"

"No. The Botanical Gardens."

"Whereabouts?"

'The Moon Viewing Garden. I know that's where she's going to be."

"It's lovely there. Very special. Have you been there before?"

"A long time ago. Remember, Freddie and I grew up on Panoramic Way in Berkeley, and Aunt Louise made it her mission to see everything there was to see in San Francisco."

"Did she accomplish her mission?"

"No. There's too much to see, and there are places in San Francisco that I hope she never sees."

"With Marie, what are you going to say or do?"

"I don't know. I'll just be there."

Stella nodded. "I understand. I'm sure Marie will appreciate that."

"Maybe I can help with the funeral arrangements."

"Maybe."

"I don't have a plan."

"Sometimes, that's a good plan. That's what I'm doing at the moment with Node Industries."

Jack shook his head as if he were trying to wake up. "I'm sorry, Stella. I'm bothering you with my introspections and not thinking about you at all."

Stella put her right palm on Jack's left cheek. "You're not a bother. You've helped me before. More than once."

Jack held her hand against his cheek. He was always willing to help Stella, and right now, he would welcome a distraction. She smiled without showing her teeth, drawing attention to her pixie-shaped, not-quite-heart-shaped face, with black hair cut to match. "So, what are you up to at Node … where you don't have a plan? Apart from Freddie, you are the most structured and organized person I know."

Stella sipped her Merlot and then grinned. "Thank you for the compliment. It's an acquisition."

"Another one. Why is this one a problem?"

"Well, the board, bar one, wants our acquisition of the company to work out as they'll make a lot of money out of it."

"And this one individual?"

"He's the founder with a majority shareholding, but we can talk about this another time." Stella raised her wineglass.

"Of course." Jack took a sip of his whiskey. He looked at the remaining contents in the glass for four seconds as if there was something in the amber liquid he couldn't quite see, and then poured it down his throat.

Stella finished her wine and placed the glass on the wooden table in front of the living room suite. "Let's go to bed."

They didn't shower, just shed their clothes. Jack knew Stella was making their lovemaking a life-affirming experience, like a spiritual practice that helps one see more goodness, truth, and beauty in the world.

Within three minutes, Stella rolled into Jack's right arm and fell asleep like a tired kitten. Jack held her against his side as he stared at the ceiling, but ceilings never provided answers.

* * *

The next morning, Jack was at the gym shortly before 6 am. This was Kenny's starting time. No excuses. The gym normally buzzed with energy as the fighters gathered for their Monday-to-Friday Mixed Martial Arts training session. The stench of sweat and determination would hang in the air, mingling with the faint aroma of disinfectant. Mats covered the floor, and gloves striking pads echoed through the room, which also served as a basketball court. With Kenny, no one stepped into the gym chasing stardom. He made sure they came for clarity. For when everything narrowed down to breath, motion, and purpose. Some came to rebuild. Others came to discover strength they never knew they had. That space held everyone like a promise. One more round, one more try, one more chance to become someone stronger.

Kenny had them all pushing the past a little further away. Every breath carved out space for something new. They didn't just train. In that hour, they transformed. In those gloves-cracking-against-pads moments, in the sting of sweat and the ache of effort, they found something rare. A sense of becoming. A sense of belonging. A reason to keep coming back.

Kenny's structured approach had many aspects. Too much to cover in the one-hour morning class. Kenny only told them what they would be doing that morning. Kept them guessing.

The session began with a warm-up, the fighters spreading out across the mats. They moved through dynamic stretching exercises, their muscles and joints gradually loosening to prepare for the rigorous workout ahead. Light stretching led to more intense movements, and the fighters transitioned to cardio activities. Jogging, jumping rope, and shadowboxing increased their heart rates and got the blood flowing.

With the warm-up concluded, the fighters gathered around Kenny, who outlined the striking segment of the training. The group broke into pairs, each ready to practice various striking techniques with an emphasis on precision. The rhythmic sounds of jabs, crosses, hooks, and uppercuts filled the gym. They delivered kicks to all parts of the body from different positions.

The fighters then moved on to combination drills, stringing together different strikes into fluid sequences. The focus was on speed and accuracy. They had to execute each movement with a purpose. Pad work followed as fighters hit focus mitts and Thai pads held by their partners. These simulated scenarios honed each strike's power, precision, and timing.

Heavy bags lined one side of the gym, the fighters taking turns working on them. The thud of strikes hitting the bags reverberated through the space as the fighters developed their striking power, endurance, and conditioning. Partner drills rounded off the striking segment, with fighters practicing techniques to improve defense and counterattacks.

The transition to grappling began, the fighters switching gears to focus on a different skill set. Technique drills involved practicing takedowns, submissions, escapes, and sweeps. Each movement was repeated meticulously, the fighters honing their skills with every repetition. Positional drills followed, with fighters working on maintaining or escaping various positions such as mount, guard, side control, and back control.

Live sparring brought a new level of intensity to the session. Controlled sparring allowed the fighters to apply their grappling techniques against resisting opponents, focusing on both offensive and defensive skills. Specific sparring scenarios added another layer of complexity, with fighters starting in predetermined positions and working to escape or submit. Clinch work closed out the grappling segment, with fighters practicing techniques such as pummeling for inside control, throwing knees, and setting up takedowns.

With grappling complete, the fighters moved on to conditioning exercises. Strength-training exercises like deadlifts, squats, bench presses, and pull-ups to build overall strength. Plyometric exercises, such as box jumps, medicine ball throws, and burpees, improved power and speed. Core work included planks, sit-ups, and Russian twists. All designed to build core stability and strength. Cardio conditioning involved high-intensity interval training (HIIT), circuit training, and sprints, enhancing cardiovascular endurance and overall fitness.

The session wound down with a cool-down period. Light stretching helped relax the muscles, while deep breathing exercises lowered heart rates and promoted relaxation. The fighters performed static stretching, holding each position for progressively longer periods to improve flexibility.

As the session concluded, the fighters would gather their gear, their faces flushed with effort and satisfaction. The structured approach of Kenny's training ensured they developed well-rounded skills in striking and grappling while maintaining peak physical conditioning. Each component of the session built on the others, creating a comprehensive workout that addressed all aspects of MMA. Each day, the fighters left the gym, ready to tackle their next challenge, a step closer to mastering their craft.

But today was different. Without Ted, the rhythm was gone. What was once routine now felt like a ritual interrupted. The usual clamor of bodies moving with purpose had thinned to presence alone. Kenny kept his voice low, guiding them through stretches and silence, not training.

It wasn't discipline. It was a pause. A moment to fill the air with breath instead of impact.

At the end, when Kenny dismissed the class, the fighters drifted off, like they were untethered. Even Jack and Freddie, who usually pounded the pavement back home, chose a slower path. No jog. Just quiet steps, side by side, heads low. As if running would've betrayed something, like moving too fast might leave Ted further behind.

CHAPTER THREE

On the way to Stella's house, Jack had picked up a sourdough loaf and was now making toast with it while he mashed avocado with two pinches of dried chili flakes in a bowl. Eggs sizzled in the pan, making a soft but distinct hiss, which Jack had always found soothing.

As Stella arrived in a white bathrobe with a white towel wrapped around her head, he spread the avocado on the toast, lowered a fried egg on each, and placed eight alfalfa shoots on the side. He pushed the plate across the counter to her as she hoisted herself onto a stool and looked at her plate of food.

"Thank you, good sir. This looks yummy." Stella cut a slice of the toast, popped it in her mouth, chewed, and nodded. "Wow, Jack, this is really good." Stella reached for the glass of kale juice. "And spicy."

Jack sat next to her as he cut a slice. Daily training with Kenny always left you feeling hungry. It was now 8 am. Breakfast was an urgent requirement. "You started to tell me about the acquisition and the founder who doesn't want to sell."

Stella put down her glass. "Carlton Engineering. George Carlton's his name. He inherited a small engineering business his father started, making automotive parts for automatic transmissions. George went to MIT, where his doctorate was on the electrification of transmission systems."

Jack swallowed. "How old is he?"

"Seventy-Three."

"He was clearly ahead of his time."

"Definitely. And the whole time, while he kept supplying the auto companies with the parts they required, he put money into R&D to further develop his ideas with prototype after prototype for which there was a limited market."

"So, the world eventually caught up with George?"

"Yep. With the swing to EVs, George now had products the auto companies wanted rather than competing with others to supply parts to them."

"Premium product, and a premium price, I would imagine."

"Correct up to a point, as other contenders and approaches exist in this area. But he does have a differentiator."

Stella took a sip of her kale. Jack kept eating as he waited for Stella to continue.

"Everything to do with transmission electrification involves energy management strategies, new designs, and shifting controls. What George has focused on are single-speed and multi-speed transmissions."

"I'm impressed. I don't recall you knowing the latest transmission technologies a few months ago."

Stella smiled. "When the opportunity arose, I had to come up to speed real fast."

"So, who is pushing George to sell?"

"His son, Danny."

"Not 'Daniel'."

"Nope. He introduces himself as Danny, but I guess Daniel is on his birth certificate. He is in charge of sales and marketing."

"Why does he want to sell what his father created?"

"In meeting him, I learned that all he wants to do is surf. Danny is a nice enough guy, but different from his father. He's the one who brought the opportunity to me. He arrived without an appointment at my office, wearing board shorts, a white T-shirt, and sandals."

"Dreadlocks?"

"No. He's a clean-cut, good-looking kid."

"Kid? How old is he?"

Stella laughed. "He's twenty-two."

"So, he wants to go off with his father's money and live the dream."

"That sounds harsh. But yes. Danny was very polite as he expressed his respect for his father and what he had accomplished. It's just not what he wants to do."

"Where's the factory?"

"The manufacturing division is in Plymouth, Michigan, because it's close to Detroit.

It's near my Plymouth Clutch and Brake PCB factory on Five Mile Road. The one where you worked for me. The engineering division is here in Palo Alto to get access to specific technical talent. He said he knew I was the owner of Node and he thought he'd pop in and have a chat."

"Can't fault his initiative."

"Not at all."

"Where do George and Danny live?"

"George has a property in Palo Alto and Danny has a cottage on the property. George is close to his engineering division and Danny's got lots of beaches where he can surf." Jack took a slice of his breakfast while he waited for Stella to continue. "Danny organized a meeting with George. That was four months ago, and over time, I've got to know them and their business much better. As a result, I found another reason Danny is pushing for this sale."

Jack finished chewing, sipped his kale juice, which barely wet his tongue, and waited.

"I told Danny that if George isn't interested in selling, I'm not interested in pursuing this. He then told me that George had been diagnosed with early Alzheimer's and that, eventually, George would have to step down from running the company. Danny had been quite open about not being interested in the business and was embarrassed when he said he felt incapable of running it. His face went pink. I gave him the Shakespeare quote. 'Some are born great, some achieve greatness, and some have greatness thrust upon them.' Danny had chuckled at this and said he would rather read Twelfth Night than concern himself with greatness."

"Sounds like he's well-read."

"In the relatively short time I've known him, I have found him able to converse on almost any topic, but the only thing he wants to do is surf. Danny was also skeptical whether anyone in the business could take on the role."

"And George, what is his view?"

"George has no other interests. He doesn't play golf and is not interested in fishing. Well-read, like Danny. That's probably where Danny got it from. Both of them are good company. George doesn't know that I know about his medical condition. His wife passed away some years ago from breast cancer, and now all he has is Danny and his work. He would continue doing what he does even if he sold the business. To George, it's not work. It's who he is. It gives him great pleasure and satisfaction."

"So now what?"

"Well, Danny stays in touch with me as he sees George's health as a ticking time bomb. He would rather see the business acquired and the handover completed before George's health reaches a point where he can't continue, or the vultures would pounce. Asset-strip it, sell off the core competency, the technology, and what George had created would no longer exist. Danny said a group had organized a meeting with him, without his father's knowledge, and were keen to buy the business. They made it clear they asset-strip. They wanted Danny to be the CEO, with a big salary, while they went about making George's life work vanish for profit. He told me he had approached me because his research on Node Industries, and me, led him to believe I would perpetuate what George had created. He asked if I would keep George on the payroll if I acquired the business. I told him I would, as it was good business, not sentimentality."

"Sounds like a good son."

"Would you like to meet him?"

"Sure. When?"

"At that café on Sutter Street. Brunch at eleven. It should be quieter at that time."

Jack knew the neighborhood restaurant and coffee house in Pacific Heights, but he hadn't been there for a while. "Wow, that was a long way to get to the invitation."

Stella smiled. "I like sneaking up on you."

"Anytime. You can sneak up on me anytime."

"Does that time work for you? I'm going to work from home and then go there."

"It does. I have to visit Marie, so from there I'll go to Sutter Street."

"Is it a guilt visit, or do you have something to do there?"

Jack shrugged.

"Ted's death wasn't your fault."

"I know. I know. But to have someone step in front of you and take a bullet that someone meant for you ... I don't have words, but what happened keeps running like a movie through my head."

"And doing wonders for your PTSD."

Stella knew about the trip switch, which kept a dark gray thing of violence in a cave-like structure at the base of his spine. She had witnessed when something tripped it, and it rushed up his spine like lava, making him fight like the Berserkers of Viking legend. It was injustice that flipped the switch. Stella knew you didn't need a degree in psychology or psychiatry to join the dots from his current state back to the death of his parents.

"No doubt."

CHAPTER FOUR

Jack had parked his ten-year-old Yukon Denali in the free parking at the Botanical Gardens, just off Lincoln Way, opposite Tenth Avenue. He arrived early for the meeting, walking through The Great Meadow where the magnolia trees perfumed the air with a mix of vanilla and citrus. Jack revisited the maze of ecosystems from the Redwood Grove, the Mediterranean, Mesoamerican, and Andean Cloud Forests, and the Ancient Plant Garden. He walked through a tapestry of nature's threads until he arrived at the delicate precision of the Moon Viewing Garden. A slight wind created a dance of light and shadow in the gnarled and manicured trees.

Marie Clark welcomed Jack, her eyes red from crying, as she stood on the wooden platform overlooking a pond with a tissue in her hand. To look at the widow, whose husband had taken a bullet for him, it was like he'd never seen her or looked at her before.

She had a heart-shaped face, a broad forehead like Ted's, high cheekbones, a narrow chin, and gracefully arched eyebrows framed by deep-set blue eyes that conveyed the intensity of her loss. Jack guessed her height as not quite five feet six inches. Her straight hair had a central parting, was black like a moonless night, and hung halfway down her back. She had the slim build of someone who ate little and exercised less. She was not quite anorexic, but she was getting there. The oversized blue jeans and tailored black shirt only highlighted the slender frame rattling around inside the clothes. Overall, one would look twice.

"Ted and I often walked in The Gardens. When the things Ted saw and had to do became overwhelming, we came here and just stood." Marie stared into the water for two minutes. "Ted would also come here with Judy, knowing that as her blindness progressed, eventually, what they saw together, one day she wouldn't." Jack waited. "The day of Ted's funeral will strike Judy like a blade to the heart. She'd lost the one man who truly wanted her to rise higher than he ever did. She knew he always silently prayed for her victories but never pushed her. It was then she felt the weight of his hopes, which were now hers to carry." Marie turned her tear-stained face to Jack. "I'm glad you came, so I can tell you I bear you no malice. I know what Ted did. He found a way out, and he was protecting me financially." Marie used her fingers to wipe the tears from her face. "Do you mind if we walk?"

"Sure. We can walk."

"And you don't have to make conversation. We can just walk."

For the next eighty minutes, they traversed The Gardens, with Marie stopping at random to look at a tree, flower, plant, or bush, which must have brought back memories, as she wiped her eyes with tissues.

* * *

They wound up at her house on Ninth Avenue, Inner Sunset, where she took Jack on a tour of the photographs on the wall. A collage of Ted, Marie, and Judy through the years.

"Isn't she beautiful?" said Marie.

People sometimes put this question to you about their children, and sometimes it is not valid. However, if you say it is true anyway, then the parents are happy. Indeed, beauty is in the eye of the beholder, and parents look at their children through magic glasses.

This time was different. Jack didn't hesitate, he even wondered if he might have answered too quickly. "She sure is." Even the black graduation gown and cap couldn't disguise it. It was a younger version of Marie, her eyes gazing into the distance, her head turned at forty-five degrees, laughing as she held her newly acquired scroll.

"I am making myself coffee, Jack. Would you care for a cup?"

Jack was already a few cups ahead of Kenny's recommendation, but it would give them something to do, as Jack still wasn't sure why he was there, but felt he should be.

"Yes, please, Marie."

Marie looked at her watch. "I'm expecting a visitor. Just a few papers I need to sign."

Jack didn't ask Marie what she had to sign, but he knew it was wise to be cautious about signing anything after such a traumatic event.

Jack sat in the kitchen as Marie got down two mugs from an over-the-counter cupboard. "You look like a mug kinda guy."

"Correct, and plain black as well."

"Same as me. Same as Ted." Marie put her left hand on the counter to steady herself, sniffed and dabbed at her eyes, sniffed again, held her head high, and continued making coffee.

"I must say, Jack, I have been impressed with the support I have received from the police department."

"Glad to hear it. Bureaucracy normally runs at the speed of a sloth."

"I know, but this morning, an accommodating man phoned me to say he is with the department's insurance company and can expedite the payout of Ted's policies. He's the visitor I'm expecting."

Maybe Freddie pulled some strings, but he questioned it. What's the expression? When something is too good to be true. Jack kept his own counsel and commented as she seemed to expect. "Wow. That's impressive."

Marie put the steaming mugs onto the table. It was too hot to drink. Marie didn't get to sit as the doorbell rang. "Marie, may I use your bathroom?"

As Marie walked, she pointed down the hallway. "Second door on the left."

Jack pulled out his phone as he walked, closed the bathroom door, and texted Freddie.

I'm with Marie Clark. A guy has arrived. He phoned Marie earlier, saying if she signs some papers, the insurance company will expedite her payout. Did you organize this?

Jack waited six seconds for the reply. *No. It's a scam. Marie must not sign anything. Record what you can. Let him go. I want further up the food chain.*

Jack didn't wait to reply but started recording with his phone. He knew enough about police procedure that Freddie would want evidence. To keep up appearances, Jack flushed the toilet, washed his hands, and walked into the living room, where a mid-forties man stood in a blue suit, white shirt, no tie, swept-back gray hair, and a smile that you had to trust. Jack held up his phone, looking as though he was reading it, until his video ran long enough to capture good visuals.

"Oh, Jack, this is Graham Hill."

Graham put out his hand and smiled at Jack, offering a handshake. Not too hard or soft. Just like in the Three Bears. Graham's other hand held a small computer. "Nice to meet you, Jack. Are you a friend of the family? You must live close by. I didn't see a car in the driveway."

Clearly, Jack's presence was not part of Graham's agenda. Jack smiled at Graham. "Yes, and yes, and I walked."

Marie gestured to the kitchen. "Jack and I were having coffee. Can I make you some?"

"No, thank you, Marie. I'm good. I'll be on my way once I get these documents signed."

"Let's all sit in the kitchen," said Marie.

Graham looked at Jack and then at Marie. "These documents are confidential. If Jack wouldn't mind waiting in the living room."

"Nonsense," said Marie as she sat at the kitchen table and tested her coffee.

Jack sat on Graham's right with his coffee and phone between them. "So Graham, I believe you're with the insurance company."

There was the smile again. "Well, Jack, to be precise, the insurance company contracts us to expedite the payout to the beneficiary in these traumatic situations. The bureaucratic process can sometimes encumber the beneficiaries."

"That's very good of them," said Jack. "Do you have a card?"

Graham reached inside his jacket. "Oops. They must be in the car." Graham opened the tablet, picked up the stylus, and pointed at a line at the bottom of the page. "Marie, if you just sign there. You can check it's your bank account details at the top."

Jack knew that once Graham had Marie's signature, it wouldn't be a technical challenge to change the account number and beneficiary name on the form and submit it.

"Is that a new model stylus?" said Jack. "Can I have a look?" Jack reached for the stylus with his left hand, knocking his coffee mug over. The contents splashed onto the tablet and onto Graham's nether regions, causing him to jump up with an expletive, which Marie, from her shocked expression, didn't appreciate. "Wow," said Jack. "Sorry, Graham. What a mess. Clumsy me. Is the tablet still working? Have a look."

Jack picked up the tablet and passed it to Graham. As Graham's fingers touched it, Jack let go, and the tablet landed on a corner, coming to rest face up, and the screen fractured. Jack put on a face that he hoped looked like a sad cocker spaniel. "Entirely my fault, Graham. I'll buy you a new one."

Graham was doing an excellent job of getting himself under control. However, if his eyes had been a machine gun, they would have shredded Jack. "Accidents happen, Jack. Marie, will you be home tomorrow? I will come back, and we can finish our business."

"Sure, I will be here in the morning."

"And I'll stay away," said Jack, "so I don't mess things up."

Marie walked Graham to the door. Jack followed, looked out at the white Toyota Camry in the driveway, memorized the license plate number, and apologized again. Graham waved off Jack's apology as he walked to the car.

Marie closed the door and looked at Jack. "You don't live with a cop for as long as I did and not pick up when something is off. You don't strike me as clumsy. What was that all about?"

"This business with this Graham Hill fellow didn't seem right. I texted Freddie from the bathroom. He said it's a scam, and you mustn't sign, and I must record as much as possible."

"What's Freddie going to do?"

Jack imagined what Freddie could do within the law's limits and what one could do outside those limits.

Sometimes, it is best to appear uninformed and unaware.

"I don't know."

CHAPTER FIVE

Danny had a gap between his top incisors. It was of a size that made Jack question whether he should have worn braces to fix it, but the rest of his teeth were perfect. Perhaps the orthodontist agonized over his decision, but his mother ultimately decided it would give her child a permanent boyish look. The gap drew your gaze when he grinned. His eyes kept smiling even when he closed his mouth.

Stella had introduced Jack as an external consultant who helped her from time to time, which was true. Danny nodded and seemed happy with Jack's job description. She also said she had told Jack about the state of their discussions and George's health issues.

"Have you surfed Maverick's yet?" Jack was referring to the legendary big wave surf spot at Pillar Point in Half Moon Bay, twenty miles south of San Francisco. Danny had the surfer's build, broad shoulders, and narrow hips. He was three inches taller than Jack and about the same weight. He looked like the archetype surfing machine.

Jack and Danny had ordered the Millionaire's Bacon with three eggs, and Stella chose Omurice, a Japanese omelet wrapped around seasoned ketchup rice. Stella gave Jack a taste, and Jack questioned his choice.

Danny watched this with interest.

Danny finished chewing before replying with his trademark smile. "Mavericks is on my bucket list. As you probably know, the waves are twenty feet high on average, and I've been there to watch guys surf them at sixty feet."

Jack was also aware of the sharks, the fog, and the cold conditions. "It is impressive."

"I don't get it," said Stella. "The risk is huge. People have died there."

"I can't argue, Stella," said Danny as his face glowed like he'd switched on a lamp. "It makes no sense, but I still want to do it. However, it does make me understand my father better. Having that inner passion to do something despite the odds stacked against you. In my case, I'm nearly ready to try Mavericks. I've got a good board, a high-impact wetsuit, an inflatable vest, and a helmet. I practice my breath-holding. It's just the mental side. To commit at that point of the takeoff. I have to assume I'll wipe out sometimes, and I want to be able to swim away and try again another day."

"Like in business," said Stella.

"Exactly," said Danny, "and that's what worries me about my father's business. There are bound to be times when, if I run it, I will wipe out. I worry I won't have the will to pick myself up, as I'm just not interested, and I will let what my father created fade away from neglect. And with his diagnosis of early-stage Alzheimer's, there is a feeling of inevitability."

"And, from my side, I've told George I would love to buy the business, and he would have a job there for as long as he liked doing what he loves. However, for a deal to work, there needs to be a willing buyer and a willing seller, and George told me he appreciated the interest but didn't want to sell. Look, you've told me about his health, and I have no intention of bringing that up unless he mentions it himself. When are you seeing your father again?"

"In a week. There are some things he wants me to do in Plymouth, but he wants me back here for my birthday."

Stella nodded. "That's nice. You'll get to spend some time together."

"It will be. I enjoy his company. We do random stuff together."

"So, Danny," said Stella. "I'm glad we had this meeting, but remember what I said about willing buyer, willing seller."

"Understood," said Danny, "but I have a new concern that's been growing for a while."

* * *

Jack knew by the way Stella's shoulders straightened that she'd tensed up, though on the surface, she was as calm as the silence between heartbeats. She wasn't expecting any wrinkles.

Danny rubbed his palms together. "Security. The IT department says they have everything under control, and my father leaves it up to them."

Jack picked up his coffee cup. "What makes you think you have a security problem?"

"I listen to my friends and hear what's happening with security at their offices, and from our IT department, I hear none of what they talk about. My concern is the intellectual property my father is developing. He's explained it to me, and it will be a quantum leap for the company."

Stella chuckled. "You are just saying that to talk up the price if George ever decides to sell."

"Not at all. You would be paying a premium for that anyway, but if someone steals the intellectual property and produces a prototype, that would greatly reduce the value of my father's business."

Stella dabbed at the corners of her mouth with the napkin. "Do you think someone has stolen something?"

"That's it. I just don't know."

Stella placed the napkin back on her lap and glanced at Jack. "Can you help out here?" She turned back to Danny. "Jack is very good at this security stuff. Like your father, I tend to leave it up to others."

What would Danny do if he knew Stella was the hacker whom many agencies had been after? She didn't have a name or a handle. Still, she was known as Numbers to government agencies because she used an algorithm to sign in using random numbers. They fed other random number generators into a daisy chain until her algorithm deemed it sufficiently random to use without attracting attention. With the advent of AI, the algorithm was even better.

"Sure," said Jack. "Happy to help."

"I'll phone Dad and let him know you're coming."

"Won't he want to meet me first?"

"No. Dad will go with my recommendation. It's not an area of the business he's interested in. He assumes it's something that's being taken care of, like housekeeping, and he likes it when I take an interest in the business. When can you go there?"

"I have to go to a funeral on Thursday. But I can go tomorrow if that's not too soon."

"Tomorrow's great. I'll let Dad know and the head of IT. Frank Lund's his name."

* * *

It was 6 pm at Stella's house when Jack's phone rang. "Before you ask, we haven't caught that guy, Graham Hill, if that was his name," Freddie said.

"What have you got so far?"

"Well, the car he was using is a rental, and they had fitted it with a tracking device, but it stopped sending a signal after it left Marie's house, which means they had pre-planned to dispose of it. It hasn't been picked up on CCTV anywhere, there are no traffic infringements, and the traffic guys haven't seen it, but it's a white Toyota Camry. There are lots of them around. It'll turn up eventually. We'll give it to the forensics team, but these insurance scammers are professionals. They won't have left any clues."

"You speak as though this has happened before."

"This is a first for someone at the Academy, but powers above my department have already tasked us to pick up on other branches of the police force where this has happened."

"By your department, you mean what we all call Area 51, as it doesn't have a name."

Jack could practically hear Freddie rolling his eyes. "It does have a name. Just not one that we share with the public. Just once, a staff member stupidly stuck up a sign saying Area 51."

"The sign was cardboard, written with an erasable whiteboard pen, and not on the wall for even one hour. The story is now legend." Jack smirked down the phone. "Nicknames are sticky. Impossible to get off."

"We do important work. It should not have a silly name."

"I don't think the military sees Area 51 as a silly name. And you do important work, although I only see a slice of it in helping your team keep abreast of what is happening in the wide, wonderful, and scurrilous world of data analytics and forensics. But back to the scam this Graham Hill attempted on Marie. What about the credit card? He must have used a credit card to get the vehicle. Was it stolen?"

"They weren't stolen. The cards are genuine. These people open an account with just enough cash to cover the cost of hiring a car. It's always a white Toyota Camry. They put a few dollars in the account and leave it there. It's a dormant account. Over sixty billion dollars is currently in bank accounts with no activity for the past year. So these small sums are less than a rounding error."

"How many cases like Marie's do you have so far?"

"I have eight, where the victims signed the bogus form and the money vanished. Marie is the first case where this didn't happen. You should keep your eyes open. We don't know who they are."

CHAPTER SIX

Frank Lund was a rumpled man in his fifties. His hair, beard, and clothes bore the same disheveled indifference as his outlook on life, which he felt he needed to share. Jack listened with one ear but got on with the job to get what he wanted.

Jack hadn't done the drive for a while. It took under an hour from the hilly streets and grand homes of Pacific Heights and onto the Bayshore Freeway. Even being mid-week, he saw sailboats racing as he caught glimpses of San Francisco Bay. With its stunning coastal views, Jack remembered picnics at Coyote Point with Uncle Alan and Aunt Louise, when he and Freddie were not even teenagers. The memory faded as he slid past Silicon Valley with the sleek modern architecture of the tech campuses. Then, the mature oak trees of Palo Alto provided a canopy of shade, placing Carlton Engineering within walking distance of Stanford University.

Frank Lund, the head of IT, was not thrilled with Jack's snooping around and made it quite clear he resented Jack's investigation. He had a no-nonsense expression, like a proper old-school headmaster, with pale, piercing blue eyes. They had dark circles under them, probably from countless late-night troubleshooting sessions. There is a view that older people couldn't, and shouldn't, wear jeans. Frank fell into that category. His white short-sleeved shirt had a coffee stain that looked like it wouldn't come out with repeated washes. He seemed ambivalent about cloud computing, and any mention of blockchain got a grunt of disapproval. Jack sat in on their morning meeting and realized that Frank's several decades of experience and knowledge would fill encyclopedias. Frank explained complex systems issues in simple terms.

His relationship with his staff was interesting in that he was a perfectionist and pointed out mistakes with sharp, sarcastic remarks delivered with an underlying dry, cynical sense of humor. His staff responded with respect for his expertise with a mixture of trepidation and admiration. Jack had seen this before, when what was sometimes referred to as The Old Guard delivered their knowledge and expertise in a grumpy, dissatisfied package, yet the insights they offered were often spot-on. Yet there was not much mention of Carlton Engineering. Frank was a technology warrior, like a samurai with a code of honor, dedicated to mastering his craft and overcoming technological obstacles with skill and precision. That Carlton Engineering was paying their salaries, they disregarded in pursuit of the code of honor.

Jack didn't meet with George Carlton because George had back-to-back meetings all day, and they were still ongoing. As he departed, the sun cast its final golden rays across the horizon, painting the sky with deep orange and violet hues. Long shadows stretched out, almost as if they were trying to pull him back to the moment he desperately wanted to leave behind. The air was heavy with the promise of dusk, a precursor to the night that would be long and unforgiving.

Tomorrow was Ted's funeral, a reality that gnawed at him with every mile. Despite the well-meaning words of comfort from those around him, the guilt was relentless, chipping away at his sanity like a tide eroding a fragile shore. The whispered assurances that "it wasn't his fault" felt empty, unable to penetrate the fortress of blame he had built within himself.

Passing car lights kept bringing everything back into sharp focus, replaying the scene in vivid, merciless detail. The weight of his remorse pressed down on him with an unrelenting force, leaving him to grapple with a sense of responsibility he couldn't shake. The world's indifference only amplified his isolation, the city's vibrancy starkly contrasting with his inner despair.

He drove on, each mile a struggle against the tide of guilt that threatened to pull him under. The night was closing in, but he knew there would be no rest, no respite from the memory that haunted him. He braced for the heart-wrenching farewell that awaited him. Would the dawn bring any solace or cast a new light on his enduring guilt?

* * *

Freddie and Kenny were among the eight pallbearers at the church. Marie stood at the front with a woman of her height, and Jack assumed it must be her daughter, Judy. They wore black suits and hats with veils obscuring their faces. In line with Ted's beliefs, he had wished for cremation and for Marie to sprinkle his ashes in The Bay. After the service, the pallbearers returned the coffin to the funeral vehicle, which drove off, followed by Marie and Judy in a black Cadillac Escalade. Everyone else left for an Irish pub that Ted liked to frequent. The department had passed the hat around and collected enough money to give Ted a good send-off.

Pubs are noisy, but the attendees had ramped up the volume as they all shouted so someone could hear them above the shouting, so they shouted louder as they made toasts to Ted. Jack and Freddie stood beside each other and had given up on talking. These events were like bonfires, roaring up to a crescendo and dissipating into ashes. Jack saw Marie and Judy walk into the pub. They had discarded the black hats and veils, making a striking pair. Marie saw Jack and walked over with Judy in tow, talking to her as Judy held onto her mother's elbow, her head half turned towards her. Undoubtedly, Judy was beautiful, a replica of Marie, and Jack looked forward to the introduction.

"Hello, Jack. Hello Freddie," said Marie.

"Freddie," said Judy without breaking stride as she held out her arms. Jack glanced at Freddie, whose face had softened like a marshmallow as he stepped forward. Freddie stepped into her embrace, and they hung onto each other like morning dew clinging to a spiderweb. Judy pointed her face at Jack, but she wasn't seeing him. Freddie and Judy stood there for two minutes until Judy broke the clinch. Freddie was an inch taller than Jack and had to reach down to hold Judy's elbow. "How are you and Marie holding up?"

"We did our crying this morning when we sat down, and each wrote a letter to Dad. Private letters. Each is sealed in an envelope and placed in the coffin before the service. Then we cried some more." Freddie held her again, then half turned her towards Jack. "This is Jack." Freddie looked at Jack. "Judy and I were in first-year law together at UC Berkeley."

Jack was in Computer Science on the same campus. Still, he had no recollection of Freddie having a girlfriend who looked like Judy. Freddie didn't need to give Jack an explanation, but Jack wanted one.

Judy put out her hand to Jack, and he took it. "Freddie was dating my best friend, who was also studying law." Judy took her attention back to Freddie. "Do you know Sally married and moved to LA?"

"Yes, lawyer to the rich and famous who need defending. Her name does come up."

Jack knew Freddie believed everyone was entitled to legal representation under the law. Still, he held a low opinion of people who defended those who had committed the worst possible crimes. Freddie also struggled with this dichotomy in the concept of ranking crimes by severity.

Judy turned her head to Jack. "Mother told me what you did with the guy who attempted to scam her. I thank you for that."

"Glad to help."

"The way Mother told me what happened sounded like some improv method-acting, with you being the clumsy guy."

It was like a cloud hanging between them. That Ted had stepped in front of Jack. Marie must have told her. Not mentioning it didn't help his guilt. Mentioning the scammer seemed like a convenient distraction.

"Maybe I am clumsy."

A crowd of Ted's colleagues had assembled around Marie, offering condolences and separating her from Judy. Marie could see she was with Freddie and Jack. Judy faced Freddie.

"Good to hear your voice again, Freddie." Before Freddie could respond, her hand found his face, and she kissed his cheek. "Now, if you could direct me back to Mother."

Freddie took Judy's elbow. He led her carefully, making sure she was safe. They inched through the crowd towards Marie, who was holding back tears.

Freddie stopped when he approached Marie, who opened her arms and hugged Judy. Freddie stepped back, letting them find comfort in a painful moment.

The wake continued long into the evening, as Ted's colleagues shared their time with Ted, surprising Marie and Judy with some and laughing at others. Stories they had never heard. A slice of Ted's life he never brought home. The barman placed tapas and paper plates on the bar counter. Chorizo, sliced tortillas, potato wedges with a spicy tomato sauce, and pastries stuffed with meat or mozzarella cheese with a dipping sauce. There was alcohol, lots of alcohol, to create a veil behind which people could submit to deaden the pain.

CHAPTER SEVEN

Jack sat at his kitchen table, the glow of his laptop screen illuminating his tired eyes. The apartment was silent except for his swivel chair's occasional creak. He glanced at the clock on his computer. Well past midnight. A half-empty mug of coffee sat beside him, its contents long gone cold. He took a deep breath and focused on the task. The IT due diligence of Carlton Engineering. He began with preparation and defining the scope and objectives of the due diligence process, outlining clear goals and specific areas he was to assess. He couldn't afford any misunderstandings.

Jack's fingers raced over the keyboard as he delved into the documentation review. He compiled an exhaustive inventory of the company's IT systems. Hardware, software, networks. Each entry felt like a small victory in an otherwise overwhelming task. He reviewed existing contracts with IT vendors, noting service agreements, costs, and terms. Step by step, Jack meticulously examined the company's IT policies, procedures, and governance structures.

The technical assessment came next. Jack evaluated the company's IT infrastructure's quality, performance, and scalability. He reviewed the software applications in use, both proprietary and third-party. Data management and security were critical components, and he assessed how the company managed and protected its data, with a focus on backup procedures and cybersecurity measures.

He paused momentarily, rubbing his temples, and sipped his cold coffee, grimacing at the bitter taste. The fatigue was setting in, but he couldn't stop now. He moved on to the IT organization and support, evaluating the skills, experience, and roles of the company's IT team. He reviewed technical maintenance procedures for IT systems and infrastructure.

Risk assessment followed. Jack identified potential risks and vulnerabilities in the IT setup, including outdated systems and security flaws. He evaluated how the company's IT strategy aligned with its overall business goals and how it supported growth and innovation. Each discovery added another layer to the puzzle he was piecing together.

The financial analysis required his full attention. Jack reviewed the IT budget and expenses to understand the company's financial commitment to IT. He conducted a cost-benefit analysis to determine the value of the IT assets. His eyes were heavy, and his vision blurred as he worked through the numbers.

Hours passed, the night slipping away unnoticed. Jack meticulously compiled his findings into a detailed report, knowing this document would be crucial in presenting his insights to George Carlton. His report needed to present a clear, easily understood picture to make informed decisions.

Integration planning was the final step. Jack developed a broad plan to integrate the company's IT systems with Stella's. He added a note, that in the event of a deal being concluded, there needed to be more detail. He addressed any issues or vulnerabilities identified during the due diligence process to ensure a smooth transition and minimize costs.

With a final keystroke, Jack saved his work and leaned back in his chair. Despite the long hours and mounting fatigue, there was a sense of accomplishment. He closed his laptop and stretched his tired muscles. Jack stood up and headed to bed, knowing he could confidently present this document to George Carlton.

* * *

After morning training with Kenny, Jack and Freddie showered and changed in the gym, and then walked across the grounds to Freddie's office. Kenny's training had focused on legs. They felt it with each step, like their shoes had lead soles.

"What happened to Judy's eyes, Freddie?"

"She has Autoimmune Retinopathy."

"What's that?"

"It's quite rare. The immune system mistakenly attacks retinal cells, leading to progressive vision loss."

"When did it start?"

"In her final year. Her night vision got worse, followed by her peripheral vision. By the time she landed her job in New York, her focus had become tunnel vision. At her work, they set her up with screen-reading software and refreshable braille displays, which convert text into braille, which she reads by touch, as she only sees shadows now."

"You seem to be very knowledgeable and up to date."

"That's what friends do, Jack."

"Does she have a boyfriend?"

"Why would I know that?"

"You said you were friends. What do you talk about?"

"We don't usually talk. It's mostly email. Why am I even discussing this with you?"

"They must have been short emails. You can't discuss your work, and Judy would be in the same boat as she's a lawyer."

"Is the concept of friends so difficult for you to grasp?"

"Friends? I saw you two together. What are you going to do about her?"

"What do you mean, what am I going to do?"

Freddie shook his head and turned his back to Jack as he opened the front door and headed for the coffee machine.

People were already in the office, but Jack had never been there when there weren't people around. Freddie flicked on the lights in his glass cubicle of an office as they entered with coffee mugs in hand. This meeting followed up on Freddie's suggestion that Jack could help with the insurance scammers.

Jack sipped the coffee. Nothing was exhilarating about the coffee. Jack grimaced at the blandness and looked at Freddie. "Don't insurance companies need a death certificate before beginning the payout process?"

"Yes, they do, and in Ted's case, it was unnatural causes, so it would have to be produced by the coroner. Also, the beneficiary or their representative must notify the insurance company, which will then request the death certificate and any other documents it requires. Not to mention insurance companies move at a snail's pace. They're in no big hurry to pay out."

"So, how did the scammer know about Ted's death so quickly?"

"We've opened a case file, but it's not complete yet. Only now do I have two officers meeting with Marie to get her statement, which you must also sign. The hospital had documented the death, which is part of the process to produce a death certificate."

Jack started to speak, but Freddie held up his hand. "Let me finish. When the scammer got to Marie's house, the hospital had recorded Ted's death in their database, but not in ours, as we were waiting on details from the hospital. Ted's file was in Pending status, and the words Death or Killed didn't appear. We need to obtain a subpoena to get access to the database. Patient records are confidential. Once we have access, we will check to see if someone has hacked into the database."

"The old dilemma of the balance between confidentiality and the public interest."

"Yes, and frustrating as it is, we are the law and can't be seen as going rogue."

"Can't be seen?"

"You know what I mean. We can't go rogue, and there must be no suspicion that we did."

"What do you want me to do?"

"Listen to what my guys have done already and maybe come up with some ideas. However, you are not to use this facility to get access to the data we have collected or hack into a network."

"With my monthly meetings, they are up to speed with the latest data analysis and hacking techniques."

"I know. Just do me a favor and listen to what they've done."

"Is the dataset just related to law enforcement?"

"That's our mandate for now. It's also a personal issue. Cops' wives live with the fear that as their husbands leave for work, they may not return. So when something like what happened to Ted occurs, the wives almost breathe a sigh of relief that they don't have to worry anymore, and that's the inevitability of it all."

* * *

Jack stepped into Marie's living room, the morning light following him through the open door. He paused in the entryway, taking in the unexpected scene. Freddie sat on the couch close to Judy, whose head turned slightly at Jack's steps. Her hand rested lightly on Freddie's knee, an unspoken connection between them.

Jack closed the door behind him. "Freddie," he said, his tone even. "I didn't think I'd see you here."

Freddie shrugged. "Had to get some paperwork signed. What's your excuse?"

Jack glanced at Marie, who sat at the dining table, reading a page she held in her hands. She looked up briefly, then returned her attention to the document in front of her.

"Didn't know I needed excuses to stop by," Jack said.

Neither mentioned the 6 am training or the meeting they'd had earlier. They had spent the morning sparring and sweating under the dark pre-dawn sky, their usual banter about who was tougher drowned out by Kenny's relentless pace. Not once had Freddie mentioned he'd be stopping by Marie's. Jack hadn't either.

Marie set down the paper and reached for a pen. She signed the bottom of the page, her movements deliberate. "That should cover it," she said, pushing the page across the table toward Freddie.

Freddie stood and took the paper. He gave it a quick once-over before holding it out to Jack. "Might as well take a look while you're here."

Jack frowned but stepped forward, his curiosity getting the better of him. He took the document and sank into the chair opposite Marie. The room went quiet, except for Judy's faint sound tracing her fingers along the edge of her cane. Jack's eyes scanned the words, focusing on the details of the events with the insurance scammer.

As he reached the middle of the second page, he stopped. His lips pressed into a thin line, and he looked up. "Marie, it says here the scammer called you the morning after Ted's death. At eight."

Marie nodded, her hands folded neatly on the table. "That's correct."

Jack leaned back slightly, holding the papers in his lap. "By then, only the hospital would have known about Ted." He spoke the words slowly, his voice steady, but there was an edge to it he couldn't entirely hide.

"Yeah, I thought the same," added Freddie.

Jack didn't look at Freddie. His focus was on Marie. "You didn't tell anyone else that night?"

"No," Marie said. "And it's all in the statement."

Judy shifted slightly, her head turning toward Jack. "What are you thinking, Jack?" She was asking in her lawyer-voice.

Jack blinked and glanced at her. "Nothing."

She smiled faintly. "Just say what you're thinking."

"The timing's odd. That's all."

Jack slid the papers back to Freddie. "There you go."

Marie stood and moved toward the kitchen. "I was about to make some coffee," she said. "Freddie's having some. Jack, do you want any?"

Jack shook his head. "No, thanks. Just came to check in."

Marie paused in the doorway, turning back to face him. "Freddie's already handled everything."

Jack stood, brushing his hands on his jeans. He glanced at Freddie, whose expression remained impassive, though there was something in his eyes that Jack recognized. It was the same look he'd seen countless times growing up, the unspoken challenge between them.

"Well," Jack said, "I'll head out then."

Freddie didn't respond, but the look he gave Jack was answer enough. The sooner he left, the better. Judy tilted her head, listening to Jack's footsteps as he walked to the door.

"Jack," she said, stopping him before he stepped outside. "Don't think too hard about it."

Jack turned back to face her. "About what?"

"Whatever it is you're turning over in your head." Her smile was small but knowing, and Jack sensed a flicker of appreciation for her insight.

He dipped his head slightly. "I'll keep that in mind."

Jack stepped outside, the sun warm on his face. He let out a breath, the tension from the room dissipating with each step he took toward his truck. Climbing into the driver's seat, he started the engine and let it rumble to life beneath him.

As he pulled away, his thoughts drifted back to Freddie. Growing up, they had been inseparable, cousins who were more like brothers. They'd shared everything. Secrets, adventures, even fights. But now, as adults, there was a subtle competition that neither would ever openly admit to. Jack smiled as he drove. Some things never changed, and some games were worth playing, even if no one declared a winner.

CHAPTER EIGHT

George Carlton would have stood the same height as Jack if he didn't have a stoop from too much time sitting at a desk looking at engineering drawings. He wore an oversized white shirt that did a poor job of hiding his paunch. Rolled-up sleeves showed his meaty forearms. His blue trousers were the bottom half of a suit. The jacket was hanging on a hat rack in the corner. The black industrial elastic-sided boots were classy enough for a business meeting, and they also served as industrial safety boots with a steel-reinforced toecap. He had an air about him, and he was well past impressing people with how he dressed. The boots were from a decade earlier and were of a quality that didn't wear out.

It was Friday at 4 pm when George had time for Jack and his report. George's mahogany desk was neat. That was the only word Jack could come up with. Neat. On it was a framed photo, which Jack could see when he walked in. He recognized George and Danny. The woman must be George's deceased wife. Danny was in the middle with everyone resting their arms on the shoulders of the person next to them. It appeared they were genuinely laughing. Not staged, as when one says, "Cheese" or "Smelly Socks." Behind George's high-backed chair was a long mahogany slab with two twenty-four-inch screens. Each had an engineering drawing. Jack sat opposite. Two cups of coffee had steam coming off them. George had his own coffee machine and made coffee while explaining its technical capabilities to Jack. Good beans make good coffee, allowing you to choose from light, medium, or dark roasts. This shiny piece of equipment ground the beans. A brown dial controlled the granularity.

Jack passed a copy of his report across the desk to George. George moved the yellow legal pad with the antique tortoiseshell-colored celluloid fountain pen to the side of the desk next to the photo.

George peered at the picture, then turned to Jack. "Well, thank you, Jack." George took the report and placed it on the desk. "I read about horror stories in the media and wonder if those big companies get hacked with all their clever people. What chance do we have here at Carlton Engineering? Why don't you walk me through it? I'm a good listener. And I must confess I know very little about the latest in system security."

Was this true, or had George read up on the topic, and this was a test? Jack had been in this rodeo before.

"Sure thing. Well, first up, I did some penetration testing. Running simulated cyber-attacks against applications and the infrastructure. It's basically ethical hacking. I have some standard automated tools that identify known security weaknesses. These tools scan the system for common vulnerabilities to identify weaknesses and assess the defenses in place. Security scanning checks for open ports, insecure protocols, and potential entry points. I then conduct a risk assessment to identify any threats and vulnerabilities these pose to the business. Then, I do a security audit, reviewing systems, processes, and controls to ensure compliance with security policies and procedures. And that security measures are implemented correctly."

"Wow, Jack, that's quite a lot. And what did you find?"

"Nothing that your IT department can't fix, but there is one thing I wanted to raise that's not in the report."

"Which is?"

"Where do you keep all your intellectual property?"

"Why do you ask?"

"Someone is hacking into your system and poking around like they are looking for something."

"Who is it?"

"It was not in my current task description, and I wanted to chat with you about it and how you would like me to proceed."

George's mobile phone rang, and he glanced at the number.

"Take it, George."

George picked up the phone, answered the call, identified himself, and listened. Jack watched as George crumpled as if a giant hand had grabbed him like a piece of paper and squeezed him, rolling him around in a massive paw.

George didn't speak, put the phone down, his face gray like the sky in a prelude to rain, and looked at Jack. His voice sounded as if he had been gripped by the throat. "Danny's dead."

* * *

Jack paced in George's living room as he phoned Stella and told her the news.

He heard Stella take a breath. "That's terrible. What happened?"

"He was at Mavericks."

Stella interrupted. "We spoke about how dangerous that place is. Did he drown?"

"No. Mavericks was massive that day, so he went to have a look.

He was walking through the car park, and he saw a guy carjacking a woman's car. Danny went to help. The guy shot Danny in the heart. The cops told George some witnesses saw the guy get in the passenger seat with the gun to the woman's head and drive away. They are still looking for the guy, the woman, and the car."

"George must be heartbroken."

"It's hard for me to describe how he transformed right before my eyes. It was like he shriveled up. It was horrific. It was sad."

"Where's George now?"

"At his house. I'm here with him. I took him to the morgue and waited while he spent time with Danny. He was like a zombie. There was no one else around to look after him, so I drove him home. He's outside in Danny's cottage. He hasn't spoken."

"What are you going to do now?"

"I can't leave him in his present state. I'll wait until he comes back in and take it from there."

"All right. Please give George my condolences. I'll speak to him when he's ready to take calls. By the way, what did your report show?"

"In the main, nothing that they can't tidy up. Someone is regularly hacking into their system. I was about to tell George about this when he got the call about Danny. My laptop's in my truck. While I wait for George, I'll try to find out who it is."

"If you need any help, you know who to call."

"I do."

"So, I'll see you when I see you."

"I'll keep you posted."

Jack returned to his truck, collected his laptop, used his phone as a hotspot, and logged into Carlton Engineering. He turned towards the back door as he heard a noise. George walked in, his shoulders back and straight, the effort of it etched on his face.

He walked over to Jack, who had stood as George approached.

George went to the window and looked across the lawn for six minutes. Jack waited. George kept staring outside as he spoke. "I used to worry, Jack, because as I got older, my days seemed to be getting shorter and shorter, giving me less time for my work and less time with Danny. Like each day was pressing on the next one. Now with Danny..." George choked on a sob, his breathing audible as he regained his composure. "...gone." The word said out loud seemed to hit him like a hammer, as if saying it out loud made it more real. "Even looking at where Danny played as a boy, the minutes already feel longer." George turned to Jack, wiping the tears from his face.

"There will be no point to these longer days. What do I do? Wait for what? To die?" Jack raised a hand to interject. George smiled at Jack like an indulgent parent. "Don't worry, Jack, I'm not considering suicide. I am in good health, and it will seem like a long time before my time is up and I get to join my wife and Danny." George went back to peering out the window. "He always had questions I was not able to answer." George looked at Jack, then his gaze returned to the lawn. "Once, we went to the pound, and he selected a dog." George made a thin-lipped smile. "The dog was already six years old. No one wanted him because he was big and he was ugly. Danny insisted on calling him Pickles. Where that name came from, I don't know. One day, Pickles was sleeping and dreaming. His legs were moving as if he were running, and he was muttering. Danny asked me if dogs can dream, and whether that proves they must have souls. I told him that I was sure it did. He then lay down on the lawn next to Pickles and closed his eyes."

George paused, controlling his emotions, although Jack remained quiet, believing George should abandon control for now.

"How could anyone truthfully know the answer to that question?"

George walked over to a liquor cabinet, pulled tissues from a box, wiped his eyes, shoved the tissues in his pocket, and picked up a bottle of Lagavulin, of which Jack approved as he did most of the whiskies made on the Isle of Islay with their distinctive smoky peat taste.

"Do you drink Scotch whisky, Jack?"

"I do."

"Two fingers, neat?"

"Yes, please."

George poured the whisky by eye into two crystal glasses and passed one to Jack.

"To Danny," said George.

"To Danny," said Jack as they clinked glasses. Jack thought people would repeat this toast many times in the coming days.

"How well do you know Stella West?"

Jack didn't want to go into detail. "Very well. Why do you ask?"

"Can you tell her I want to sell Carlton Engineering to her?"

CHAPTER NINE

Once a month, on a Saturday, Kenny ran a class that covered advanced MMA techniques. Today was one of those Saturdays. It was by invitation only. That meant you had to attend. Freddie jogged with Jack as they returned to their apartment block.

"It's probably outside your jurisdiction, Freddie, but do you know if the police have found the carjacker who killed that surfer at Mavericks?"

Freddie snapped his head around to Jack. "What do you know about that?"

"Chill, Freddie. Why are you so tense? I was with George Carlton, Danny's father, when the police phoned him about his son's death."

"You're talking about Danny Carlton?"

"Yes."

Freddie half-closed one eye as if this would help him understand. "But the father lives in Palo Alto. What were you doing there?"

"I do work outside San Francisco, you know. Sometimes, I even leave the country for my work. My life is not all about doing pro-bono work for your department."

"Did you ever meet Danny Carlton?"

"Yes. A nice guy. He seemed decent in the old-fashioned use of that word. It was through him that I wound up doing the assignment at Carlton Engineering." Stella's involvement not to be mentioned, Jack put his hand on Freddie's shoulder and pulled him from a jog to a walk. "What's going on, Freddie? George's impression is that Danny got caught up in a carjacking that went wrong. Why is this in your domain?"

"Sorry for being snappy, Jack, but this case has certain characteristics we've seen over the last year."

Jack's attention picked up like a gundog on the scent. The curiosity bug had bitten him, and in Jack's case, it didn't have to bite too hard. "Like what?"

"You realize that whatever I tell you now falls under the Non-Disclosure Agreement you signed."

One's view of what constitutes disclosure depends on what is in the public domain, yet who is this public, and what is the domain? Upon this premise, Jack could tell Stella when he sensed it was in the public good, but he didn't disclose this to Freddie. A dichotomy with which he could be comfortable. "Of course."

They arrived back at their apartment block and walked up the stairs. "Maybe," said Freddie, "you can help my team analyze the data we have so far. You were going to come in and help with the scam on Ted Clark's insurance policy."

"More pro-bono work, Freddie, but yes, I'll help. I'll come in today."

Freddie opened his apartment door. "Coffee?"

"Yes, please. So tell me what I don't know about the Danny Carlton case."

* * *

Freddie put the coffee mugs on the four-seater table. Freddie's apartment was a replica of his office with a queen-sized bed. "Witnesses," said Freddie, "identified the vehicle used in the carjacking as a white Toyota Corolla. It was a rental, paid for with a credit card, with just enough money for a one-day hire. The cardholder's details are bogus, as is the copy of the driver's license provided to the rental company. Shortly after arriving at the parking lot, someone disconnected the GPS tracker in the car. It's like they only wanted it to track them up to the point of the carjacking, then to come off the radar."

Freddie took a mouthful of coffee, and Jack did the same.

"They drove the car back to the Tenderloin and parked it on the side of the road with the keys in the ignition, the doors unlocked, and the windows down. Predictably, it got stolen, and the police pulled it over for speeding. Apparently, the driver was acting odd. I don't have the details, but there was sufficient cause to phone in the car's details. As a result of the feedback, they arrested the driver and impounded the car."

Jack frowned. "What was the driver going to do with the car?"

"He's known to us. Works for Ragnall Restorations, which is also known to us. The owner has links to chop shops. That's probably where she told the driver to take it."

"She?"

"Freya Ragnall."

"At the risk of sounding sexist, isn't that unusual? A woman taking cars to chop shops?"

"It is, but Freya grew up doing it. Her father did it, and she's been doing it since she learned to drive. She doesn't do the driving herself anymore. One of her staff does that. We wouldn't have caught him if he'd just driven quietly to the chop shop and walked away. The chop shop guys would have turned the car into a heap of parts within a few hours and would have sold them while dismantling."

"What did the driver have to say?"

"The report said he saw the car standing at the side of the road, looked in the glove box, saw it was a rental, and phoned the rental company, who said they would pay him fifty dollars if he delivered the car back to them. There is a phone call to the rental company on his cell phone, but no one at the rental company recalls taking such a call. The rental company's office, which he phoned, is at San Francisco International Airport. It takes a lot of calls. That's not enough to make a case in court. Ragnall's lawyer escorted the driver from the holding cells."

"Anything else of interest on his phone?"

"Nothing, except a call from a burner phone, which lasted less than two minutes."

"Any idea where he was taking the car?"

"Most chop shops are backyard operators, hot rod builders, and small car repair shops. There's a whole underground supply chain. She would have known which chop shop would be interested in that particular car."

"Sounds knowledgeable."

"She is. She took over the garage from her father when he became ill. It specializes in restoring classic cars to their original condition. Maybe you should meet her, Jack, and see what you can find out."

"If it helps find Danny's killer, I'm in. Text me the details later." Jack laughed. "My ten-year-old Yukon Denali could do with some work. The perfect cover."

"She deals in classic vehicles. There's a difference between a classic truck and a truck that's simply old."

"Point taken. I'll plead ignorance when I get there. What can you tell me about her besides the very Irish name?"

"Both names are Irish versions of Viking names."

"Have you found the woman who was supposedly being carjacked?"

"No. And from witnesses, we have very sketchy descriptions of her and the gunman. What the witnesses told us is that the woman had been sitting in the car for some time, and they'd seen the gunman loitering around the parking lot, as if he was waiting for someone. When Danny arrived, the gunman made his move. Danny had arrived with another guy, but only Danny got involved when the carjacking took place."

"The guy who was with Danny, what has he had to say?"

"He's vanished."

"Do you have a sketch of him?"

"Yes, but like the others, the reliability is questionable. We think Danny must have come to Mavericks with this guy, as Danny's car was not in the parking lot."

"So you don't think this is all a coincidence?"

"If it was just a one-off, I would probably have said it was just a matter of someone being in the wrong place at the wrong time. It happens."

"But?"

"There have been others reported with similar characteristics."

"If you are saying that this is a murder, not a coincidence, it's a very complicated way to go about it."

Freddie gave Jack a look as hard as winter ground. "Not if you didn't want it to look like a murder."

CHAPTER TEN

The morning spent with Freddie's team was as frustrating as standing in a long, unmoving queue. Access to the hospital database was pending the submission of proper paperwork to the hospital, which justified the police's "need to know" over patient confidentiality. The data on Freya Ragnall was also minimal. No criminal record, not even a speeding ticket. Not even a social media presence. Time to see the lioness in her lair. The website said Ragnall Restoration was open on Saturdays. He phoned to check. It was open all day.

It took twenty minutes to get to Bryant Street, which was not bad considering the traffic. The Ragnall Restoration building had its signage in block black letters. It was difficult to tell if the walls had changed into what now looked like a pale attempt at camouflage using a caramel pastel shade, or if someone had chosen this color for a reason known only to themselves. Jack found a parking spot between a 1969 canary-yellow Camaro and a 1972 dark-blue Pontiac Firebird TransAm. Both looked like they were fresh from the showroom floor. Both were in their original condition.

The entrance was a roller door big enough for a Mack truck to drive through. Inside was petrol-head heaven with several classic cars in various stages of restoration. Classical music was emanating from hidden speakers, filling the air. Aunt Louise had instilled an interest, not necessarily a love, of classical music. When he heard classical music, he couldn't always remember the composer's name or the piece's title. However, the iconic opening notes of Beethoven's Symphony No. 5 were instantly recognizable. At the risk of appearing to assign stereotypes, Jack was expecting something more rock and roll or country and western. Also, the volume was such that Beethoven provided a powerful, motivating backdrop to keep everyone focused, and you could have a conversation without shouting.

"I'm looking for Freya Ragnall," said Jack to the mid-fifties man in dark-blue overalls and a cap with a logo for the San Francisco 49ers.

The man pointed. "She's in the back."

Jack walked across the green-painted concrete flooring, edging between the cars and the mechanics until he got to the back, where a middle-aged blonde woman was talking to a twenty-something guy, both wearing dark-blue overalls, standing in front of a red Plymouth Barracuda with the hood up.

Jack could hear her talking, but not what she was saying. The guy would listen and respond with, "Yes, Ma'am," like she was a quietly spoken drill sergeant. When they noticed his presence, they stopped talking and turned to Jack.

"May I help you?" said the woman, who seemed to take Jack in with a glance, like some human MRI who was not pleased with what she saw.

"Are you Freya Ragnall?"

"Ha," said the woman with a noise that sounded like a crow. "Over there, buddy. See the red truck?"

"Thanks." Jack walked over to what turned out to be a first-generation F-series Ford. The engine was rumbling, and a woman with a ponytail was behind the wheel. "Freya Ragnall."

She turned to Jack with a smile that would have launched a thousand F-series Fords, but it didn't reach her eyes. "Yes. May I help you?"

"I have a truck I'd like to get back to its original condition. Like you've done with this truck. It's a first generation, right?"

"Correct, 1949, this one."

Freya exited the truck, the door closing with a solid clunk. She was also wearing blue overalls that covered her figure. He guessed she was around five feet ten inches tall. Her hair appeared undecided whether it was blonde or platinum. Her face was symmetrical, the softness of her cheeks emphasizing her high cheekbones. Jack couldn't determine whether her eyes were blue or gray.

"What can I do for you?"

"I have a ten-year-old Yukon Denali that I bought from my uncle. It came off his ranch in Texas, where maintenance means getting it back on the road as soon as possible, with whatever it takes."

"Where's the truck?"

"Outside?"

Freya looked at her watch. "I'm trying to get out of here to go for a run." She seemed to do some calculations or considerations in her head, then looked at Jack. "Bring it in, and let's put it up on a hoist."

Jack followed her as she walked to the middle-aged woman. "Sandra, I need that hoist at the front. That Chevelle that's on it can go outside for now."

Sandra didn't speak, but went to the hoist, lowered the Chevelle, and drove it outside, making the tiniest squeaks like a mouse as the oversized rear tires took traction on the green floor. Jack navigated the Denali onto the hoist. Freya got inside, looked around, started the engine, lifted the hood, looked and listened, turned off the engine, got out, and smacked the hoist button. She watched it rise until she had enough head clearance to walk underneath.

She turned to Jack. "There's nothing wrong with the maintenance except where they've gone cheap and not used genuine parts, like the fuel pump, but under here, where they didn't repair, it still does the job."

She signaled Jack to come under the vehicle, which Jack did. Up close, Freya smelled like freshly washed sheets. Maybe they were new overalls, but there was a hint of jasmine. She pointed to the rear of the exhaust system.

"Looks like someone drove over a stump or a big rock. See the bend in the pipe."

Jack knew about the bend in the pipe. It happened when he and Freddie took the Denali out to check on some steers, as instructed by Uncle Alan. They had taken the Denali cross-country and went over a stump that was hiding in the grass. "I do."

"Haven't you noticed the noise?"

The exhaust noise sounded different after the stump episode, and it was not long after that incident that Jack expressed a desire to buy the Denali. "It's always sounded like that. I thought that's what it was supposed to sound like."

Freya looked at him. Jack could see her shaking her head inside her mind, but her face was still like a marble sculpture; her eyes now looked grayer than blue. "I can give you an estimate to bring it back to its original condition, and you can think about it."

"Sounds good."

Freya called out to Sandra, indicating with her head. "Let's go to my office."

As they walked, Freya didn't offer any conversation.

"Ragnall is an Irish name, isn't it?"

"Yes and no. It's a contraction of a Viking name, dating back to when the Vikings decided to spend a few years visiting Ireland."

Jack glanced at Freya's profile.

Sandra sat behind the desk as Freya outlined the tasks and their associated prices. She did this while pulling off her safety boots and heavy-duty socks, unbuttoning her overalls, and letting them fall to the floor, revealing her blue running shorts, a yellow tank top, and a midriff that looked like it was on its way to having a six-pack. As she put on ankle-high socks and running shoes, Jack guessed her to be one hundred and thirty pounds. Judging by the muscles on her arms and legs, this was no skinny marathon runner. This was like watching a Viking shield maiden.

Sandra tore off the page, handed it to Jack, and left the office. Jack looked at the estimate. It wasn't cheap. "How do I pay you? Cash or card?"

"We can talk about that another time. I have to get going for my run."

"Where do you run?" He kept his tone conversational so she wouldn't feel threatened by his question. A wise woman was wary of strange men, and Freya seemed to understand that.

"Today, I'm going to Golden Gate Park. Last week, it was The Presidio." Freya looked up from tying her shoelaces. "As soon as I'm bored with a place, I move on."

Did her reasoning only work with places or people as well?

* * *

Jack had been at the desk in his apartment all afternoon. He had phoned Marie to see how she was doing. She'd said she was doing fine, but her voice sounded sad, which was understandable, so Jack invited himself over. He wasn't sure how his presence would help, but he knew it was his way of dealing with the guilt still consuming him. Even though no one blamed Jack for Ted's death, the guilt was on him, like barnacles on a boat. His focus was unfettered as he worked on his laptop.

Discovering if the hospital's system had been hacked was Jack's aim. He was not overly concerned about patient confidentiality, as he would send any data he had to his electronic trash can. In his software toolbox, he has standard products, his developments, and some unique pieces of software given to him by Stella. It was one thing to get into the hospital system, but finding any hidden code was another story. He assumed someone was collecting data on hospital deaths and sending it elsewhere. He had to find the code that was doing this. To do this, he had to track backward.

He had runtime monitoring in place to see what the hospital system was sending. A deluge of data was part of the hospital's ordinary operations. In searching the database, there was a table specifically to record a death linked to the patient's profile. It was clear that the documentation of a death in a hospital was a regular event occurring at random intervals. Jack wrote code that monitored the table for the creation of a new record. When someone created a new record, his runtime monitor kicked in, recording all instances of where the information had been sent. His code would ping his phone when this happened and store the destination result in his search history.

When it was all in place, Jack stood to make coffee and felt as uncomfortable as having a rash in the middle of a heatwave as he waited for someone in the hospital to die. At that point, that person would soon become well-known to Jack.

Jack put his coffee on the desk and looked around his apartment. He had designed the layout and acquired the furniture, making it resemble any of the world's four-star hotels, which invariably was where customers placed him. So, no matter where he was, it felt like home. Well, at least a reasonable facsimile. Some tidying up and housework would keep his mind off his ghoulish endeavor.

He took a basket of clothes downstairs to the laundry in the basement and was putting them in the machine when his phone pinged like a pinball machine. Then it stopped. Jack started the washing machine and went upstairs.

The deceased, Peter Bain, had died from a myocardial infarction. A heart attack. He was forty-six years of age at the time of death. The link to his profile listed his address, his occupation as a lawyer, and his next of kin, his wife, Evelyn. One by one, Jack checked on the recipients of the data. As expected, this information has gone to several government departments. Jack was looking for something that looked out of place, like someone playing the wrong chord on a guitar in a well-remembered song.

He found four that looked questionable, parked them to one side, and kept working through the rest. When he had completed the list, he went back to the four. Upon digging deeper, three were government agencies with unusual names, but were legitimate. The fourth one used the Tor network. The open-source network enabled anonymous communication by routing internet traffic through a network of volunteer-operated servers. Each of these relays encrypted the data. Multiple encryptions of the same data. Getting to the raw data was like peeling the layers of an onion. Hence, it was called The Onion Router. He'd need help with that.

CHAPTER ELEVEN

Jack recognized Freddie's white F-150 truck standing in Marie's driveway. Like Jack's Denali, it also came from Uncle Alan's ranch in Texas. Jack parked on the street in case Freddie needed to leave before him. It turned out to be a good decision, for as he got to the door, Judy came out, holding Freddie's arm. Marie stood in the doorway.

"Hello, Jack," said Marie.

"Oh, Jack," said Judy, who turned to Jack's voice, reaching for him with her free arm.

Freddie's eyes flashed a warning to Jack like a semaphore, making Jack engage in an awkward hug with Judy.

"Freddie and I are off to a restaurant he's been telling me about."

"Great," said Jack. "Well, enjoy."

Jack stood with Marie while Freddie guided Judy into his truck, and they drove away.

"Come inside, Jack. If you're hungry, I've got a leftover black bean and chipotle pizza from last night."

"Sounds great to me."

While Marie microwaved pizza slices and made coffee, Jack felt guilt coursing through him like a relentless river, its icy currents chilling him to the bone. It surged and swirled within him, an unyielding force that eroded his peace and left him adrift in a sea of remorse. Ted should be the one in the kitchen sharing pizza with Marie.

Jack's mind wandered back to the events that had led to this moment. He could still hear Ted's laughter, see his easy smile, and feel the camaraderie that had once bound them together. Then he remembered Ted stepping in front of him, the loud *bang* of the gun, catching Ted as he fell back, leaving Marie and Judy to pick up the pieces of their lives.

Marie turned from the microwave, her eyes meeting Jack's. She offered a smile that barely showed on her face, which didn't conceal her sadness and only deepened the guilt that clung to him like a cloak.

"Jack, are you okay?" Marie's voice was soft, filled with concern.

Jack's eyes filled with tears. "I didn't mean for it to happen. I let him down. I let you both down. And Judy."

Marie crossed the room, wrapping her arms around Jack. "No, you haven't. You just happened to be there. Ted had been undertaking high-risk activities. On his record, he looked fantastic, but that was not what he wanted. I talked to him about it, and Ted said he was just doing his job. In the end, it was the job he loved that killed him. Sending him into a depression he couldn't get out of. The morning training sessions with Kenny were helpful, but they still weren't enough. I'm grateful to Freddie for documenting it as he did. Let's sit."

Jack sat while Marie put the pizza and coffee on the table and joined him. "I came here with a vague thought to comfort you, but now the roles have been reversed."

"I've done my fair share of comforting cops' wives over the years, and as I said, it's not like this was unexpected. It sounds terrible, but it's almost a relief because I knew he was looking for the opportunity each time he walked out the door, despite what he said to me."

"How's Judy coping?"

"Not well. Freddie's been fantastic with her."

How much was Freddie comforting Judy, and how much did he find her attractive, though? Probably a bit of both.

"We'll get through this, Jack."

Marie patted Jack's hand. "It'll be a team effort."

Sometimes, changing the topic is better to get oneself back onto less emotional ground.

"Have any more bogus insurance people contacted you?"

Marie laughed. It was good to hear her laugh. "Not since you spilled coffee in the last one's lap and broke his tablet. Maybe the word got out about you."

Jack smiled without showing his teeth. Laughing right now would be like retrieving a sunken ship from the ocean floor. He bit into the spicy and smoky-tasting pizza. He chewed the requisite number of times, as Aunt Louise had reinforced it as a habit for him and Freddie, particularly when in company, then swallowed before speaking.

"Is there anything I can help you with?"

Marie finished sipping her coffee and held the cup in two hands. "What do you know about cars?"

"Well, I like driving them."

"Ted's sanctuary was his garage, where he tinkered with old cars." Marie smiled at a memory with her eyes. "That was our private joke. I called them old cars. He called them classics. The latest one he was working on is in the garage."

"What is it?"

"It's a 1964 Ford Mustang convertible in Wimbledon White, the year they first made the Mustang."

"You're very knowledgeable. Did you also do tinkering?"

"Not at all. I was just a good listener. Would you like to see it?"

"I'd love to."

"Bring your coffee."

Marie pulled a key from a hook at the back door, and Jack followed her across a thirty-foot strip of grass to a brick shed two stories high and two garage doors wide. The key snapped the lock on the metal door open. Inside was room for four cars, and in one corner was a hoist on which rested the Mustang's chassis with a steering wheel but without wheels.

Marie moved her arm in an arc like a ballerina to take in the whole shed. There was only one vehicle. The Mustang's motor was on a pallet. Its doors rested against the bench. The bumper bars were missing. On the bench was a clutch kit. Jack gazed at all the tools, neatly attached to their correct positions on the wall.

"Ted never got much past this stage, as he continuously decided some parts were not in good enough condition and would order new parts. They had to be original."

"Understood. Car enthusiasts can be very particular."

"I'm not explaining myself properly. Ted never intended to finish this car. This was his safe place. I think he feared completing it."

"Did you help?"

"You're kidding. I know next to nothing about cars." Marie pointed at a tired-looking three-seater leather couch with a side table. "I sat over there with a glass of wine and a book and waited for him to talk."

"What do you want to do with the Mustang?"

"I'd like to get it finished."

"Then what?"

"I'd keep it. Maybe drive it on a sunny day. But first, I must find someone who can complete the build as Ted would have liked, at a reasonable price."

"I'll take some photos, and let's see what I can find."

Jack left Marie's home and dialed as he walked to his truck. Stella answered in three rings.

"Hello, Jack. Are you free to come to my place?"

"Well, that answers why I phoned you. I have two things for you, which I'd rather not talk about on the phone."

* * *

"What are the two things you want to chat about?" said Stella.

"Freddie's team is treating Danny Carlton's death as a murder case."

"The press is circulating a story that Danny was just a good guy coming to the rescue."

"Freddie wants it like that so they can continue their investigation without alerting the perpetrators."

"What are Freddie and his team doing?"

"They are doing their best as they work within their constraints."

"And what have you been doing?"

Jack smiled. "Am I that predictable?"

"When something is bugging you. So, what have you done?"

Jack explained the car used in the hijacking, how Freya Ragnall had arranged for the vehicle to be collected and disposed of, and how the police had picked up the driver. And how he had taken the Denali for a quote.

"How much is the quote?"

Jack passed the quote to Stella. "Nine thousand dollars. What's the Denali worth?"

"About seventeen thousand dollars. As the quote points out, there is a lot of work to do to get it back to its original condition."

"Are you going to do it?"

"No. She's not that interested in doing it anyway. Even though she gave me a quote, she said there are other people better suited to take on work on a Denali."

"So now what?"

"Look at these photos."

Jack held his phone next to Stella and scrolled through the pictures. "What are you asking me to do, Jack? Identify it."

"No need, I know what it is. It's a 1964 Mustang. This was what Ted Clark worked on. Marie wants it completed."

Stella frowned at Jack. "You want to get Freya Ragnall to do the work? Isn't that putting Marie at risk? This Freya Ragnall is a criminal."

"She clearly runs a legitimate business that does good quality work as a front for her criminal activities. And yes, I must get Marie's agreement before doing this. She might like the idea of Ted's Mustang being used to catch a crook. But I wanted to tell you about it before I went any further."

"I take it this won't involve anyone at SFPD."

"Definitely not. After some convincing, Freddie might go for a sting operation, but the paperwork and approvals will take ages. This way, I might have a chance to find Danny's killer. Then I can involve Freddie."

Stella pursed her lips. "You'll be careful, right?"

"Of course."

"What was the other thing you wanted to talk about?"

"Have you ever cracked a Tor network?"

Stella smiled. "Once before, just to see if I could."

"Just for fun?"

"Just for the challenge."

"As one does."

"As one does. Who is this for?"

"I'm hoping to track down the guys who did the attempted insurance scam on Marie."

"What have you achieved so far?"

Jack told Stella about his efforts to date and waited for her response. "You'll have to help me. As you know, a Tor network involves many relays and many encryptions along the way."

"Glad to help."

Stella's face brightened up like a sunrise punching through smog. "I've also got some news."

"What?"

"George Carlton is in San Francisco."

"Why?"

"George called me yesterday to follow up on his wish to sell his company to me. He said that the SFPD had asked him to come to San Francisco as they had further information about Danny's death, which they wanted to discuss face-to-face. He arrived from Palo Alto this morning and met with Sergeant Kenny Braithwaite, who told him they were treating Danny's death as a murder case, and they had questions about who or why someone would do this. Then he phoned me and told me. He is devastated. I have invited him here." Stella looked at her watch. "He should be here in about twenty minutes. While we wait for him, let's have a look at that Tor network you want to crack." Stella's eyes sparkled like sunlight on snow crystals, and she smiled. "I haven't had a proper challenge for a while."

They adjourned to Stella's workspace, where they spoke as Stella's fingers danced across the keyboards until the doorbell made its mute sound like an oversized Tibetan gong. A single frequency permeated the house like smoke. Outside, all one heard was a buzzing sound. Stella looked at Jack. "That'll be George. We didn't get very far with cracking this Tor, but I didn't expect to. I'll bring George through to the living room."

* * *

Jack waited in the living room as Stella brought George through. He seemed to have shrunk. His posture was no longer upright, and he had dark rings under his puffy eyes. They sat, and George told them what Kenny had said. When he finished, he looked back and forth from Stella to Jack and frowned. "You two are not surprised at this news."

Stella looked at Jack, then back at George. "Jack can explain, but what he tells you must stay in this room. Are you comfortable with that?"

George swallowed and waited for one second. "Absolutely."

"George," said Jack. "Occasionally, I assist the unit Sergeant Braithwaite is in with hacking and data analysis advice. Not unlike what I did for your firm. The guy who runs the unit, to whom Sergeant Braithwaite reports, is my cousin. He has taken an interest in this case because it shares similarities with other cases. Unfortunately, they get hamstrung by their own creation, the law, and the policies and procedures they have to follow."

"But you, Jack," said George, "are not encumbered by such things."

Jack didn't reply, as the statement was rhetorical.

George looked at Jack. "I will pay you to find Danny's killer."

"That won't be necessary, as I'd planned to help my cousin anyway."

"At least let me pay for any expenses. And I will read your report on my business." George looked at Stella. "You should also read it. That's if you are still interested in acquiring my company."

"I am still interested, but let's not rush. I want you as a partner, not as an employee."

George nodded. "Understood." George turned his attention to Jack. "Did Danny mention that other people were interested in acquiring my company?"

"He did."

"Maybe you should have a look at one of them."

"Why?"

"They remade contact just before the police made Danny's death public."

"Coincidence?" said Stella.

"It probably is. But earlier, I'd said I was not interested, and I did again. Quite persistent this time, bordering on rudeness, so I cut the conversation short."

"Who are they?" said Stella. "Maybe I've heard of them and can comment."

"The firm is called VT Equity. The individual who has been phoning is Victor Thornfield. It's his firm."

Stella shrugged. "Never heard of him. What do you know about him, George?"

"I know a little bit about him. Not a lot. I've met him. He talks like he has money, and from what Danny said …" George's eyes welled up. He coughed twice with his hand over his mouth. "You must excuse me."

Stella gave George a hug. "It's all right, George. Take your time."

George blinked and gave Stella a thin-lipped smile. "Danny found out that he has money based on the acquisitions he has made to date. However, all the companies purchased were asset-stripped and sold off in pieces until they no longer existed. He seems to know his way around, letting all the competitors in the acquisition know what he now has, and it becomes almost like an auction. The whole process is relatively quick. My company, what I've created, would vanish in six months or less. He is very keen to do a deal. Pushy."

"What if the company has intellectual property like yours?"

"Same process. Sells it to the highest bidder."

"Is this Victor Thornfield running a profitable business? I mean, is the sale of the stripped assets greater than what he purchased for the whole business?"

"I can't comment. Danny did all the research. I can give you his computer. All the information he collected is on it."

"When did Thornfield first approach you?"

"Over the years, there have been overtures from competitors to buy my company, but I've politely refused them. However, it gave me a good feeling that other people saw sufficient value in the business to make me an offer. The case with Thornfield was different in the timing, as his initial contact came about a week after I first got my Alzheimer's results. It seemed rather fortuitous, perhaps divine intervention, or the universe telling me something. I took the time to meet with Victor. Danny attended these meetings but didn't participate. Just sat and listened. At the end of the first meeting, after Thornfield had left, Danny told me he didn't trust him. There was something about him that he felt was off. No evidence. Just his gut feeling. But Danny's feelings about people were always good. So I took note of what he said." George smiled with his eyes at Stella. "Danny's gut feeling about you was what brought us here today."

"Where did you have your tests done, George?" said Stella.

"At the hospital. There are resident neurologists and geriatricians there."

"When did you last hear from Thornfield?" said Jack.

"He called to offer his condolences and to see if we could do business. Again, it seemed like an opportunity as I was not being fair to the business." George paused. "When I started the business, my father gave me some advice. Negotiate when you have a strong position, and when you have a weak position, litigate. It sounds counterintuitive. However, he argued that when you have a strong position, you should aim to resolve disputes through negotiation and find a mutually beneficial solution. When your position is weak, litigation might be a strategic move to protect your interests or achieve a fair outcome. Right now, all things considered, I do not know if I am in a strong or a weak position, but I gave myself time to consider Danny's view of Victor and you, Stella." George spread his arms wide. "And here I am."

"You will always be welcome here, George," said Stella. "It's a pity that we are getting to know each other under such sad circumstances."

"I agree, Stella. I have taken up enough of your time. We shall meet again, I'm sure."

George shook hands with Jack, and Stella escorted George to the door. When she returned, she kept walking. "Let's continue having a look at that Tor. It's got my interest."

They sat back at Stella's terminal. "What now?" said Jack.

Stella clapped her hands together in front of her face like she was praying. "Let's recap on what we know." Jack waited. "The traffic is routed through a series of volunteer-operated servers, or nodes, as they like to call them. There may be a weakness where someone has incorrectly configured that node. Suppose I can control or monitor a significant number of nodes by finding the entry and exit nodes. In that case, I can give you the data. Then you can perform traffic correlation, and I can use that to do an attack. With any luck, the users will no longer be anonymous. They call it de-anonymization. Can you believe that's a word?"

"I like the word. It says it better than a sentence."

Stella's face shifted gears, from intrigued to deadly. "I'm going to do some digging on this Victor Thornfield character."

"That would be worthwhile. The way George explained his dealings with him, it's unclear whether Thornfield is overly keen on doing his job or if there is something else at play. It sounded a bit off, didn't it? Anyway, I know when you like to work alone, so I'm off to see Marie."

"Will I see you later?"

Jack took Stella's head in his hands and kissed her mouth. "That's why I'm going to get a change of clothes from my apartment before seeing Marie."

CHAPTER TWELVE

Jack walked along the hallway to his apartment, sweat still clinging to him from Monday morning's training session with Kenny. A great way to start the week. Because of Kenny's expectations, the surprise of Freddie's absence from training hung over him. He reached for his keys, ready to unlock his door, but paused as Freddie's door opened.

Freddie stepped out with Judy on his arm, her fingers lightly gripping his elbow. A suitcase followed them, its wheels softly scraping the floor. Jack stared, surprised by their sudden appearance.

"Hello, Judy. Hello Freddie," Jack said, his voice steady but his curiosity undeniable.

Judy turned her head toward his voice, her lips curving into a smile. "Hello, Jack. Freddie told me you lived next door."

"That's right," Jack said, nodding reflexively. "Just like when we were kids."

Freddie acknowledged Jack with a curt nod. "Jack."

For a moment, the three of them stood in awkward silence, the weight of unspoken thoughts hanging in the air. Jack's gaze fell on the suitcase by Freddie's side. Freddie didn't volunteer an explanation, and Jack didn't ask.

Freddie broke the silence first. He glanced at his watch. "We need to get going, Judy."

Judy adjusted her grip on Freddie's arm, her head tilting slightly toward Jack as she spoke.

"Bye, Jack."

"Bye, Judy, bye, Freddie."

Freddie didn't reply immediately. His expression guarded as he guided Judy down the hallway. Finally, he said, "See you around."

Jack watched them walk away, Judy's cane lightly tapping the floor as the suitcase wheels clicked softly in rhythm. When they disappeared around the corner, Jack turned back to his door, unlocking it with a sharp twist. He stepped inside, letting the door click shut behind him.

The apartment greeted him with its usual mix of order and chaos. It wasn't tidy enough to appease Aunt Louise, who would undoubtedly feel compelled to organize his life. Still, it wasn't messy enough for Uncle Alan to notice anything out of place. Jack dropped his bag onto the couch and sat down heavily. His thoughts refused to settle.

Freddie had been tight-lipped about Judy. Was it serious? Was Freddie finally letting someone in? He doubted he'd get answers. Freddie had always guarded his secrets, even when they were kids.

Jack rubbed his temples, remembering the last time Freddie poked his nose into his private life. "You and Stella seem close," Freddie had said once. Implication had laced his tone. Jack had waved him off, refusing to entertain the suggestion. Freddie was constantly probing, always pushing boundaries without revealing anything of his own. Maybe that's why he became a lawyer and then found a home in the SPFD, running his "unnamed" unit.

Jack exhaled and leaned back. He wouldn't press Freddie about Judy. Not today. Whatever Freddie was hiding would eventually come to light. It always did.

* * *

Jack had picked up two Bahn Mi sandwiches from a Vietnamese restaurant and put them on the kitchen table. He'd purchased one chicken and one pork as he didn't know Marie's preference. Marie placed two mugs of coffee on the table.

"I've found a place that can put Ted's Mustang back together. It's called Ragnall Restorations. However, I have a reason for suggesting this particular place."

"Go on."

"Did you read about an attempted hijacking at the parking lot at Maverick's?"

"I heard or read something about it. The story didn't make sense, and I had other things on my mind, so I really didn't pay much attention. Why do you ask?"

"Freddie and his team are treating it as murder."

"Lots of murders in San Francisco. That's what I know was wearing Ted down into a state of depression. He saw just one too many. But carry on. I interrupted."

"That's all right. Ragnall Restorations runs two businesses. The restoration of classic cars, which she inherited from her father."

"She?"

"Freya Ragnall. She doesn't just manage the place. She is actively involved."

"You've been there? To see if they would do a good job on Ted's car?"

"That thought came later. The other business that Freya Ragnall operates is the disposal of vehicles to chop shops. The car used in the supposed hijacking was en route to Ragnall Restoration when, because of the driver's poor judgment, the police pulled him over. He revealed the car's intended destination. Someone had contacted Freya Ragnall to arrange the disposal of the car. That person could be the person who killed Danny, or will lead to the person who organized it, or did it. I tried to get closer to her by saying I wanted to get my Denali restored." Marie raised her eyebrows. "I know, I know, but it was worth a try. She gave me a quote but said other places would be more interested in doing the work."

"And as I've said, I wanted to get Ted's Mustang restored. You thought you could solve two problems with one action."

"It sounds opportunistic. And it is."

"I know, and I'm on board with the idea."

Jack paused as he was unsure how Marie would feel about his idea, but he was not expecting such a quick agreement.

"There is a risk that you could be in harm's way as, let's be clear, Freya Ragnall is a crook."

"Ted would have liked the idea of his Mustang being used to catch a crook." Marie unwrapped her Bahn Mi. "When and how do we start?"

Jack sipped his coffee. "I will visit her with the photos, then she'll probably want to come around and see for herself."

"Bring her. I'd like to see a crook up close." Marie took a bite of her Bahn Mi, chewed, swallowed, took a sip from her mug, and gave Jack a look as wistful as an echo. "Judy and Freddie are spending a lot of time together. I wonder if that would have surprised Ted?"

* * *

Jack leaned against the edge of the desk, watching Stella as she worked. He asked her about her progress with the Tor. Her fingers guided the mouse, and her focus was on unraveling it, so he moved to another topic.

"Marie isn't just willing to use Ted's Mustang to get closer to Freya Ragnall," said Jack. "She wants to do it."

Stella didn't look up, her eyes fixed on the screen. "That's good of her."

"It's more than that," Jack said. "It's like she's making sure Ted's legacy doesn't fade away as if it were of no consequence."

Stella paused, her left hand reaching up to rub the back of her neck. "Is she comfortable being that close to criminals?"

Jack tilted his head, considering her question. "She welcomes it."

Stella let out a small sigh, her fingers stilling on the mouse. She rolled her neck, trying to ease the tension that had built up, then looked at the watch. "It's two o'clock already."

Jack stepped behind her without a word, his hands finding her shoulders. He kneaded the tight muscles in her neck and trapezius, his thumbs pressing into the knots he found there.

Stella let her hands fall away from the mouse, her head lowering slightly. "That's good," she murmured. "You can press harder."

Jack obliged, his hands working with more pressure. Stella made a sound somewhere between relief and discomfort, her body relaxing under his touch.

"I need to soak in a hot bath."

Jack chuckled. "You probably should get off the internet before Freddie's people start tracking Numbers."

Stella's head leaned to her left, with lips curving into a faint smile. "You're right." Her right hand moved back to the mouse, clicking a few times before the system shut down with a quiet hum. She leaned back in her chair, her neck arching as she looked up at Jack.

"You asked about the Tor," she said, her tone thoughtful. "The answer is, it's slow work."

Jack nodded, his hands still resting lightly on her shoulders. "Figured as much."

Stella sighed, her gaze lingering on him. "Care to join me in the bath?"

CHAPTER THIRTEEN

"This Mustang's not mine. It belonged to a friend of mine, who died and his wife wants it restored. I've learned you don't work on my old Denali but you do work on classic Mustangs."

Freya looked at the photos on Jack's phone. "What year is it?"

The workshop buzzed with activity, already more than an hour into the day. A symphony of sounds created a lively atmosphere. The clang of wrenches and hammers against metal parts echoed through the space, mingling with the hiss and hum of air compressors. Mechanics moved swiftly, their industrial boots a discordant rhythm on the concrete floor. Engines roared to life, their deep rumble reverberating off the walls as mechanics tested and tuned them. The rapid staccato bursts of impact wrenches punctuated the air, tightening and loosening bolts with precision. In the corner, a grinder whirred abrasively, shaping metal parts with sparks flying.

Amid the cacophony, conversations flowed, blending into the background chatter. Mechanics exchanged instructions, jokes, and updates on their progress, their voices a constant undercurrent. A radio played country and western softly in the background, the music providing a steady beat to the workshop's activity. Overhead, the garage door creaked open, allowing a brief burst of fresh air to mix with the oil and metal. Hydraulic lifts squeaked as they raised cars, adding to the symphony of sounds. Papers shuffled, manuals consulted, the rustle of pages adding a softer note to the mix.

Freya had moved through the workshop, her presence a calming force amid the noise. She inspected the cars, her hands deftly checking oil levels and tightening bolts. As she worked, the familiar sounds surrounded her, each one a testament to the hard work and dedication that filled the workshop. The clang of tools, the hum of compressors, and the roar of engines blended into a chorus that spoke of skill and passion. It was a place where cars came back to life, and Freya was at the heart of it all.

Her hair was wet. She must have come back from a run. She smelled of soap and hair shampoo, adding a touch of freshness to the air.

"1964. The year the Mustang was first introduced."

Freya sighed. "I know when the Mustang was released. I'll need to see it so I can give you a quote."

"When suits you?"

Freya looked around at the assortment of cars. "I can't come during the day. Too much work on the go. I shut at five. Can I come after that?"

"That works. I'll text you the address."

Freya watched Jack as he typed on his phone, and Freya's phone pinged. Freya looked at the address. "I should be there by six o'clock."

"My Denali will be in the driveway."

"Hmph. I look forward to seeing it again."

Clearly, a ten-year-old Denali was not on Freya's list of must-sees. Aunt Louise had always advised him and Freddie that it was best to ignore or be amused at other people's prejudices unless they presented a threat. This time, he chuckled to himself.

"Great. See you then."

Freya nodded and returned to her work, her freshly washed hair's scent lingering in the air as she resumed her tasks in the garage. Jack watched her momentarily, thinking about the Mustang and the work it would need. He was looking forward to seeing what Freya could do with it.

* * *

Jack had parked in Marie's driveway for six minutes past the agreed time when Freya pulled in behind him in a white F-150. It was not a new model. Jack got out and stood by the door. Freya got out of the truck and walked to Jack.

"Sorry, I'm a bit late. I squeezed in a short run, then I had to shower, and my hair needed a wash."

Jack had already taken in the blue jeans, white T-shirt, white trainers, and hair pulled back into a damp ponytail. No makeup. A floral hint of soap and hair shampoo. "No problem." Jack held up his phone. "Gave me a chance to catch up on some emails and messages." Jack pointed at the F-150. "I was expecting to see you in one of your restorations. That looks about the same age as my truck."

Freya smiled. "It is. It's a workhorse. Sometimes, I need to collect parts."

Jack looked at the truck, which wouldn't care if it transported stolen parts. It was as unremarkable as a cloudy day in winter. Then he looked at Freya. "Let's look at the Mustang, shall we? It's in a shed out the back."

Together, they walked to the front door. Jack pressed the buzzer, and they waited until nineteen seconds had gone by. Jack knocked on the door with his knuckles. He heard movement inside, then a voice. "Who's there?"

Jack recognized the voice. "Judy, it's Jack. I'm here with a lady to look at the Mustang."

Judy opened the door and let them in. She reached for Jack, who reacted and stepped in for a hug. "Sorry about that, Jack. A New York habit, and I can't exactly look through the peephole."

"Judy, this is Freya."

Judy held out her hand. "Nice to meet you, Freya."

Freya hesitated, then shook her hand. "And nice to meet you."

Judy inhaled. "I use the same hair shampoo. Nice. Sorry, I'm being intrusive. When you go blind, your other faculties get enhanced, or you try harder with them. I'm not sure which."

Freya smiled as gently as a whispering breeze on a tranquil summer evening. "You are not intrusive, and the shampoo has a wonderful fragrance."

"Judy, where's Marie? We were to meet her here."

"I don't know. Freddie dropped me off about half an hour ago. He had things to do, and I expected Mom to be here."

"Did Marie mention restoring the Mustang to you?"

"She did, in passing, but didn't go into details." Judy turned to Freya. "Is this what you do, Freya?"

"Yes, it is."

"I thought that would have been a male-dominated sector?"

"It is, but I inherited the business from my father and worked on cars with him almost since I could walk. I had my own toolbox. The tools were plastic so that I couldn't damage any of the vehicles."

"Do you do restorations on all vehicles?"

"I do, but personally, I prefer classic American muscle cars."

Freya looked at Jack and smiled. "Jack brought in his old Denali for a quote, which I gave him, but it's not what I like to do."

"Freya told me to take my Denali elsewhere."

"I was not quite that blunt, but yes."

Judy laughed. "Good on you, Freya. But tell me, wouldn't it be easier to work on a recent model where parts are more available?"

Jack realized it was Judy's lawyer training, where one question led to another. On this question, Freya hesitated. "The parts are available. You have to know where to look and who to ask. It's an informal network."

Jack was interested in seeing if Freya would hint at her criminal activities. She cut the conversation short, glancing at her watch and then at Jack.

"Can I see the Mustang? I need to get to another meeting."

"Sorry, Freya," said Judy. "Here I am chatting away."

"It's fine, Judy. I'm just under a bit of time pressure today."

* * *

Jack led Freya through the side entrance of the garage, where the dis-assembled Mustang awaited inspection. As they stepped inside, the familiar aroma of oil and metal mingled with the floral scent that clung to Freya. Freya's eyes sparkled with curiosity as she approached the Mustang, taking in every detail of the classic car.

Freya spent seventeen minutes meticulously inspecting the Mustang, her expert gaze assessing the quality of the work already done. "He did a good job," she said, straightening. "Not much for me to do but to put it together. If I can do some of the rebuilds here, I can get it on the road with temporary plates and drive it to my shop. Then I can finish it there. With the transport of the parts to my shop, labor, and a few materials, it'll be four thousand dollars."

Jack nodded, appreciating the thoroughness of Freya's assessment. "Sounds more than fair. When do you want to start?"

"I can bring one of my guys here tomorrow. Explain what he needs to do. It should take him two days, and we can get it on the road. I've got some temporary plates we can use, and over the next two days, I'll complete two cars at my shop. So they'll be gone, and there'll be space for this Mustang. We just need access. I saw from the front that there was a side entrance. Can we use that? I don't want to be tracking our dirty boots through the house."

Jack smiled, glad that Freya was already thinking ahead. "I can organize that. The owner is normally here. She's not right now, but she should be back shortly. In the meantime, let me give you my number. Give me a call when you get here tomorrow. What time would that be?"

"About eight o'clock," Freya said, her tone efficient and businesslike.

Jack pulled out his phone and quickly exchanged numbers with Freya. He watched as she returned to her inspection, noting how she moved with purpose and confidence, like a leopard stalking an impala. It was clear she was a professional, and he felt reassured that the Mustang was in good hands.

Freya glanced around the garage, appreciating its organized chaos, and turned to Jack with a satisfied smile. "I'll see you tomorrow at eight then," she said, her eyes glinting with determination.

"Looking forward to it," Jack said, feeling a surge of excitement about the project ahead. As he left the garage, he couldn't help but feel optimistic about the Mustang's future. With Freya's expertise and the plan in place, it wouldn't be long before the classic car was back on the road, restored to its former glory. And hopefully, he would get a clue who shot Danny Carlton.

* * *

Jack escorted Freya to her car. Not just a car enthusiast or a runner, but an enigma who lived in the fast lane, literally and figuratively. Her movements were self-assured and unhurried like fog rolling in, as she climbed into her truck. Her demeanor was calm and composed. As she bid Jack goodbye, he felt a mixture of admiration and unease. Despite her quiet exterior, there was an intensity about Freya that set him on edge. Jack saw the paradox in this woman whose passion for classic cars and dedication to her fitness belied a deeper, more complex character who could handle the running of an illegal activity.

He watched her drive away, then turned back towards the house.

He found Judy in the kitchen, her brow furrowed in concern. "It's strange that Marie's not here. We had agreed to meet Freya at this time," he said, his voice tinged with unease.

Judy nodded, her hands resting on the kitchen counter. "It is odd. When I'm back in town, Mom keeps track of me and keeps me informed if she goes anywhere. Even if she's going to the local shops to fetch something quickly." She paused. "I rang her and found her phone on the kitchen table. Both her and Dad's cars are in the garage. I put my hand on the hoods. Both are cold."

Jack felt a knot of concern tightening in his chest. "When did you last speak to her?"

"Yesterday afternoon, about four, when I told her I'd be staying at Freddie's place."

Judy had the phone in her hand, and Jack had to remind himself that cell phones had braille settings. "Judy ... she may be at the Japanese Gardens. It's a special place for her, I learned. She could have lost track of time. Left her phone behind. Your dad's passing has undoubtedly had an effect on her, which may not be visible."

Judy's shoulders sank, the weight of Jack's words settling heavily on her. "You're probably right. I'm worrying for no reason." She drew a breath, exhaled, and seemed to perk up. "I'll make us some coffee. There should be some blueberry muffins on the counter. Can you please locate them? And do you take your coffee the same way Freddie does? Black, no sugar, in a mug?"

"That's right," Jack said, his voice gentle.

As Judy busied herself with the coffee, Jack placed the muffins on the table and searched the cupboards until he found the small plates. They each ate a muffin. The sweet, crumbly texture was a comforting distraction. They sipped their coffee until it was gone, made more coffee, and discussed trivia. Judy never mentioned Freddie, and Jack left the topic alone. Almost two hours had gone by when Judy's worry resurfaced.

"Something is wrong, Jack. My mom does not go missing like this. How long must I wait before I can report her as a missing person?"

Jack knew the answer from some lectures at the SFPD Academy he'd been privy to attend.

"There is no waiting period. All you need to do is report that you believe that person is at risk."

"Can you call Freddie?"

"He's always busy. Let me text him. That will work better."

Jack texted the situation to Freddie, who phoned back in three minutes. "How long has Marie been missing?"

"Let me give the phone to Judy."

Jack placed the phone in Judy's hand. "Hello, Freddie. My mom does not go missing. We always know where the other person is."

Jack was close enough to the phone to hear Freddie. "Has this ever happened before?"

"Never. That's why I'm worried."

"Is she on any medication?"

"If she were, she would have told me. You know how close I am to my mom."

"I do. All right. Judy, give the phone to Jack."

Judy passed the phone to Jack. "Jack," said Freddie, "in the hallway, there is a photo of Marie and Ted. It looks fairly recent. Take a photo of Marie's head and send it to me. I can fill in the rest of Marie's details to get her loaded as a missing person. I'll organize us to conduct standard hospital checks, especially for recent accidents. Then I'm coming over there."

"I'm going to take a walk around the Botanical Gardens and see if she's there. It's a favorite spot of Marie's."

"All right, I'll see you at Marie's place," Freddie said.

Jack ended the call and turned to Judy, his expression resolute. "I'll go check the Botanical Gardens. You stay here in case she comes back."

Judy nodded, her eyes filled with hope and fear. "Be careful, Jack."

Jack stepped out, the weight of the situation pressing heavily on his shoulders. The Botanical Gardens were a short walk away, and he hurried, his thoughts racing. Marie's disappearance was out of character, and the more he thought about it, the more uneasy he felt.

* * *

The path to the Golden Gate Park Loop was well-trodden, familiar beneath his feet. As he entered the gardens, blooming flowers mingled with the damp earth, creating a heady aroma. The Japanese Tea Garden's serene setting loomed ahead, its tranquility a stark contrast to the turmoil in his mind. Jack scanned the area, searching for any sign of Marie. The carefully manicured plants and tranquil water features provided no clues. Marie was not there.

He pressed on, nature's music accompanying him on his journey. Birds chirped softly in the trees, leaves rustled gently in the breeze, and the distant hum of city life created a subtle backdrop. Halfway between Stow Lake and the Conservatory of Flowers, he felt a light tap on his shoulder.

Jack spun around, his senses heightened. The faint scent of sweat and jasmine filled his nostrils. "Hello, Freya," he said, recognizing the runner. She wore the same athletic attire as before, her wraparound glasses with yellow frames masking her eyes.

"Hello, Jack. I didn't figure you to be the type to go ambling through the Botanical Gardens," she said, a playful smirk on her lips. He realized she had nice lips.

Jack managed a small smile. "Appearances can be deceiving," he said, his voice calm despite the rapid thump of his heart. Jack considered saying he was looking for Marie. The description would fit many older women, and no one knew what she was wearing.

Freya's face remained impassive, her eyes hidden behind the sunglasses. "I guess so. Anyway, I must keep moving. Enjoy your walk," she said, her tone light but brisk.

He watched as she jogged away, her movements fluid and purposeful. Jasmine lingered in the air, a reminder of their brief encounter. Jack knew she was aware of his gaze, yet she didn't look back. She disappeared around a bend, leaving him alone with his thoughts.

Returning to his search, Jack continued toward the Conservatory of Flowers. The grand glass structure stood ahead, its beauty somewhat diminished by the worry gnawing at him. He called out Marie's name, his voice echoing in the quiet evening, but there was no response. The garden's emptiness mirrored his growing sense of dread. After what felt like hours, Jack returned to Marie's house. The journey back was slower as he continued searching, each step heavy with concern.

It had taken him eighty minutes from when he had left to when he returned and saw Freddie's truck in the driveway. Inside, Jack saw Freddie sitting on the couch with his arm around Judy's shoulders. Her right hand held a fistful of tissues, and her face registered hope. They had both looked up as he closed the door. A flicker of hope, like sunlight appearing briefly through winter's clouds, illuminated Judy's face, and a tentative smile formed at the corners of her lips. When she realized it was Jack, hope dashed away like glass dropped onto rocks.

"No sign of her?" said Jack.

"I have no reports of sightings," said Freddie. "I'm going to stay here tonight, but I have to be at work early tomorrow. Can you bring me back some clothes?"

Jack and Freddie had keys to each other's apartments.

"Sure thing. Then tomorrow I'll wait here until you or Marie return. What time suits you?"

"Six. Kenny's leading the search for Marie. I'll tell him what we're doing."

"I'll get going then. Judy, maybe you want to tell Freddie that we're getting Ted's Mustang restored."

CHAPTER FOURTEEN

Jack parked his car in Stella's garage and walked through the connecting door into the kitchen. Chimes like tinkling bells rang when he passed through the doorway. It was a house where you wouldn't hear a sound if you stood and listened. He had installed the chimes so Stella would know when someone came through from the garage. This way, he wouldn't frighten her upon arriving, and it was not the type of house where one shouted. In the living room, Stella sat on the living room suite facing The Bay. The sun had set an hour earlier, and the city's nightlights were on. He kissed her. She reciprocated. The kissing continued until Jack paused it, as he needed to talk to Stella.

"Hmm," said Stella. "I was enjoying that."

"Marie Clark is missing," said Jack.

"What? When?"

"Sometime today. It's odd, as apparently Marie always keeps Judy informed of what she's doing and where she's going while Judy is in San Francisco, and vice versa. Freddie has organized a missing persons alert and is with Judy at the house. Judy is distraught, of course, and says this is totally out of character."

"Has Marie ever shown signs of dementia?"

"I've seen nothing that would indicate that. Her memory's good. Never noticed any disorientation. She communicates well. Look, I'm not an expert on the subject, but she seems fine to me."

"So, Judy and Freddie sit and wait?"

"Not much else they can do. Freddie no doubt used his influence to see that the search for Marie got priority, and she didn't just become one of the more than one thousand missing persons."

"How come you know that number?"

"Working with Freddie's guys on the missing persons dataset. At the last count, one thousand four hundred people were missing. Eighty percent are found or have returned home in the first twenty-four hours. If they have not turned up in two days after that, the probability of finding them drops significantly, and they are most likely to become a cold case file. Freddie will focus on the next twenty-four hours. I must be back at six tomorrow morning so Freddie can go to his office."

"Well, my day has not been without its ups and downs. I've been working on the Tor network, and it still hasn't cracked, so I gave it a rest and sat down here to read the report prepared for me on Carlton Engineering."

"I thought you had already read the report."

"I have read several reports on the business, but George Carlton prepared this one."

"And?"

"It makes for fascinating reading. There is a far bigger upside to this business than I knew. George has documented what is currently happening and the prototypes he's working on. It's like peeling an onion, each layer revealing the true depth of George's genius, and none of this will happen without him."

"Where does George stand on staying involved?"

"He's undecided. However, what has been particularly annoying is that Victor Thornfield keeps calling him and pressuring him to sell Carlton Engineering to him. George became irritable with him and let it slip that he was talking to me. Thornfield has phoned me and left a message that he wants to meet for breakfast, lunch, or dinner to discuss it."

"What do you want to do?"

"I'll meet him. I'd appreciate it if you could be there."

"I'll be there."

"The name Thornfield was familiar, and I've done a bit of digging. He grew up here in Pacific Heights."

"What else do you know?"

"Not much more, but I will before the meeting."

"Forewarned is forearmed."

"You going to use your hacking skills?"

"That, and I still have a few acquaintances in Pacific Heights with whom I stay in touch. I want to find the stuff that's not on the internet."

* * *

Jack had arranged with Freddie what time he needed to leave for work. Jack arrived fifteen minutes early. Freddie shook his head. A slight movement that carried the weight of unspoken words. Marie was still missing. Judy was a mess. Eyes puffy and red, the skin around them tender and swollen. Tear tracks glistened on her cheeks like a map of sorrow. Hair disheveled. Strands stuck to her damp face. As though the weight of the world had etched them, lines of worry and sadness settled in her fine features. Jack had no words to offer that would help. He hugged her.

Just over an hour later, Freya texted to say she was out the front.

Jack went out the back and around to the side gate and let in Freya and Logan, who looked like he was about eighteen. Together, they walked to the shed, which opened with a clunk, and switched on the lights. Logan was thrilled with what he saw. Freya's phone pinged, and she looked at it. "Excuse me, Jack, I need to phone the workshop. Logan, check out the parts you have to assemble."

Freya walked to the back of the shed, and they could hear her talking about an Oldsmobile that needed new piston rings.

Jack looked at his phone as if checking for texts or emails. His Bluetooth was on, and he looked for others nearby. Logan and Freya appeared on his screen. He connected to Freya, bypassing any permission requirements, opened his hacking app, and started downloading her phone calls and text messages to the Cloud. He didn't need years of data. Jack had tweaked the app to give him the last six months, starting with the most recent.

Freya finished her phone call and came back to explain to Logan what he had to do to get the Mustang on the road so they could drive it to Freya's workshop. Logan's head bobbed up and down as he ran his eyes over the disassembled vehicle. Jack looked at his phone. The app was still running.

Freya told Logan she'd be back at five to pick him up and see his progress. Jack walked Freya to her vehicle. She seemed impressed and surprised by Jack's gentlemanly behavior. As she drove off, Jack looked at his phone. The app was still running. Freya drove away and out of range of the Bluetooth link, leaving Jack to wonder how much data he had received.

He walked back to the shed.

* * *

"I'm making coffee, Logan. You want one?"

"Yes, please. That'd be great. I had to bounce out of bed and didn't have a chance to make coffee."

"And a blueberry muffin."

"The breakfast of champions. Thanks, Jack."

Jack made three coffees in mugs. One he placed in Judy's hands. His and Logan's he balanced on a dinner plate with a muffin. He put them down on the shed's bench and picked up a mug. Logan didn't need an invitation to pick up the remaining mug and sip it. He found it too hot, reached for the muffin, and took a bite with his teeth bared like a leopard.

"Where are you from, Logan?"

Logan replied while chewing as if he had always done it. "Here in San Francisco. Raised by my dad. I know nothing about my mother. He remarried. My dad and stepmother played favorites with my step-mother's two kids, so I left. I lived on the street for over a year. I slept in Freya's office doorway one night, as it had a big awning that kept the rain off me. She found me there. Took me in. Gave me a cup of coffee, then went looking in the staff fridge for something for me to eat." Logan laughed. "There was only a half-eaten cheeseburger that one guy had left there. She was shocked when she saw it, as she eats super-healthy. I ate it cold. The best burger I've ever had."

No doubt he had told this story many times. Was happy to share this in one rush of words. His loyalty to Freya hung in the air like a shadow on wet asphalt.

"Hunger is the best sauce," said Jack.

"Never heard that before, but you're right." Logan finished his muffin and rubbed his hands against his shorts to remove the crumbs. "Is that your Denali in the driveway?"

"It is."

"An oldie but a goodie."

"It needs some work. Freya gave me a quote that blew my socks off. She was upfront about it, though, and said she wasn't interested in doing the work."

"Sounds like her. She has her niche, and she sticks to it."

"So, Logan, if I needed a cheaper part for my Denali, could you source it for me?"

"You're not a cop, are you?"

Jack put on what he hoped was his incredulous face. "Me? A cop?" Jack thought he would add to this. "If you knew me better, Logan, you'd realize how unlikely that is. Why do you ask?"

"Well, sometimes if a part is hard to find, you have to go looking in more, let's call them unconventional places. You know what I mean?"

Jack nodded and waited to see where this conversation would go.

"I could get you parts, Jack, but that's what Freya does, and I won't do anything behind her back. I owe her a lot. How do you think I learned to work on cars? And she gave me a place to stay for free."

"For free? Where do you stay?"

"There's a mezzanine floor in the shop. If you walk past all the tires, there's a one-bedroom apartment."

"Which goes against the building codes but doesn't bother me. Fact is, I have friends who have done the same thing."

"My girlfriend thinks it's pretty cool. She said it's like the Bat Cave but with lots of cars." Logan winked at Jack. "Also, when I put the shutters down, I know I won't be disturbed."

"I can see the attraction."

"Well, let me get to work. I reckon I should have this on the road by tomorrow. That is, it will be good enough to drive to the workshop."

"Good work. I'll see you later."

* * *

Jack stood between the shed and the house and phoned Freddie, who answered on the fourth ring.

"Hi Freddie, no news on Marie?"

"Nothing. As soon as I have anything, I'll let Judy and you know."

Jack knew this was Freddie's way of telling him to get off the phone and let him get on with his job. Jack went inside and downloaded Freya's phone calls and texts from his phone to his laptop. Judy stayed in the living room, holding her phone. He made coffee for Logan four times. He talked with Jack about the cost of getting parts for the Denali. It was clear he enjoyed sharing his knowledge.

Jack found a text with a time eleven minutes after the car used in the bogus hijacking left the car park. *Incoming white Toyota Corolla. Make it disappear.*

Jack phoned the number. It didn't connect. Most probably a burner phone. Freya should know who this is.

But right now, he had to go on an errand with Stella.

CHAPTER FIFTEEN

Jack rapped on the brass knocker. Above the door were fluorescent tubes spelling out the word, Vortex. Jack wondered what color they became at night. A man with a broken nose, the cartilage squashed onto his face, and a mop of black curly hair opened the club's door. He wore jeans, a denim shirt with black hair protruding from the neckline, under the cuffs, and down to his wrists, and a Celtic tartan scarf hanging to his waist. "We're here to see Victor."

The bouncer held onto both ends of his scarf and looked them over, letting them see his two hundred and fifty pounds. Given that his fights had not been kind to his face, it was hard to guess his age. Maybe five years on either side of fifty. A delivery van pulled up. The bouncer scoped the van and then looked back at Jack and Stella. "Follow me."

The accent was not from around San Francisco. He then turned his attention to the van driver, who had gotten out and lifted the roller shutter on the back. "Bring your stuff in and close the door on your way out." The accent was Brooklyn, New York.

The driver raised his hand in acknowledgment. "Sure, Lenny." He reached inside the van.

Now, they had a name. Lenny, the bouncer who hadn't introduced himself, walked off into the club with a rolling gait. For Jack and Stella, it was like following a five-foot, ten-inch black bear.

The club was bathed in white light, then switched to a pale purple light that gave the illusion of warmth but didn't, bathing the entire club in a glow that invited you to enter. A pleasant moment for the guests as they arrived. A place where you wanted to be. The lights flickered, and they went back to white. A man moved his ladder under the offending bulb. A mixture of rhythmic beats filled the air as someone did a sound check.

The bar stood as the breathtaking centerpiece of the room, gleaming like a jewel in a crown. Its sleek, polished marble surface caught the light, casting a shimmer across the room. Bottles of top-shelf liquor were displayed with precision, creating a spectrum of colors. Crystal glasses hung overhead, glinting like stars. Not just a bar, it was the venue's heart pulsating with life and luxury.

Scattered around the bar were seating areas with plush red velvet couches and dark leather booths, providing intimate spots for whispered conversations or people-watching. The dance floor probably pulsed with energy as elegantly dressed patrons moved to the music, lost in the moment. The floor, a polished dark wood, reflected the lights above and added to the sense of timeless elegance.

They walked past people mopping floors and wiping down countertops, tables, and anything that might have had dust or debris, to a tall, lean man wearing an impeccably tailored black suit with a pocket square in classic white. He'd paired it with a white shirt as crisp as a frosty winter's morning, complete with polished dress shoes that would reflect your face if you stooped to look at them. A woman had her arms draped around his neck. They were talking. Jack didn't recognize the language until they got closer. Russian.

"Victor," said Lenny, "these two say they are here to see you. Is that true, or should I throw them out?"

Jack didn't bother to look at Lenny. Somehow, belligerent bouncers seem to come from the same gene pool. Jack was sure Victor had told Lenny to expect them. Best to let Lenny have his moment in the spotlight.

The woman spun as if she were expecting imminent danger, revealing pale blue eyes above high cheekbones. Although poised, she looked elegant, like a cat, as her cream silk blouse flowed lightly with her movements, as though a tailor had adjusted the fit just enough to highlight her elegant posture. The sleeves were rolled up neatly to her elbows, revealing delicate gold bracelets that caught the light in subtle flashes. Her high-waisted, dark-wash jeans hugged her figure, and she wore tan suede loafers. Her hair was a cascade of dark curls, swept to the side in a style that suggested she hadn't tried too hard, although every strand seemed perfectly in place. Added to this was a touch of mascara, a hint of blush, lips painted in a soft mauve shade, and tiny pearl earrings that framed her face. It looked like she wanted to blend into a crowd while still turning heads.

Victor turned as if he had all the time in the world, his sharp, chiseled features and neatly styled dark hair and black eyes, focusing on Stella with a glint as if he knew some naughty secret about her. "That won't be necessary, Lenny. I was expecting them." Victor smiled, showing all his teeth. "Stella West and Jack Rhodes, I presume."

He held out his hand to Stella, then to Jack, focusing his eyes on each of them as he shook their hands. Stella nodded and let go of his hand. Jack felt a firm grip, neither weak nor bone-crushing.

"Call me Victor. May I call you Stella and Jack?" They both nodded. Victor extended his arm sideways. "Shall we sit in one of the booths? They are very comfortable."

The delivery guy walked past Lenny, carrying a box labeled

champagne. A guy in a gray hoodie followed him. He wasn't carrying anything. When passing, Mr. Gray Hoodie pointed a gun at Victor and screamed something in Russian.

Jack recognized obscenities about Victor. It wasn't the time to chuckle but Russian obscenities were detailed with taboo topics more than anything in English. The Russian woman screamed. Jack moved Stella behind him. The gunman should have kept Lenny in his field of vision. Lenny didn't wait for introductions but grabbed the guy by the back of his hoodie and continued the motion downwards as he dropped to one knee, bringing the gunman's head with him. The gun went off, causing the delivery guy to look back and stumble, losing his parcel, which hit the floor as Lenny slammed the gunman's forehead into the floor. Lenny rested his knee on the guy's back, reached over, and took the gun from the inert fingers.

Victor spoke Russian to the woman. Jack's Russian wasn't great, but he knew enough to hear him call her Olga and tell her to leave. Olga blinked rapidly, like a flickering candle in a gusty wind. She didn't need further instruction or advice and stalked to a staircase, glancing back once before walking up.

Victor turned on his all-teeth smile. "As I was saying, shall we sit in one of the booths? They are very comfortable. Sorry about the intrusion, I trust it wasn't too upsetting."

"We've seen worse," said Stella.

"But," said Jack. "Only during gang wars and at weddings."

Jack and Stella followed Victor and seated themselves. Lenny dragged the gunman by the hoodie through the swing doors to the kitchen. The delivery guy was doing his best to pick up the pieces of his parcel and apologize for the mess. Cleaners arrived with mops to clean up the champagne and blood. A waiter appeared. "Something to drink?"

They both replied in the negative. Victor waved the waiter away with the slightest twitch of his fingertips. "It's not every day I have the CEO of an illustrious enterprise like Node Industries coming to my club, as well as an international forensic data analyst."

Jack and Stella didn't look at each other, but they knew Victor had put some time into researching their backgrounds. Not unexpected.

"Thank you, Victor," said Stella, "Let's discuss Carlton Engineering."

Victor smiled with a gleam like a poker player with an unbeatable hand. "Of course. Let's leap right in."

"George Carlton wants me to buy his business."

Victor shrugged in a Gallic manner. "I, on the other hand, would like to own his business."

"But you just want to break it up and sell the pieces."

Victor held up his index finger. "I am not a silly businessman. There is considerable intellectual property in that business, which I would like to retain."

"Which will go no further without George Carlton."

Victor made a movement with his shoulders, which could have been a shrug. "Are you asking me to walk away from acquiring Carlton Engineering?"

Stella clasped her hands together and placed them on the table. "George is going through a heartbreaking time at the moment with the death of his son. He came to me saying he wanted me to buy his business. George would stay on, investing his time and energy into product development. With what he is going through at the moment, with his son's death now being declared a murder case, he does not need more stress or grief in his life right now."

Victor smiled at Stella like he was an indulgent parent. "Your humanity is admirable. George may be the majority shareholder, however, under Californian law, a minority shareholder can object to the sale of a privately held business if they believe it is not in the company's or its shareholders' best interest."

"But George would have the first right of refusal on the sale of any shares," said Stella.

Victor shook his head slowly, as though he were addressing a naïve pupil while applying a layer of condescension. "Back when they drew up and agreed to the shareholders' agreement, there was more faith in one's fellow man. I've learned that such an agreement was word of mouth and a handshake."

"So George has no knowledge of this?" said Jack.

"Correct," said Victor, "and as soon as I have the paperwork, I will call for a board meeting to table my objection to selling to Node Industries."

Stella's eyes didn't narrow and enlarge. She may have been checking what brand of coffee to buy. "Well, Victor, thank you for your time. We have nothing else to discuss."

"Oh, but Stella, there is more."

Victor signaled Lenny, who had been behind the bar and now stopped putting glasses away and ambled out.

"Sorry, Victor, I've heard enough. This meeting is over."

Jack slid out of the booth when Lenny blocked his way and put his hand on Jack's shoulder. Jack looked at Victor. "Tell him to get out of the way."

"Sorry, Jack. Now Stella." Victor put his hand on Stella's arm and stopped her from moving.

This action was all it took to trigger Jack, whose eyes narrowed as he grabbed Lenny's Celtic scarf with both hands. His left hand gripped one end near Lenny's neck while his right hand seized the scarf halfway up. With a swift, practiced motion, Jack pushed his right hand past Lenny's throat, transforming the scarf into a garrote. A favorite move in judo. Lenny's eyes widened in shock as he staggered back, yanking Jack with him, clawing desperately at the scarf as it cut off the blood supply to his head. Jack was ready. He drove his left knee into Lenny's groin with brutal force. Lenny bellowed, his face contorting in pain. A sound that was marrow-deep. He dropped his hands to his groin, hoping to ease the agony and fend off further attacks. Jack didn't relent.

He twisted the scarf tighter, forcing Lenny to stumble backward. Lenny's legs wobbled, and he crashed into a nearby table, sending dishes and cutlery flying. The noise drew the attention of the cleaners in the room, but Jack remained focused. None of them had rushed to Lenny's aid. Maybe Lenny's belligerent bouncer persona had been applied to them and they were keen to see him get a comeuppance. Jack released the scarf and delivered a swift punch to Lenny's jaw, sending him sprawling to the floor. Lenny lay there, gasping for breath, his hands still clutching his groin. While Lenny's brain focused on the pain, Jack reapplied the garrote. Lenny's face was turning pink like he had a mouthful of Habanero chilies, and his eyes bulged, but he was conscious. Jack turned his attention to Victor and Stella.

Victor's eyes seemed like an X-ray as he watched the fight. His dour expression suggested his estimate of Jack was changing, and he was dissatisfied with the fight's progression. Victor slid a stiletto-looking knife from the inside of his jacket and slid out from the booth.

"Stay in your seat," Stella said.

Victor turned to her, Stella now holding a Glock 42 with her hand resting on the table.

"I have a concealed carry license," said Stella, "and the instructor taught me to shoot twice, at the center of mass. Double-tap, it's called, but it will feel more than two taps. Now throw the knife over near the bar."

Victor grinned and shook his head as he looked at his employees, his eyes now had a twinkle like a mischievous boy. "Oh dear, look at you. It seems I brought a knife to a gunfight." Victor put the knife on the table, and his hands were well clear of it. "I'd rather not throw it, as it is a Fairbairn-Sykes fighting knife, which has been in the family since WWII. The British Commandos were the first to use them. I would hate to see it damaged. It has sentimental value. No commercial value."

Stella looked at the double-edged blade with a handle that was almost as long. Jack knew enough about Stella's interests that she was aware of the knife's history and capability.

"Knife on the floor, now or I shoot you in the stomach, which may or may not kill you, but can be difficult to repair depending on what organs and blood vessels get damaged, but it will make holes in your colon. Use two fingers to get rid of the knife, then put your hands flat on the table."

Victor rolled his eyes and sighed, and there was a clattering sound as the knife landed. Stella didn't take her eyes off Victor. "Will you be much longer, Jack?"

"Give me a minute." Jack lay sprawled across Lenny, who'd recovered enough to alternate between grabbing at his scarf and throwing punches at Jack's head, which he twisted each time to take them on his shoulder. "He's got a thick neck."

"Take all the time you need, Jack. I have my pistol focused on Victor. He is behaving very well." Stella chuckled. "He reminds me of those bored patients you see in a doctor's waiting room."

"Finished," said Jack as Lenny's eyes closed and his arms went limp like old lettuce. Jack let go of the scarf and stood.

Stella slid out from the booth and walked past the inert Lenny. Victor didn't move. His palms were still resting on the table, watching them leave. Outside the club, Jack's breathing was slowing down. They jogged across the street and stopped a taxi. As Jack opened the door for Stella, she turned to him.

"I need to send some messages."

* * *

Stella gave the taxi driver her address. Jack slid the partition closed between them and the driver. The cab moved smoothly through the bustling city streets. Jack glanced at Stella, who was typing a message on her phone. She texted George Carlton: *When is a good time to call you?* The anxiety in her eyes mirrored Jack's feelings.

"That was interesting," said Jack. "Why would Thornfield want to stop us from leaving?"

Stella looked at Jack. "Thornfield's words were, 'as soon as he has the paperwork,' which makes me think he has nothing in writing as yet."

"But he must have a shareholder in his pocket for some reason. It can't be just money, because if Thornfield made him an offer above the fair value of his shares, he could have taken it to George and played Thornfield off against him. Another thing I don't understand is that even if there is no first right of refusal in the agreement, a sale of shares in a private company still has to be approved by the board."

"That's correct if an individual holds the shares in their name."

Jack scratched his head as he waited for Stella to continue. "However, if a trust owns the shares, then you buy the trust, and you own all the assets in the trust. I need to get to my home office to see who has their shares in a trust."

"Is this recorded in a state database?"

"In some other states, yes, but in California, no. The company holds all records of shares and share transactions."

Jack clasped his hand to his forehead in a show of mock reprieve. "Wow, that's a relief. You don't have to hack into a state database, just into Carlton Engineering's database."

"Very funny. I just hope the records are on their database, not elsewhere, like with their auditor. We need to move before Thornfield and whoever is the shareholder sign a sale agreement."

The taxi moved through the city, the engine a steady hum against the backdrop of their collective silence. Jack could feel the tension radiating off Stella. There was nothing else they could do but sit in frustration as they drove, trapped in the confines of the backseat with their thoughts and worries.

Jack tried to distract himself by looking out the window. The streets were alive with activity, people bustling along the sidewalks, shopping, chatting, and going about their day. Neon signs above storefronts added splashes of color to the urban landscape. The city seemed indifferent to their plight, its relentless pace unchanged by their personal crises.

He pulled out his phone and texted Freddie: *Have you found Marie?* He didn't expect an immediate reply, knowing Freddie would be busy with the search, plus his other cases and duties.

With a sigh, Jack opened another message thread and texted Freya: *How is the Mustang progressing?* He knew she was probably in the middle of her work, covered in grease and sweat, focused entirely on the car. The chance of her replying immediately was slim.

Stella shifted in her seat, breaking the silence. "Do you think Freddie has any leads?" she asked, her voice barely above a whisper.

Jack shrugged, trying to keep his own doubts at bay. "I hope so. He's resourceful. If anyone can find her, it's him."

Stella nodded, her fingers drumming nervously on her knee. "And Freya? The Mustang? Any leads regarding Danny Carlton?"

"None."

They lapsed back into silence, the weight of their unanswered messages pressing down on them. The taxi continued its journey, the driver oblivious to the storm of emotions brewing in the backseat.

As they neared Stella's address, the neighborhood grew quieter, the hustle and bustle of the city fading into a more residential tranquility.

The taxi finally pulled up in front of Stella's house with its bay windows and understated grandeur, which reeked of money. Jack opened the door and helped Stella out into the warm sun.

CHAPTER SIXTEEN

Once home, Stella went straight to her workroom and started hacking into Carlton Engineering. Jack put a hand on Stella's shoulder. "I know you're angry but be careful. Freddie and his team are always on the lookout for Numbers."

"I know, I know. I'll be quick."

Stella's phone pinged, and she glanced at it. "George says I can phone him anytime."

Stella hammered away at the keyboard with the speed and precision of a concert pianist playing a rapid, intricate piece. Her fingers danced across the keys, each stroke purposeful and exact.

Jack's phone pinged, and he glanced at it. "Freddie says Marie's still missing."

Stella nodded but kept working the keyboard, then stopped like a tripped circuit breaker.

"There are two trusts holding shares. One is George's trust, which holds other assets. Who's Frank Lund?"

Jack leaned in to read the name. "He's the IT guy. I met him when I did that work for George."

Stella pointed at the screen. "There are two beneficiaries. Matthew and Nicholas Lund. No mention of a Mrs. Lund. Maybe that's the holdup of why Thornfield has not got his paws on the trust. The beneficiaries would have to approve the sale of the trust."

Stella started shutting down all the hacking apps she had running. "We need to speak to George."

Stella made a video call from her laptop. After eleven rings, George appeared on the screen. "Hello, Stella. Hello Jack. Nice to hear from you."

"Hello, George. As you can see, I'm with Jack, and this call is encrypted."

"How can I help you both?"

"If I can cut to the chase."

"By all means, Stella. What's up?"

"It has come to our attention that Frank Lund plans to sell his shares to Victor Thornfield."

George was silent for seven seconds. "Frank has been with me for over twenty years, but of late, he has become disgruntled, as you saw, Jack, when you did that due diligence work for me. His wife died, and his two sons have estranged themselves, so he has no one here. We had an agreement that shareholders would grant me the right of first refusal. I never changed the shareholders' agreement to reflect that. I didn't think I'd have to." George paused for three seconds. "I wonder why Frank didn't come to me if he wanted to sell his shares. I would have given him a fair price."

"Does he have any weaknesses?" said Jack. "Drugs, gambling, women?"

"Well, he regularly went to Las Vegas for a weekend. And you know what they say about Vegas? What happens in Vegas stays in Vegas. He's obsessed with mathematics and statistics. He's somewhat of a savant with statistics. Particularly fond of Probability Theory, specifically Conditional Probability. Are you familiar with that?"

"Yes," said Jack. "It's the probability of an event occurring, given that another event has already happened. It's a standard test for computer science students that requires them to develop software that updates probabilities as new information becomes available. They must also consider Bayes' Theorem, which relates to the conditional and marginal probabilities of random events. It's a powerful tool for updating the probability of a hypothesis as more evidence or information becomes available."

"I recall him mentioning Baye's Theorem as he told me one time at a social event at the office that, in his spare time, he had developed software that would beat anyone at Blackjack, and he had memorized the process. He'd had a few drinks and challenged anyone in the room to Blackjack with the proviso that they had to play fast. There were plenty of takers, and he beat them all. Sometimes playing three at a time."

"I understand," said Jack, "that he could memorize what he had done with the software, but to make it work, he would have had to do what they call card counting."

"That's what he whispered to me in his drunken state. To me, it sounded dangerous and I told him so."

"It's a strategy," said Jack, "to track the ratio of high cards to low cards remaining in the deck. The idea is that high cards, tens, face cards, and Aces, are more favorable to the player, while low cards, two to six, are more favorable to the dealer. Players can make more informed decisions about their bets and playing strategy by keeping track of which cards the dealer has dealt."

"Sounds complicated."

"In principle," said Stella, "it's not. You just have to be good at watching the cards and keep numbers in your head. Let me explain. Cards two to six are assigned a value of plus one. High cards, that is, the ten, face cards, and Aces, are assigned a value of minus one. Cards seven to nine are assigned a value of zero. You keep a running count in your head. As the card dealer distributes the cards, you add or subtract the assigned value from the running count."

"That would be easy for Frank to do," said George.

"But," said Jack, "while card counting itself is not illegal, most casinos do not allow it and take measures to prevent it. Casinos are private establishments and have the right to refuse service to anyone they suspect of card counting. And the measure may be to ask you to leave, ban you, or have some large gentlemen escort you into an alley."

George let out a sigh like the wind dying down after a storm. "None of this explains why he didn't first come to me, and it presents us with a huge problem."

"George, Frank's shares are held in a trust."

"I know that." George narrowed his eyes. "How do you know that?"

"That's not relevant right now," said Stella. "What we need to do is get hold of Frank's sons, as they are the beneficiaries and would have to approve the sale."

There was silence on the phone for nine seconds, where you could almost hear the wheels turning in George's brain. "I am assuming, Jack. This is something you took care of?"

Stella smiled but didn't look at Jack. Once again, the assumption was that only men were hackers. "Yes, George, but we don't want this to go any further than the three of us."

"I wholeheartedly agree, but what do we do now?"

"Well, George," said Stella, "if you are still keen to sell me your business, let's agree on the terms of the sale for you and the minority shareholders, as well as a role in the business for you going forward that you're happy with. In parallel with this, I need to meet with Lund's sons and get them to agree to my buying the shares. I will buy them in my personal capacity for now, as I don't need board approval. Once the sale goes through, I will sell my shares to Node Industries."

George chuckled. "This will leave Frank with a problem. He will have to come clean and explain that he's talking to Victor Thornfield."

"And why," said Jack.

"I wonder," said George, "if Thornfield paid Frank a deposit. In which case, he will have to return it, supposing he hasn't spent it already. Frank needs to be careful, Thornfield is a dangerous man." George grimaced like the past just walked in.

Jack looked at George thinking about telling him about their run in with Thornfield, but George had enough on his plate and seemed to be aware of the risk Thornfield presented. "Thanks for letting us know George," said Jack.

Goerge waved this off with a hand gesture like he was chasing a fly. "Anyway, that's all supposition at this stage. Thank you both for updating me and thank you for your efforts."

"Before you go, George," said Stella, "can you please send me the contact details for Matthew and Nicholas Lund?"

"I will, but you don't have to travel far to see them. They're in Silicon Valley. They've created their own cybersecurity firm. Frank told me Matthew calls himself Erebus, and Nicholas calls himself Moros."

"How do you know that?" said Jack.

"When they were in high school, they were already very active on the internet. They got expelled for hacking into the school's database and changing student records. Mainly exam results. They did this for money. I had to go to the principal's office with Frank. I made a substantial donation to the school. A loan that Frank still hasn't repaid."

"Are you going to confront Frank?"

George raised his chin and looked to the side, making him look like a Roman emperor on a coin. "Yes. And Jack, I'd like you to be there. We can cover your report, and then I shall ask him why he didn't come to me to buy his shares."

"You'll catch him unawares," said Stella.

"Exactly. I've had a thought running around in the back of my head while we've been talking. I am hopeful that he will blurt out what prevented him from coming to me."

"When do you want to do this, George?"

"Jack." George paused.

Jack could almost see him scrolling through his calendar in his mind.

"I have some things to do tomorrow morning, but my afternoon is free. Can we make it for one o'clock?"

"Works for me. I'll see you then."

They bid their goodbyes, and Stella's screen went blank as she stared at it. She tapped her index finger on the keyboard like a metronome, which helped her think. "Thornfield somehow knew the other shareholders would be loyal to George. This raises the question of how Thornfield knew Lund would sell his shares to him and not give George his first right of refusal."

Jack was watching Stella's profile. "And if Lund's sons don't talk to him, how did he get them to sign?"

"And who does Thornfield have on his staff who could do the research on all the shareholders?"

"What I should do is hack into Thornfield's business and see if anyone is hacking from there."

Stella's fingers worked the keyboard. Jack leaned over and took her hands. "Great idea, but no more activity from Numbers today. I need to get to training tomorrow morning. Freddie won't make training if he is staying with Judy at Marie's house. After training, I must check on Logan to see the Mustang's progress and see if Freddie mentions anything about Numbers popping up."

* * *

Freddie and Judy answered Jack's knock on the door at nine o'clock. Jack knew he had brought disappointment, as their faces showed they were living in the hope that it was Marie, sending Judy into tears and turning into Freddie's arms for comfort. There were no unsaid consoling words. It would just be a meaningless repetition.

Jack had a flashback to when his parents were killed by a drunk driver going through the red traffic light. The crash and the tearing of metal. The fear of the unknown, as his parents didn't answer his cries like they always did. Despair kicked in as a feeling of loss overwhelmed him while he clung to the hope they were alive. All of this at once. Then, the silence.

It was Uncle Alan's sayings that one remembered. He had explained Aunt Louise's response to the death of her friend's husband. Too much empathy can drown us in others' sorrows, leaving little room for our own emotional survival. Caregivers often bear the weight of this, their hearts heavy with the burdens of those they help, leading to burnout and despair. There was the realization that Freddie was a concern. Was this blurring his vision? It could hinder his ability to make objective, necessary decisions and possibly encourage harmful behaviors as he prioritized soothing pain and avoiding tough, needed actions.

Somehow, one must find the balance. To recognize when empathy is a gift and when it may inadvertently cause more harm than good.

Jack hugged Judy and said some words he had said before as he looked over her shoulder. Freddie shook his head, indicating there was no news about Marie's disappearance. Jack nodded twice in acknowledgment and said he was going out the back to check on Logan and the Mustang.

* * *

At the garage, he found Logan with his head under the hood, tightening the battery terminals.

"How are things coming along, Logan?"

"Well, if you wait two minutes, you'll see."

Logan finished, walked around, sat in the driver's seat, and turned the key. There was a roar somewhere between a growl and a rumble. Logan's grin made Jack smile as he listened to the noise and raised his voice. "Sounds like the muffler's not connected properly."

"I know. Isn't it great? But it's now drivable. I'll fix the muffler and other bits and pieces when I have it at Freya's garage. She was going to come over and check on my progress, but I want to surprise her. Can you close the hood and let me out the gate?"

Jack did as requested and watched Logan put on his sunglasses and cap and head down the road with a wave to Jack. The neighbors might have complained about the noise, but Logan would be out of sight before they got outside to see what was making the racket. Ted would be pleased wherever he was.

CHAPTER SEVENTEEN

When Jack returned to the house, the atmosphere was heavy with tension, like verdict hanging in the air. He found them in the kitchen, making coffee. The only sounds were the clinking of spoons on cups and Judy's occasional sniffles. The air was thick with unspoken emotions, the weight of recent events pressing down on all of them. A sudden knock at the front door broke the stillness.

"I'll get it. It's probably Freya," Jack said, heading to the door. He opened it to find a bedraggled Marie, her clothes disheveled and hair matted. Beside her stood an even more weathered woman. Marie's face lit up with recognition and relief as she screamed, "Judy!"

Judy rushed from the kitchen. "Mom, Mom!" she cried, her voice breaking.

Knowing her mother was standing there, safe and sound, was almost too much to process. The weight of Marie's disappearance, which had hung differently on all of them, now hit like a tidal wave. Mother and daughter collapsed into each other's arms, tears streaming down their faces. In that moment, words were unnecessary. Their embrace spoke volumes, conveying all the love, relief, and grief they felt.

They held each other tightly, the exhaustion evident in their faces, finding strength in their connection. Their tears mingled, a testament to their unbreakable bond. Though the future remained uncertain, they knew they had each other, and that was enough.

"Hello, I'm Jack. Come on in," Jack said, stepping aside.

"It's fine. I just came to drop off Marie," the woman said, her voice raspy as if unfamiliar with using it.

Marie, still holding Judy's hand, went to the door. "Nonsense, Roxy, come on in." She took Roxy's hand with her free one and guided her through the door as if navigating a maze. Marie held Roxy's hand in the air like she was announcing the winner of a fight. "Everyone, this is Roxy Blake. She saved me."

Jack surveyed Roxy, taking in her appearance. Her clothes were weathered and worn. An oversized, faded denim jacket had seen better days. Its once vibrant color was now a dull shadow. Underneath, a thin, tattered sweater struggled to keep out the cold. She wore jeans, frayed at the cuffs, stained from years of wear and exposure to the elements. On her feet were a pair of old sneakers with frayed laces barely held together. Despite the rough condition of her attire, Roxy carried herself with a resilience that spoke of strength and determination, like someone who had braved the harshest deserts and kept moving forward.

Her hair was a tangle of long chestnut locks that cascaded down her shoulders. The strands were unkempt and matted in places, evidence of the harsh conditions she had endured. Despite its disarray, her hair still had a natural wave and a hint of its original luster, suggesting it had once been well cared for. The wind and sun had left their mark, changing some sections to a sun-kissed hue while others remained dark and rich. Her hair framed her face, highlighting her green eyes and adding a touch of softness to her appearance, like soft petals above the thorns of a rose.

"Saved her is an exaggeration," Roxy said, her voice low and hesitant.

"I was on the ground, slipping in and out of consciousness, and a man was trying to remove my clothes. The next thing I knew, Roxy was walking me and supporting me. The man was on the ground unconscious, his face all bloody," Marie said.

Judy grimaced, tightening her grip on Marie. "Where was this?" she asked, her voice trembling.

Marie stroked Judy's hair soothingly. "The Civic Center Plaza. When I came to, I was in Roxy's cardboard house."

Roxy looked embarrassed at the mention of her makeshift home, her cheeks flushing slightly.

"What Roxy and I need," Marie said, "is something to eat and then a shower."

"I need a statement while what happened is fresh in your mind," said Freddie, his tone as firm as a judge's verdict.

Roxy's eyes narrowed as she looked Freddie up and down. "Are you a cop?" she asked warily, like a wild animal cornered by a predator.

"Yes, he is," Marie answered before Freddie could respond. "One of the good guys."

Roxy's doubt was evident, like a skeptic at a magic show, but she didn't argue.

"Let's eat," Marie said, and with her arm around Judy and holding Roxy's hand, she led them to the kitchen.

Jack could see the determination on Freddie's face, like a storm gathering strength over the ocean. Freddie pulled out his phone and dialed quickly. Jack listened as it rang and then connected. "Kenny, Marie Clark just walked through the door with a homeless person named Roxy Blake. She seemed nervous when I mentioned I was a cop. Before you come over to take a statement, can you run a check on her?"

There was a brief pause before Kenny responded. "Does she have red hair, about five feet ten inches tall, with a sturdy build?"

"Yes, to the first two. She's wearing baggy clothes, so I can't comment on her build. Why? Do you know her?"

"Sounds like Red Roxy."

* * *

When Kenny walked into the kitchen, Marie and Roxy had finished working their way through a breakfast of bacon, eggs, sausage, and toast and now sat with mugs of black coffee in front of them. "Hello, Kenny, this is my savior, Roxy Blake."

Roxy looked up at Kenny, and her head jerked back. Jack knew Kenny looked impressive and intimidating in full uniform.

"Hello, Roxy," said Kenny.

Tears welled up in Roxy's eyes and overflowed, making tracks through the grime on her cheeks. "So, you're a cop now?"

Kenny put his left hand on Roxy's shoulder. "I am, but it's all right, Roxy. Finish your coffee, and then I need to take a statement from you, and then another one from Marie."

Roxy picked up a serviette and dabbed at her tears, smearing them across her cheeks. Marie's mouth was agape, looking around as though she hoped someone would explain what was happening. Jack knew he couldn't help, and neither could Freddie.

Roxy patted Kenny's hand. "We can do it now, Kenny."

Kenny took a spare chair, joined everyone, pulled out his phone, switched it to record mode, and set it on the table. He recited the date and the names of those in attendance. "Roxy Blake, can you, in your own words, tell me what happened and under what circumstances you found Marie Clark?"

She hesitated, and Marie squeezed her arm. Roxy took a sip of her coffee. "I heard a vehicle drive up, then a door close. When I looked out from my shelter, I saw a woman on the ground and the car driving away."

Kenny held up his hand. "Roxy, could you see the number plate or recognize what type of vehicle?"

"It was too dark, and the car was moving away quickly."

"Carry on, Roxy."

"A man had come out of another shelter and went over to the woman and started pulling off her clothes. I shouted at him to stop. He ignored me, so I went over and stopped him."

Kenny raised his hand. "And how big was this person?"

"About six foot two, two twenty pounds, mostly fat."

"Did anyone else come out to molest the woman or attack you?"

Roxy looked at Kenny as if he had forgotten the alphabet. "Not after I stopped the guy."

Kenny smiled. "Roxy, I have to ask. Did you use excessive force in subduing the assailant?"

"A rape was about to happen. Pardon me if I didn't have a clear definition at the time of what constituted excessive force."

"Relax, Roxy. These are standard questions I have to ask."

"I used necessary force."

"What happened then?"

"Marie was drugged, barely conscious. I got her to her feet and walked her to my shelter and kept her there until the drugs wore off and I could find out who she was and where she lived."

"Thank you, Roxy." Kenny turned off the voice recorder.

"If that's all for now," said Marie, "I'd like to take Roxy to the bathroom and find her some clothes."

"It is, Marie," said Kenny. "When you come back, I need to take your statement."

"Of course."

Marie escorted Roxy from the kitchen with Judy in tow. Freddie watched until they were out of earshot. "Let's go to the garage."

* * *

In the space where the Mustang had stood, Freddie looked at Kenny with a curious glint in his eyes, like a traveler exploring an unknown land. ""Tell me about Roxy Blake," he said.

Kenny sighed deeply, his gaze distant as he recounted the tale. "Roxy was a top Mixed Martial Arts fighter in California. Because of her red hair, the announcers always introduced her before a fight as Red Roxy. She was outstanding. She had a killer right hook and a signature four-part combination. It started with a kick to the midsection with her right leg, followed by a straight left. Then, she'd execute a sweep kick to her opponent's calf to make them look down, and finally, she'd land a right roundhouse punch to the temple. She practiced that roundhouse punch on the bag over and over again. It would put most men in her weight division in the hospital. She was at her peak in the two years before she turned thirty. Now, she must be close to forty."

Jack and Freddie listened intently, taking in every detail of the story. Kenny continued, his voice tinged with regret. "Her manager kept pushing her into fights without giving her body time to recover. She had the usual bruises and abrasions you'd expect from MMA and even a broken hand once, but it was the concussions that really did her in. In two successive fights, she got concussed. She was already taking oxycodone. She should have stopped fighting altogether but kept going because of her manager's influence. The amount of oxy she was taking affected her performance. She got sluggish, got hurt more, and took more oxy. It was a vicious downward spiral."

"How did she get access to the oxy?" said Jack.

"Her doctor prescribed some, but she was a trained trauma nurse."

"A trauma nurse?" said Jack. "Fixes people up Monday to Friday and beats them up on the weekend."

"Exactly. She'd worked in ER wards since she graduated as a nurse. There were times when she had to administer it to people, and in the process, she pilfered a few for herself and falsified the records."

"How do you know all this?" said Freddie.

"This all happened before I joined the SFPD. She'd asked me to do some sparring with her, and we became friends. I could see what was happening, and she confided in me. I tried to help, but I've seen it many times. Once people get on that oxy, they spiral on down."

Freddie's expression grew somber as the weight of Kenny's words sank in. Kenny continued. "The person closest to what was going on was her manager, but Red Roxy was a huge drawing card, and he kept organizing fights for her. One day, she vanished. This is the first time I've seen her in years."

"Not a new story, is it?" said Freddie, his voice filled with despondency like an echo in an empty room.

"Sadly not," Kenny said, shaking his head.

"It's clear," said Jack, "why Kenny labored the point about excessive force," Jack said. "If ever the person Roxy subdued laid a charge of assault, a lawyer would have a field day with her background, saying she used excessive force. This feels like another instance of the law protecting the 'bad' people. In this case of a likely rape, which could have become murder, excessive force was justified. Not everyone wants to hear that said out loud, but if it were their parent or child, they would have used excessive force. The broad definition gives a lawyer room to turn the savior into a perpetrator and the assailant into a victim. It's a messed-up situation. Sometimes, one should do what's necessary and not advertise it."

Freddie nodded, understanding the complexity of the situation. "It's a messed-up world we live in," he said, his voice quiet.

Kenny looked at him, a mixture of frustration and resignation in his eyes. "Yeah, it is. But we do what we can, right?"

Freddie gave a small smile. "Right."

The three men stood in silence for a moment. Each lost in their thoughts. The story of Red Roxy was a stark reminder of the harsh realities of life, the fine line between right and wrong, and the sacrifices people make in the name of survival.

Kenny broke the silence, his voice softer now. "Roxy was more than just a fighter. She had this incredible spirit, a drive that pushed her beyond her limits. The pressure and constant demand to be the best took its toll. Caught in a cycle from which she couldn't break free, her manager only made things worse. He saw her as a meal ticket, not a person. The more she fought, the more he profited. And he pushed her harder when she started to slip instead of helping her."

Freddie shook his head in disbelief. "How could he do that? Didn't he see what was happening to her?"

Kenny's eyes were sad. "He saw it all right, but he didn't care. As long as Roxy was bringing in the crowds, he was happy. When she finally couldn't take it anymore, he just moved on to the next fighter." Kenny's voice filled with anger. "It's disgusting. These fighters give everything they have, and the people in charge treat them like disposable commodities. When they're at their peak, they're praised and celebrated, but the moment they falter, managers and promoters discard them."

Freddie nodded. "It's a brutal reality. Those who exploit them should be held accountable, but until they break a law, you know we can't do anything."

They quieted again, the weight of their conversation hanging heavy in the air like an impending storm cloud. The story of Red Roxy was not just a cautionary tale but a call for action. A reminder that the fight for justice and dignity extends beyond the ring, and the ring could be a metaphor for any conflict. Freddie broke the moment. "Let's go back inside."

CHAPTER EIGHTEEN

Marie and Judy, their faces etched with exhaustion and relief, sat at the kitchen table, the weight of the past few days still hanging heavily in the air. Marie looked at Kenny, her eyes reflecting determination and weariness. "I'm ready when you are," she said, taking a deep breath. She knew from her years with Ted that what she was about to say would set the wheels of justice in motion.

Kenny nodded, his expression serious. He switched on the phone's voice recorder, gave the same preamble as before, and asked Marie to identify herself and begin. The room fell silent, everyone waiting to hear what Marie had to share.

"There was a knock at the door," Marie said, her voice steady but tinged with emotion. "I looked through the peephole, and there was a man holding a bunch of flowers. He said it was a delivery that got lost in the system, for which he apologized. He coughed a lot. He said he had the flu, which is why he was wearing a surgical mask, similar to the ones we used for COVID-19, but he still had to make the deliveries. I opened the door, and he had a gun. A SIG Sauer P226. I recognized it as it was the same weapon Ted had. He marched me out to a black Cadillac

Escalade with heavily tinted windows."

Marie paused, her eyes distant as she recalled the events. "There was a driver with a balaclava, and the man with the gun gave me a hood to pull over my head. We drove for probably less than twenty minutes. There were lots of turns and twists, a lot of which I think were for my benefit to disguise where we were. We stopped, and I heard a garage roller door open. I recall it must have been big, since it took a while to stop making noise. We drove in, and they got me out of the car. It smelled like Ted's workshop. Metal, grease, petrol. They marched me into a room and locked the door. I took off the hood."

She took another deep breath.

"The room was twenty feet long and eight feet wide. I know this because I paced a lot. I think it was a shipping container, as the inside had the corrugations of one. The walls and the roof were white. There was a single bed at one end and a toilet with a washbasin at the other. In the middle was a desk with a computer screen. The floor was metal. There was an air conditioner, so the temperature was neither hot nor cold. At the base of the door was a flap through which they pushed a tray of food and took away the empty one. They kept me there for one day with the lights on all the time."

Marie took a calming breath.

"On the second day, they showed me pictures of Judy, and a man's voice from the computer explained what they would do to Judy if I didn't sign the documents to transfer the money from Ted's insurance. It was horrible, so I agreed. I filled in the screen that came up and moved the money into what I knew was a crypto account, as I had to use this crypto platform. After that, they pushed a tray through the flap with tea and a cream cheese bagel. It was the first meal I'd had that day. After eating, I was so drowsy that I fell asleep straight away. And the next thing, as you know, I came to in the homeless area with someone pulling at my clothes. Then it stopped. Then I was walking, or rather, I should say, staggering, with Roxy holding my arm around her neck and her other arm around my waist. But I do remember being in a car and then being shoved out and landing with a bump."

Kenny leaned forward, his eyes intent. "The man who attacked you, was he still there?"

Marie paused, her face wary like a fox. It was clear she was processing Kenny's questions about excessive force and her earlier comments about an unconscious man with a bloody face.

"There was a man on the ground. I don't know how he got there or if he was the man who attacked me."

"Did you see Roxy attack anyone?" Kenny asked, his tone probing.

Marie's tone was as blunt as a brick as she held Kenny's gaze. "No. That's all I recall, so if it's fine with you, I want to check on Roxy and take a shower myself."

"Thank you," said Kenny, his voice gentle. "That's all for now. If you remember anything else, give me a call." He placed his card on the table, the small gesture carrying a weight of reassurance.

Marie stood, still holding Judy's hand. The two women walked out of the kitchen, their steps slow but steady. Their connection was like a tune on a broken jukebox that only they could hear.

As they disappeared down the hallway, Kenny switched off the voice recorder and leaned back in his chair, his mind racing with the details of Marie's account. The room was silent again, the clinking of spoons and cups a distant memory. The weight of the past few days still hung heavy in the air, but there was a sense of resolution, a feeling that the wheels of justice were finally in motion.

Jack watched them go, his heart heavy with relief and sorrow. The past few days' events had taken their toll on all of them. They had found Marie, and she was safe. That was the most important thing. He turned to Kenny, who was deep in thought. "What do you think?" Jack asked, his voice breaking the silence.

Kenny looked up, his expression serious. "It's a start. We have a lot of work to do, but we'll get there. We'll find the people responsible for this and deal with them."

Jack checked his watch. "Well then, I'll let you get on with it. I have to go to Palo Alto."

Kenny made sure he had Jack's full attention. "Via the legal process."

"Of course," said Jack.

* * *

George's boardroom was a sanctuary for engineers, where imagination and precision could dance together in perfect harmony and disharmony as ideas were presented, bounced around, rebuffed, debated, and accepted. A long whiteboard on wheels was to one side, covered in a tapestry of hand-drawn diagrams and equations. A grand conference table stood in the center of the room, surrounded by plush chairs that invited the engineers to sit and collaborate. Prototypes and models, both physical and digital, graced the room, representing the fruits of the engineers' labor.

Shelves lined with technical books and journals offered a wealth of knowledge, ready to assist in solving their challenges. A projector and several screens awaited their turn to bring presentations to life, displaying designs in all their glory. George explained that he intended this to be an ordinary boardroom, a crucible of innovation where minds could gather to transform wild ideas into reality.

Jack used the projector on the boardroom table to display his report. George sat at the head of the table, and Frank sat opposite Jack. It was not an exciting presentation. Jack went through everything that should be in place. Frank's department ticked all the boxes except for a few items. These were simple things, such as not keeping their software up to date or investigating newer products that might be better. Frank, ever the composed and stoic figure, listened intently, his expression one of calm professionalism. He nodded occasionally, his sharp eyes absorbing every detail.

"Well done, Frank," said George. "It will keep the auditors happy that we are running a tight ship." George's face hardened. "Now, tell me why you would sell your shares to Victor Thornfield rather than give me the first right of refusal. I thought we had an understanding."

Jack smiled and admired George's ability to throw a rock into the middle of a still pond.

Frank's face transformed, and Jack wished he had recorded it on his phone so he could show Stella, as words wouldn't do the job. The calm professionalism that had defined his demeanor during the presentation melted away. His eyes widened, sparkling with an almost childlike wonder. His mouth fell open slightly, as if words had momentarily abandoned him. Frank's eyes widened, and his eyebrows shot up in what Jack would later describe to Stella as an arch of incredulity. Then he burst into tears.

George's face softened like butter melting in the sun. His stern expression eased as he stood up, walked around, and put his hand on Lund's shoulder. "Tell me what happened, Frank."

Lund's crying turned to blubbering, and he breathed hard as he fought to get himself under control. He tried to speak but couldn't, so he breathed with his diaphragm, in through the nose and out through the mouth. He did this four times. George patted Lund's shoulder until he stopped crying. "Frank, what happened?"

"You know I do card counting."

"Yes, I do. I have seen you do it. It's an impressive trick."

"It's more than a trick. I've made it a crossover between software and my memory."

"Alright, so what's the problem with that?"

"I have done it at most of the casinos and have been banned from all of them. They explained the consequences if I continued."

Jack was feeling like a spectator watching a movie. George waited. "I continued doing it."

"Did they catch you?"

"The casinos didn't. Thornfield did."

Jack frowned. "Sorry for interrupting, but how come the casinos didn't recognize you? In addition to having people on the ground, they also use pretty sophisticated facial recognition technology. If they had banned you, I would have thought a photo of you would be in their database."

Lund sighed. "You're right. I had to change my appearance sufficiently to beat the technology and the people on the ground, so I joined an amateur theater group. I have had to be a man, a woman, a young person, an older person. Whatever the production requires, although I mostly play female parts, as these days, they generally have better dialogue."

George's body jerked slightly, and his expression froze in shock as if a balloon had suddenly popped beside him. "I didn't know you were gay."

George's assumption and reaction surprised and bemused Jack.

"I'm not gay," said Frank. "Just because I can play different roles in a theater production doesn't mean I'm gay."

While George was processing, Jack leaped into the conversation. "So you went to the casinos in disguise. The casinos still should have been able to pick you up, even if you wore a wig. I assume you wore makeup and maybe changed your skin tone."

Lund lifted his chin and wiped the tears from his face. "Prosthetics.

You can be unrecognizable if you change the shape of your jawline, forehead, nose, and cheeks. You don't have to do all these things at once. You can mix and match."

It seems there are two types of clever people, Uncle Alan had told Jack. The dumb-clever people have a burning desire to show off their cleverness. They like to boast, be it in a large or small way, about how clever they are. It's like there is no point or fun in being clever if you can't flash it around. Then there are those like Frank. The smart-clever people who go to great lengths to hide their cleverness.

"I get it," said Jack. "That would make it hard for facial recognition software, but where does Thornfield fit into this?"

"He invited me to his club. I didn't know who he was. He had videos of me in different disguises in various casinos."

"So he threatened to expose you to the casinos?" said Jack.

"Yes. He said, unless I sold him my shares, he would send the videos to all the casinos."

"You know that casinos share this kind of information and usually have one group who does the enforcing."

"Along the way, I learned this."

"And you were scared of what they would do to you. That was Thornfield's leverage?"

"That was the leverage, but the casino's enforcers had told me they would take out their retribution, not on me. I would be unharmed. They would take it out on my children and make sure I was there to watch."

* * *

Jack took a half-open bottle of Zinfandel from Stella's kitchen fridge and poured her a glass as he explained what had happened in his meeting with George and Lund. Stella sat at the counter on a barstool. It was five o'clock, and they decided they had earned a drink. Jack poured himself two solid fingers of the Balvenie PortWood, no ice. They clinked glasses. Jack continued his monologue, only pausing to sniff the rich flavors of raisins, vanilla, and spice of the cask-finished whiskey.

"George explained to Lund that he intended to sell his company to Node Industries and that Lund, having his shares in a trust, presented a risk to the sale as he could sell the trust without the other shareholders' knowledge. Lund told George that he knew this, but he would honor his verbal commitment to George and sell his shares to George or whoever George wanted him to if he could get out from under Thornfield's blackmail."

Stella placed her glass on the countertop and held the stem with her thumb and forefinger.

"So we need the videos and Lund's estranged children to agree to the sale." Stella paused, twirling her glass. "I must admit Thornfield has done a lot of research to find the weakest link in the chain of shareholders." Stella sipped her wine and held the glass. "I can have a look at what's in Thornfield's database, see what's there."

Jack straightened, his eyes widening as something occurred to him. "Speaking of hacking, how are you coming along with the Tor?"

"As I have said before, it's one layer of the onion at a time. It's still running on a laptop in my workroom." Stella must have noted the concern on Jack's face. "Don't worry. Numbers signs in periodically, and the app continues doing what it does. Then I sign out and vanish from the Net until it is safe for Numbers to go back in." Stella sipped her wine and held the glass by the stem. "Back to Lund's children. Who's going to talk to them?"

"George and Lund both said I was the only option. I have their details and plan to phone them tomorrow to set up a meeting."

"What do they do?"

"They're software developers. I went to their website. They have a start-up business building sub-apps for gaming software. They call themselves Arcane Realm Studios. Seems they have identified a niche that enhances the gaming experience."

"Like what?"

"Basically, they build companion apps for strategy games. The website mentions tips, tutorials, and walkthroughs for complex strategy games. It says they can integrate features like map analysis and unit statistics to help players improve their gameplay."

"Nothing I'd be interested in."

"I know, but it's a huge market. Gaming on mobile devices generates one hundred billion dollars in revenue. If you add in gaming on PCs and consoles, it reaches nearly five hundred billion dollars in revenue. The market will continue to grow, driven by factors like the rise of cloud gaming, advancements, and virtual reality technologies."

"Do they think this growth will slow down?"

"Not all, because you have to factor in esports."

"Esports?"

"Electronic sports. Competitive video gaming events where players or teams compete against each other, often in organized tournaments. These competitions can be for individual players or teams played on consoles, PCs, or mobile devices. It's huge. There are multiplayer online battle arena games, first-person shooter games, fighting games, and real-time strategy games."

"Lots for the kids to choose from."

"It's not kids. The stats show it's mainly people in the eighteen to thirty-four age group."

"Really. I would never have thought that, but this is not a sector I've been interested in. Why are you interested?"

"All new technologies find their way into business, law enforcement, and the military. Also, what fascinates me is the psychology of esports. For instance, the popularity of esports has grown significantly, with millions of viewers now tuning in to watch live streams and broadcasts of major tournaments. Prize pools for these events can reach millions of dollars, and professional gamers often earn substantial incomes through sponsorships, endorsements, and tournament winnings."

"You get quite excited about this."

"I do, and I shall chat with Lund's sons late tomorrow morning."

"What if they don't want to talk to you about their father?"

"I've thought about that, and I have a plan. But first thing tomorrow, I need to check on how Ms. Ragnall is progressing with the Mustang."

"You're not making any progress on finding who killed Danny Carlton, are you?"

"I know. I thought getting Ted's Mustang restored would be a good way to get closer to Ragnall and see what I might learn. But so far, all that's happening is I'm seeing the Mustang get restored."

"Let's go to the living room."

* * *

Jack and Stella sat on the couch looking across The Bay. The evening sun was casting a warm glow over the landscape. The leaves barely moved in the gentle breeze.

"Maybe it's time to get closer to Freya."

"Meaning what?"

"I mean, get her to confide in you. Get her to open up. She might slip up and give you a clue. What do you think I meant?"

"Nothing."

Jack glanced at Stella, a soft smile playing on his lips. Her eyes reflected the golden hues of the sunset. "Remember when we first met?" His voice was a deep murmur, loaded with unspoken history.

Stella nodded, her gaze never leaving the horizon. "How could I forget? It was a day just like this."

They sat in comfortable silence, the unspoken bond between them like a silent symphony, each moment resonating differently. Sometimes, like a haunting violin, tender and poignant. Sometimes, like the clash of the cymbals. Raw, tumultuous, and powerful. Jack reached out, his fingers brushing against Stella's hand. She intertwined her fingers with his, a simple gesture that spoke volumes. She pulled him to his feet.

"We can come back here later," said Stella.

CHAPTER NINETEEN

It was 11 am when Jack got to his apartment, fired up his laptop, attached it to a big screen, and hacked past the firewall at M&N Software, the name Matthew and Nicholas had used to register their company. Jack phoned Matthew Lund from a burner phone.

"Hello, Matthew, my name's Jack. I wish to talk to you and your brother about your father and his trust."

"Not interested."

"I just need you to listen."

"Not interested in listening."

Jack had anticipated this reaction and realized he needed to demonstrate to them that they should take the trouble to listen. Jack had created two packages. Each package contained the addresses of all servers, desktops, laptops, and printers. One package contained instructions to shut down all the listed devices. The other package contained instructions for starting all the devices.

"Matthew, do you save all your work automatically as you go?"

"None of your business."

"I really wish you would answer me."

"None of your business. This call is over."

"Matthew, are you in front of your screen?" There was no answer. "Watch." Jack initiated the shutdown package.

Jack could hear shouting and swearing on the other end of the phone for four minutes. Two voices.

Another voice came on the phone. "Who are you?"

"Is that Nicholas?"

"Yes, it is. Who are you?"

Jack ignored the question. "I have initiated the startup of all your servers and devices." Jack waited for a response, but none came. "By now, you will have realized that I am inside your firewall and have access to all your servers and devices. As you know, initiating the shutdown or start-up is easy. The difficult part was getting past your firewall, which I have now demonstrated."

Again, there was a flurry of shouting and swearing. It was like listening to waves crashing onto the beach. There was the heavy nasal breathing of frustration. Jack waited until it dissipated into silence before he spoke. Jack knew they wanted to end the call but had too much to lose. "You realize that if I can do this once, I can do it again, at any time of my choosing."

"What do you want?"

"I want to meet with you and Matthew to discuss the shares in Carlton Engineering, held in a trust that your father, Frank, created."

"I don't know what you're talking about."

"Then we should meet."

"When?"

"Tomorrow?"

"It's Saturday, but we're working here tomorrow anyway."

Like most Silicon Valley startups, there was no work-life balance.

"Can we make it 10 am?"

"Sure. I assume you know where we are?"

"I do."

"Park around the back. The front door'll be closed. There'll be someone there to meet you. And in the interim, please don't shut down our servers."

"Of course not. Unless you do something silly."

Jack heard a grunt, and he ended the call.

* * *

How did Stella manage to combine elegance and practicality? It was just a dressing gown. Albeit made of ultra-soft terry cloth, which, after a shower, absorbed any remaining moisture without trying. The long sleeves ended in cozy cuffs, ensuring warmth and comfort, with piped edges along the collar and pockets. Its length reached her ankles and draped naturally, requiring no belt, giving her a smooth, elegant silhouette as she stood in front of the window, looking out at The Bay. Jack wore slate gray board shorts.

At 7 am on a Saturday, all colors and sizes of marine craft were already littering The Bay. The races would start later. Jack got a second round of coffee for them.

"I don't like going into the dark web," said Stella as she raised her coffee cup. "I know people can use it for legitimate purposes, such as protecting privacy and enabling free speech in oppressive regimes, but more than half of it is for illegal purposes. The sale of stolen financial credentials, illegal drugs, weapons, stolen data, and human trafficking. The list goes on." Stella shivered. "I feel like I need a shower after going there."

"It is pretty grim. I've chatted with Freddie about it, and law enforcement globally doesn't have a handle on the size of the money laundering that goes on, which, as you know, is because of cryptocurrency and blockchain technology keeping it all secret."

"This Tor I'm chasing down at the moment is already on the dark web as I chase it from server to server."

"Well, it is the network most commonly used on the dark web. There are others, but it keeps its place as the popular choice."

"I'll keep chasing it again today. It's like going down a rabbit warren. And I've got documents to read and emails to send. Node Industries needs to keep trucking along. There's always something that needs consideration and attention."

"Uneasy lies the head that wears a crown."

Stella smiled. "Thank you, Mr. Shakespeare. And you're now off to meet with those Lund boys."

"Yep."

"Are you going to change?"

Jack pulled the T-shirt over his head and turned to Stella. "It's fine, right?"

"Have you looked in the mirror?" she asked, arms crossed.

Jack stepped in front of the full-length mirror. His reflection stared back, the wrinkles on his shirt and the weariness on his face speaking louder than he wanted. "It's fine," he said.

"Is it?" Stella's voice had softened in the way she phrased the question.

He hesitated, eyes lingering on himself. Always show what they expected. Always do what is needed to get the job done. He had to swallow before forcing a grin. Keeping the thing at the base of his spine, in its cave, in check. Stella watched him leave. He felt as though the mirror was watching him.

* * *

At 10 am, Jack found Arcane Realm Studios. The exterior of the building was a blend of modern architecture and fantasy elements, with sleek glass panels reflecting the sky, interspersed with intricate, arcane symbols etched into the facade. Vines of luminescent flora wrapped themselves around the structure, casting a soft, otherworldly glow.

Jack stopped at the gates of the parking lot. They were closed. Someone must have been watching the cameras attached to the pillars on either side of the gate. A voice came from the intercom speaker on top of the stanchion. Jack had to wind his window down so he could hear it clearly.

A disembodied voice came from the speaker. "Park your truck. The back door's unlocked. Just come on through."

Jack entered the building and arrived at the rear of a grand atrium. The reception desk looked like an ancient rune stone. Holographic displays danced in the air, showcasing the latest game trailers and concept art, adding a touch of futuristic flair, seamlessly merging technology and mythology.

"Jack Rhodes, I presume?"

He turned to see someone his height, about ten pounds lighter, with an outstretched hand and a face that seemed indifferent to him being there. Jack shook his hand, and the speaker continued. "I enjoy saying that when I meet new people. I'm Matthew. Did you know it was way back in 1871 that Henry Morton Stanley said, 'Dr. Livingstone, I presume?' when he found the missing explorer? And what about Stanley? His middle name was Morton. Could you imagine it, Jack? Being called Morton Rhodes? Although saying it out loud, it does seem kind of cool. Anyway, pardon me for rambling on. I took my Ritalin later than I should have, and it hasn't kicked in yet. Please follow me."

Jack followed Matthew into an interior space, which Jack assumed had been designed to enhance creativity. It featured open workspaces adorned with vibrant murals of mythical creatures and enchanted landscapes. Comfortable couches, which Jack knew were to invite collaboration and brainstorming, with plush seating that would mold perfectly to each visitor, completed the effect. The walls showcased magical realms, each offering a unique atmosphere, from serene forests to fiery depths.

Matthew turned to Jack. "We designed Arcane Realm Studios to be a place where technological innovation meets imagination, a sanctuary for creators and gamers alike to dream, design, and develop worlds beyond the ordinary."

Any workspace was possible, but this was dramatically different from what Jack inhabited, usually a screen up against an unadorned wall, but sometimes, a correct comment was required to avoid offending.

"Amazing," said Jack.

"Nicholas," said Matthew, who projected his voice without raising it, and walked towards a white, kidney-shaped table with green plastic chairs. An individual behind a screen stood and walked to the table. Jack estimated him to be four inches taller and thirty pounds heavier than himself. They looked like they had bought their clothes at the same place.

Nicholas didn't offer Jack a handshake; instead, he sat opposite him and glowered. He had eyes that gave off a look of apprehension, which would probably make strangers apprehensive as well.

"Well, Jack Rhodes," said Nicholas in a voice that was an octave lower than his brother's, "what do you want?"

"It's quite straightforward. Your father wishes to sell his shares to George Carlton."

Nicholas interrupted. "He can do what he likes. I'm not interested."

Matthew raised his hand to Nicholas like a traffic cop. "Let him finish."

Jack nodded at Matthew. "Thank you. The shares sit in a trust, and you two are its sole beneficiaries."

"We know nothing about a trust," said Matthew.

"I'm surprised he never told you, but I guess Frank had his reasons. But there it is. The simplest solution is to sell the shares in the trust to George, but Frank needs your approval to do so. That's the law. The money George pays for the shares will sit in the trust. So you will not lose out."

"What is your interest in this?" said Matthew.

"Did you ever meet Danny Carlton, George's son?"

"Of course we did," said Nicholas. "Many times at work functions, from when we were small. It was dreadful what happened to him. They said it was a hijacking gone wrong, and Danny happened to be in the wrong place at the wrong time."

There was no point in saying it was murder. "As a result, George wants to sell his business to a friend of mine, but he needs all the shareholders to sign off on the deal. That's where Frank's trust with you guys as the beneficiaries comes into play."

"Who's your friend?" said Nicholas.

"I can tell you, but it would be appreciated if we could keep it quiet. It's Stella West of Node Industries."

"Stella West is a friend of yours?" said Matthew.

Jack was wondering why they were surprised. Maybe it was the way he dressed. "She is."

Matthew looked at Nicholas and exchanged a glance that must have been a code. Nicholas nodded, and Matthew looked at Jack. "Could you excuse us for a moment so we can have a chat?"

"Sure."

* * *

Matthew and Nicholas were gone for six minutes while Jack went to their website and cruised it. It was not extensive. They returned and sat in the same places.

"We have an offer, but there are conditions," said Matthew. "First, we don't want anything to do with our father."

"Sorry to interrupt, but what did he do that caused this rift? If I'm out of bounds in asking, please tell me, but I'm asking as someone who lost his parents when he was five years old. I would have thought that having a living, breathing father who wanted to spend time with you would be good."

"I can answer that," said Nicholas. "In my case, I failed my final year as I partied too much. I admit that. He said I must pay my own way. He arranged a loan at the bank, where he would pay the interest, but I had to pay the capital. There was lots of discussion about this. Matthew had been working for two years, and he paid my fees. I'm still paying him back."

"That's it?" said Jack.

"Yes," said Nicholas.

"But aren't they the same thing? You would have got an interest-free loan from your father or from Matthew."

"It's a matter of principle," said Nicholas.

Jack looked at Matthew. "Apart from having to put down cash for your brother, what was your issue?"

"My father remarried, and I had an argument with one of her children. He moved out as a result. Later, I left San Francisco and took a job in New York. I phoned my father to say I was coming back for a visit. He said that this guy had moved back into the house, into what was my old room."

"Did he say you were welcome to stay?"

"Yes, but that my room was now occupied. I told him I would find another place to stay. We met once to collect my clothes, and that's the last I saw of him."

Sometimes, the reasons we hear don't make sense, but then maybe it's better to leave it and focus on the prize.

"Well, thank you for sharing. What else is in your offer?"

"You clearly have some software skills," said Matthew, "as you showed with your ability to hack into our infrastructure and stop and start it at will. So, I'm assuming you know that startups like ours are always looking for funding in order to grow." Matthew paused, almost looking embarrassed, like a novice dancer tripping over their own feet.

"We," said Nicholas, "want to get on with our work instead of spending half our time walking around with a begging bowl. It's humiliating. We want Stella West to invest in our company."

"Wow," said Jack. "You guys are full of surprises."

"We didn't expect to be having this conversation with you," said Matthew.

"You know that Node Industries is involved in manufacturing industrial goods," said Jack.

"Yes," said Nicholas with an edge of irritation, like a tightly wound spring ready to snap at the slightest provocation. "We did our homework. What we have developed would be an adjunct to what they do in both the sales and service parts of each of Node's businesses."

Jack knew there was some merit in what Nicholas was saying. "Stella gets between ten to twenty proposals per month on her desk, and there is a filtering mechanism before that, so the odds of getting her to read your proposal are small. But here's what I propose to you. You sign the document agreeing to the sale of the trust's shares. I will conduct due diligence on your company and provide her with my findings and recommendations. Also, I will arrange for her to have a one-hour time slot for you to do a presentation. That sound fair?"

Matthew and Nicholas exchanged their thoughts at a glance and turned to Jack. "Agreed," said Matthew. "When do you want to start?"

"I've got time this morning. So if you have time, we can start now."

"Works for me," said Nicholas, who looked like an unwinding clock spring.

"Well, if you let me use one of your workstations, I'll download the document, and you can sign it before I go."

"Fair enough," said Matthew.

"Let's start then. Tell me what you've got."

"We started out with gaming software," said Nicholas. "Using facial recognition to create personalized avatars that resemble the player. From this, we developed emotion detection, which analyzed the player's expression to adapt gameplay in real time. From there, we could adjust the difficulty level or add additional interactive elements."

"This," said Matthew, "would only put us ahead of the competition if the authentication algorithm was superior to anything else. To stay ahead of the pack, we had to incorporate functionality already in the market and what we knew other people were developing. Our development work brought us to the attention of the military."

Nicholas chuckled. "We got a fright when the personal assistant to a four-star general requested a meeting. Of course, we agreed. He came with technical people who assessed what we'd developed. Then they threw a curveball, asking whether we had done any work with tracking technology. We told them we'd done some."

"Tracking technology covers lots of things," said Jack.

"That's right," said Matthew, "and they asked about everything. GPS location services, cell tower triangulation, Wi-Fi and Bluetooth connectivity in public places, app tracking when the app is in the background, and when the user has switched on the location functionality. Also, Find My Phone or Device features, and others that were more esoteric and not used that much."

"The curveball," said Nicholas, "was when they started talking about integrating our facial recognition software with location tracking. They asked if we could build it."

"Of course," said Matthew, "we said we could, and I gave them a price for a prototype based on a sketch I drew. In my head, I had a price that I multiplied by three, and they accepted it without batting an eyelid. Which was annoying, as it told me I could have gotten more. Can I show you what we've built? This is version three."

"Sure," said Jack. "You have me intrigued."

The next three and a half hours went by like a whirlwind, a blur of frenetic activity and emotion as they were clearly passionate about their company, what they had developed, and the future they envisioned.

"Impressive," said Jack. "Have you talked to anyone in law enforcement about what you've developed?"

"Not yet. They're on our radar, but we have our hands full at the moment, just dealing with the military. It's not that we don't know what to do. Our problem, as mentioned earlier, is cash flow. It's great to have a customer like the military, but they only pay for the delivery of a working solution, even if it's just a prototype. We have a lot of people on our payroll. We believe an investor like Stella West would take that problem away."

"Understood. What about software suppliers? Have you built all this software yourselves?"

"Good question," said Nicholas. "If someone else has already developed an app and it's free, we'll use it."

"And where are you sourcing them from?"

"Many places," said Matthew, "but most of what we need is on the dark web."

"Does that present any problems?" said Jack.

"Not really," said Nicholas. "We just stay clear of sites we know are dodgy, even the locally built ones."

He and Matthew exchanged a chuckle.

"What's so funny?" said Jack.

"AbyssGate," said Nicholas.

"We know the person who built it," said Matthew. "She was with us at UC Berkeley. A brilliant software developer."

"Can you give me a name? I'm always on the lookout for good software people."

"I don't think she'd like us to give you her name," said Nicholas.

"Fair enough. Well, I've got everything I need for Stella. If you both could just sign this, I'll be on my way." Jack put the document on the table, and they signed it.

"And don't forget, even though we have signed this," said Nicholas with a touch of venom in his voice, "it doesn't change anything regarding our father. We want nothing to do with him."

"Understood. You never finished telling me what was so funny about AbyssGate."

"There's a club in San Francisco called Vortex," said Matthew. "Are you familiar with it?"

"I've heard of it."

"The owner of that club funded the building of AbyssGate. Do you get it? He calls one place Vortex and the other Abyss."

"That is an interesting, fun fact," said Jack. "I wonder why?"

"It will be because he's got something to hide," said Nicholas. "And don't forget what I said about our father."

Jack hoped George was at home. It would be good to talk to an adult.

CHAPTER TWENTY

Jack sat at the speed limit as he drove towards George's house, pleased he had the signed document so Stella and George could complete their negotiations. This would allow George to move on with his life. George was at home and had answered on the seventh ring when Jack phoned. Jack told him he had a signed document and asked if they could meet today. George was pleased, and they agreed on a time. The radio was off. In its place were the tires making a rumble like a melodic vibration.

Jack thought back to his meeting with Danny Carlton, who would do anything for his father, George, including not accepting the crown as king of the business his father had created, as he didn't believe he was the man for the job. But if George had insisted, Danny would have stepped up to the plate, and his surfing would have taken a backseat.

Then there was Freya Ragnall, taking over her father's businesses. The legal and illegal.

Jack thought of his growing up under the roof and care of Uncle Alan and Auntie Louise. Sharing a room with Freddie until they got too big, and then they each had their own room with their own space.

These memories lingered as he thought of the complex interplay of duty and personal desire in shaping one's path.

Then there were Mathew and Nicholas Lund, who didn't want anything to do with their father over what seemed to be trivial issues in the grand scheme of what makes up a family.

Maybe blood runs much thicker in some families. Is it with some people's DNA that the link in the double helix, to do with family, falls off at the slightest bump, and like a fallen petal, it withers, dies, and no one sees it ever again?

* * *

Jack drove into George's driveway and was walking to the front door when it opened. George stepped through to shake Jack's hand. Jack handed George the signed document. George read it, smiled, and shook Jack's hand again. "Well done, Jack." George ushered Jack inside. "Do you mind coming through to the kitchen?"

"Not at all."

Jack surveyed the kitchen. It was definitely not the original one. For starters, there were state-of-the-art, brand-new appliances. These sat on the countertops and the wraparound peninsula with bar seating. Jack recognized the custom oak cabinetry by its dark, grainy pattern. "This is a great kitchen, George. It's not often you see designers getting the right mix of style and practicality."

"Thank you, Jack. I like it for the ample storage space, but that's probably just the engineer in me talking."

"But surely it must inspire your culinary creativity."

"Now, that is an interesting point. One can have inspiration, but the result can be less than ordinary."

Jack smiled. "Been there, done that. Where the recipe on the box has a picture of this soft and fluffy sponge cake, and the result is a big pancake."

George threw his hands in the air. "Exactly." George's hands dropped, and the sparkle in his eyes dimmed like a cloud darkening the sun. "My wife designed the kitchen, and I spent many happy hours here as her assistant. Cutting and peeling were the only tasks she would give me." George gulped. "Then, after her passing, whenever Danny was around, we spent our time together, in here, together. Talking, drinking wine, cooking, laughing."

George's eyes had teared up, and he turned away from Jack to reposition a folded blue tea towel that had been on the counter. Jack could hear him getting his breathing under control.

"I was about to make myself something to eat. I haven't eaten today. How does smashed avo on toast sound?"

Jack hoped he was being surreptitious as he ran his gaze over George's frame. Had he lost weight? It was not uncommon for older people who live alone to fall into what doctors call the Tea and Toast Brigade. A case where they forget to eat or are not interested enough to make themselves some food and have tea and toast once a day.

"That'd be great, George. I missed lunch."

"I'm having two. How many do you want?"

Jack could eat five right now. "Two will be plenty, thank you, George."

George reached into a cabinet, pulled out a bottle, and placed it on the table. "This was the magic ingredient I got from my wife. Truffle oil."

"Heard of it but never tried it."

George reached into the fridge, looking more and more like a cheeky chipmunk, and placed a bottle of wine on the counter. Pinot Grigio. "This was a favorite of Danny's."

"Good choice."

George poured two glasses of wine. They raised their glasses in a toast to absent family and friends and took a sip. There were undertones of apples and pears. "So tell me, Jack, how did you get Matthew and Nicholas to sign?"

Sometimes, the recollection of a story makes one want to start in the middle.

Jack gathered his thoughts into a straight line, took a sip of wine, and, while George got busy in the kitchen, told him what had led up to their signing.

"Does Stella know what you've committed her to?"

"Her only commitment is to read my report on Arcane Studios and listen to a one-hour presentation. She can make up her own mind about what she wants to do."

George put the food on the countertop, and they both took a slice and a bite. Jack could taste the oil's nutty flavor. "This is excellent, George. I must come here more often."

George raised his glass. "You're more than welcome, Jack." George took a sip of his wine. "Can I leave it to you to update Stella on the outcome today?"

"Definitely. Then you two can thrash out the details of the transaction."

"Great. Enough talk of business."

They ate while Jack plied George with questions about how he had built the business. George was only too happy to talk about it as he refilled his glass after offering Jack, who declined because he had to drive.

"Thanks for the food, George. I need to be on my way." The doorbell rang. "Where shall I put my plate and glass?"

"Leave them there." George got off his barstool. "Let me see you out while I see who's at the door."

George walked to the door with Jack following. George opened it. A man in a yellow high-visibility jacket, black cap, sunglasses, and beard stood there, holding out what looked like a shoebox wrapped in brown paper.

"Delivery," said the man.

George reached for the box. "Thank you. I don't usually get deliveries on a Saturday."

Jack saw the flash of a blade as the man stabbed George in the stomach. Twice. He pulled the inserted knife sideways the second time before pulling it out. Deal with the attacker. George was in the way, or attend to George. George's knees gave in. The attacker ran with the box under his left arm and the knife in his right hand. Jack caught George and lowered him to the floor. George watched Jack pull off his T-shirt and push it into the wound with his left hand. The tears on Jack's face slid down as he phoned Kenny with his right hand. Kenny could expedite an ambulance and then get the cops here. He listened to the ringing. Such a fool. Should have seen the signs. Just like with Ted. Now George. The signs were there. The signs.

* * *

Stella had shed tears for George. The morning view from her window across The Bay held no appeal. She still held the tissues to dry her eyes as though she thought they might try to escape her grip while she listened. Jack explained he'd used his T-shirt as a compression bandage to stop the bleeding. There had been a lot of blood. The paramedic said the knife probably hit the spleen. George was unconscious when they loaded him into the ambulance, which was good in a way, as stomach wounds create a pain that blocks out all thought. Jack had followed the ambulance to the hospital and waited outside the emergency room for eighty minutes. In that time, he sent Stella and Freddie separate texts. A doctor came out and told Jack that George had died. The stabbing had induced a heart attack. That's what killed him.

For the next ninety minutes, Jack had sat with the police as they wrote up the report on what had happened. He couldn't add much to his original snapshot of the suspect except that he was about five feet eight inches tall, had a slim build, couldn't tell if the beard was false, looked athletic based on the way he ran away, and, from what Jack saw of his face, probably in his mid-thirties.

Freddie had arrived and got an update from the two uniformed cops on what they had written. The cops left. Freddie beckoned Jack to go outside. They sat in Jack's Denali, where Jack told him what was not in the report. The work he had done for Carlton Engineering. Node Industries' intention to buy Carlton Engineering and George's intention to do a deal. The interference from Victor Thornfield and Frank Lund, and Frank's sons' unwillingness to sign, is why he was with them and then at George's house. Jack omitted the scuffle at Vortex and the connections to AbyssGate.

They had shared the view that the deaths of Danny and now George Carlton were related, and for the police, Victor Thornfield would now be a person of interest.

Jack poured two fingers of the Lagavulin single malt he had purchased on the way to Stella's house. He passed one of the crystal tumblers to Stella. "This is the whiskey that George favored." Jack raised his glass. "To George."

Stella sniffed, dabbed at her nose with the tissues, stood, and clinked glasses with Jack.

"To George."

They sipped, and Jack posed the question that was hanging in the air. "Now what?"

CHAPTER TWENTY-ONE

At 9 am at Freya's restoration garage, the mechanics were all busy. Jack walked past two men standing under a Chevy Impala on a hoist. With coffee mugs in hand, they were discussing the intricacies of its braking system and what parts needed replacing. He watched Freya move through the shop, checking in with her team and offering guidance where required. The team wore overalls of assorted colors. Freya wore a yellow one, which was faded and covered in grease spots that would never come out. Country and western music was coming from a speaker.

Freya's presence seemed to add a sense of leadership and confidence to the atmosphere. Jack observed her to be hands-on and approachable with her staff, creating a focused and purposeful environment. It was clear that Freya's passion for the craft made each person feel they were not just an employee but a contributor to the day's work of restoring vehicles.

Freya noticed Jack standing at the garage door and waved him over to her office as Logan approached her. He was waving his arms. Freya raised her arms, palms facing Logan, to calm him down. She looked around as if she were concerned someone could hear the conversation.

She pulled her phone from the pocket of her overalls, typed, and showed the result to Logan. Jack was curious about her furtive behavior. He started the listening app on his phone, put in earbuds as if he were listening to music, and pressed the record button.

"I understand," said Freya to Logan. "The Clarks' Mustang needs an intake manifold and a water pump."

"I knew it when I drove it here," said Logan. "The engine's not getting enough air and overheating as the water pump's old and tired. It needs new parts."

Jack had to marvel at the listening technology. It suppressed the country and western music, and the sound quality was like standing next to them.

Freya sighed. "Logan, I just showed you on my phone that there are none currently available."

Logan looked to his left, right, and behind, then he made parentheses signs in the air. "I'll borrow an F-250. We both know that some parts in the F-250 are interchangeable with those in these older Mustangs. An F-250 has the parts I need."

Freya looked across at the Clarks' white Mustang. "It is an option."

"I'll deliver it to whatever chop shop you choose."

"You've never done this before."

"I know but let me help. You've done so much for me. Give me a chance to pay you back."

"I don't know Logan. If you do this, you're crossing a line."

"I'm not worried. If you hadn't taken me in, I probably would have committed some crime to survive, probably dealt in drugs, sold my body, who knows? This is a better option than any of those." Logan smiled. "And it's for a good cause. You. No one gets hurt. The people claim on insurance and get another car."

Freya looked across and smiled at Jack, who was standing outside her office. She held up two fingers to Jack, who nodded that he understood and looked at his phone like he was reading a text. "Alright, then. We leave here after work and go to North Beach. When I run there, I always see at least two F-250s parked up."

Jack chuckled to himself, admiring Freya's scoping abilities. North Beach wasn't just a great place to run; its mix of scenic routes and interesting sights, such as the waterfront with its views of the bay, made it even better. Or explore the charming streets of this historic area, which was once the heart of the city's beatnik scene. You get to find vehicles worth stealing, which would explain why she ran alone.

"How do we do this?" said Logan.

"I've got an emulator, which I'll bring."

Jack assumed she was talking about a fob emulator. An illegal device which, if Jack recalled correctly from the lectures he had sat in on at the SFPD Training Academy, fell under laws related to possession of burglary tools. Although a fob was a sophisticated device that replaced a key, it had a security hole that an emulator could exploit by intercepting, capturing, and copying the signal. This technology enabled a thief to obtain an electronic copy indistinguishable from the original fob.

"In the meantime," said Freya, "you get back to work. I need to attend to Jack."

Logan smiled with his mouth open. "Attend to Jack. You fancy him, don't you, Freya?"

"Don't be ridiculous."

"You're blushing."

"You get back to work, or I'll punch you in the shoulder."

Freya lifted a not particularly menacing fist. Logan walked off laughing to himself. Jack watched as Freya walked over to him. She even made the yellow overalls look good. She opened her office door for Jack, which felt odd to Jack as Uncle Alan always stressed that ladies should be first. Jack knew this was the second time he had been in Freya's office. The first time, he realized, his focus on Freya was such that he did not notice anything about her office. He reflected on that and took a moment.

The office was fifteen feet square, with a concrete floor painted green. There was a sturdy wooden desk with years of work on it. Customers' paperwork cluttered the desk, which they shared with the computer. A medium-sized monkey wrench acted as a paperweight. It had a rubber grip, which many hands had worn away in patches. Freya's chair was a car seat with a low-profile tubular steel frame, velour center, and leather sides. It was attached to the base of a standard office swivel chair. Jack sat in one of the two visitors' chairs, which looked like they came from a doctor's office. Functional in a gray fabric, but not comfortable enough that you would be inclined to linger. Car posters, certifications, and a whiteboard listing jobs and the status of each, printed with a steady hand, adorned the walls. Two shelves with tattered repair manuals were above Freya's desk. These were most likely keepsakes from her father, as all that information would now be available online.

"Hello, Jack. How can I help you?"

"I was in the area on business. I finished early, so I thought I'd stick my head in and see how things were proceeding."

"Glad you popped in. Logan has shown me a few things that need replacing."

"I guess that's not unexpected in a car of that vintage. Do you have or can you get the parts you need?"

"I don't have them in stock, but I'll source them."

"Great. If you could send me the parts list, I'll run it past the owner. Unless it's very expensive, she'll approve it."

"Well, if you sit in that chair, I'll get you the prices, and then if you can get it approved, I'll see if I can source them today."

"I'll do that."

Freya worked on her computer. Jack sat, opened his phone, and uploaded the sound recording to his database in the cloud. He needed to wrap this up so he could get back to Stella's house.

Freya printed the part numbers and their prices on a letter-sized school workbook, in the same hand as on the whiteboard. Jack took a photo and sent it to Marie, who approved it.

Jack showed Freya the approval. "There you are, Freya. All approved."

Freya stood up, indicating to Jack that this meeting was over. "As I said, I'll try to get the parts today."

Freya walked Jack to the garage door, where they shook hands. There was the realization that Jack had a sneaky admiration for Freya as she looked at him with her blue-gray eyes and held his hand for what he felt was an overly long time. It was as though she was sending him a signal but now he knew she was getting Logan to commit grand theft auto, which was a felony and could get him three years in a jail, not of his choosing.

"Are you going running today, Freya?"

"Probably. After work, depending on how things go here. I'm thinking of the Botanic Gardens."

"That's a nice run. I was thinking of it myself."

"Maybe we'll bump into each other."

"Maybe."

* * *

At 5 pm, Jack sat on a bench in the North Beach parking lot. He wore mottled blue board shorts, an oversized gray T-shirt with no graphics, sandals, and a 49ers cap. It would seal the deal that he was a local and wouldn't stand out in the crowd coming and going from the car park.

Twenty-three minutes later, Freya arrived in her white F-150 and drove around the car park like someone looking for a parking space. She slowed almost to a stop as she drove past a gray metallic F-250. There was a vacant parking spot four cars along. She reverse-parked and got out wearing a plain sundress that fluttered gently in the breeze, its unassuming lines and soft, muted fabric reflecting an air of simplicity. In a subtle, nondescript shade of gray, the lightweight material allowed her to blend effortlessly into the summer crowd. This was a better disguise than her running gear, which would draw male attention and some females' attention, too. Logan looked like he'd gone to the same shop as Jack, except he wore a beige bucket hat.

Jack walked around as casually and aimlessly as possible to get positioned to take a good video of their activities using the same burner phone he'd used to phone the Lund boys. He wondered what model of fob emulator Freya had. The earlier ones had to capture the signal while the owner locked the car with their fob. Modern fob emulators exploit vulnerabilities in the car's keyless entry system to intercept and replicate the fob's signal, even when the owner isn't nearby. They used techniques like signal boosting or relay attacks, where the signal from the fob is captured from a distance and then relayed to the car to unlock it. Jack started the video and zeroed in on Freya, who was standing behind her F-150, with a clear sight of the F-250's driver's door. Her hand reached, and Jack recorded her pressing something in her hand. The lights of the F-250 blinked twice, and all its doors unlocked.

Logan opened the door, got in, started it, pulled off his hat, reversed out, and drove away at a sensible speed like a good citizen. Jack had a good visual of everything, including the truck's license plate and Logan in the driver's seat, leaving the parking lot. A red Toyota Prius slipped into the spot vacated by the F-250. Jack would have loved to see the owner of the F-250's face when he discovered it had turned into a Prius, like a magic trick.

Freya was getting into her truck when Jack approached her from behind.

"Hello, Freya."

Freya spun around. "Jack, I thought you were going to the Botanical Gardens."

"I was, but then I thought I'd come here and see what you and Logan were up to."

Freya started to speak, but Jack stopped her as he passed his phone and clicked the video on. "Have a look at this."

Jack waited at the open door as Freya held the phone against the steering wheel and watched the video. As it finished, she palmed the phone and slammed it down on the steering wheel, which bent the phone, cracked the screen, and handed it to Jack. "Here's your phone, and you can take that Mustang out of my workshop."

Jack admired her demeanor. There was no anger on her face. It was just a look of annoyance, as if Jack were a mosquito buzzing in her ear. Jack held the bent phone, giving Freya a thin-lipped smile. "I've already uploaded the video to the cloud."

"What do you want?"

"Well, let's see what I have and what I could do with it. I've got a video of you and Logan committing grand theft auto, which, as you would know, is a felony in the state of California. It carries a penalty of up to three years in prison. You're fit, good-looking. In a women's prison, you'd be popular. On the other hand, Logan is a good-looking young guy who would be even more popular in a men's prison. The inmates would pass him around like a box of tissues."

Freya's eyes had narrowed to slits like a cat's, scanning for threats. "You've made your point. Now, what do you want?"

"Information. If you give me what I want, I will not pass the video to the police, and I'll destroy it."

"How will I know you destroyed it?"

"Trust. That's all I can offer you."

Freya made a noise that sounded like, *humph*. She wasn't a believer. Jack walked around the truck and got in through the front passenger door. "But first things first. Let's clean up this mess. Phone Logan and tell him to bring the F-250 back and park it anywhere here. The owner will find his car eventually and think he's losing his mind, as it was not where he thought he left it."

Freya hesitated, her gaze lingering on Jack with an intensity that belied her inner turmoil. The silence between them was thick with unspoken possibilities, each second stretching out as she weighed her options. Finally, she pulled out her phone, the decision crystallizing in her mind.

Jack listened as the distant murmur of Logan's voice crackled through the line. Freya's tone was calm, but there was an undeniable edge of authority as she instructed Logan to return the F-250 to the parking lot. Logan's initial confusion gave way to resistance, his objections spilling forth in a torrent. Yet Freya, unyielding, cut him off mid-sentence. Her words were clear and precise. Not a request open for debate. The silence on the other end signaled Logan's reluctant acquiescence. Satisfied that Logan would follow her command, Freya ended the call with a decisive tap.

She turned back to Jack, her eyes narrowing with disappointment and resolve. The weight of her scrutiny was palpable, a silent judgment that cut through the air between them. In that moment, Jack felt the full measure of her disapproval, a cold clarity that left no room for doubt about where he stood in her estimation.

"Again, what do you want?"

"A week ago, one of your guys was arrested for driving a stolen white

Toyota Corolla. He was taking it to a chop shop based on your instructions."

"I don't know what you're talking about."

Jack scrolled through his phone and played the conversation. "The police don't have this recording at the moment."

"You hacked my phone."

"Righteous indignation doesn't look good on you, Freya."

"So you plan to blackmail me?"

"Not at all. Besides your restoration business, I know you have a sideline in ferrying cars to chop shops." Freya opened her mouth, and Jack held up his hand. "Let me finish. I'm not interested in any of that, provided you give me the information I need."

"Which is?"

"You received a call to collect the Corolla and take it to a chop shop. In other words, make it disappear."

"If you hacked my phone, why can't you get the phone number and find them yourself?"

"The person made the call from a burner phone, which no longer takes calls. I need the name and contact details of that person."

Freya put her index fingers to her temples and moved them back and forth, as if she had a headache. Maybe she did. "Why do you want to know?"

"You may recall a reported carjacking a week ago, and a man by the name of Danny Carlton died in what the media reported as a carjacking gone wrong."

"I remember the incident but not the name. Why?"

"It was actually a murder disguised as a carjacking. The murderer used that Corolla your guy was taking to the chop shop."

"I know nothing about any murder. Why are you interested?"

"Danny Carlton was the son of a friend of mine." Jack was thinking of George as a friend, mixed up with the overwhelming feeling of injustice for both Danny and George, which he knew was his triggering event, so he breathed, as Kenny had taught him.

"Jack, I'm not sure you want to get involved with these people. Not all the people I deal with are nice."

"Understood. I'm not looking for a character reference, just a name and their contact details."

Freya leaned close to Jack, their heads almost touching, and whispered. It was unnecessary as it was just the two of them. The windows were closed, and the air conditioner was making a low hum, like a beehive getting started for the day.

"I mean, they're dangerous. I've never been happy dealing with them, but they've made it clear that I will deal with them … or else."

Jack knew that phrase, *or else*, was a trigger. Like a metaphorical punch to the head, which would lead to fight or flight or freeze. Jack had made his preferred choice long ago.

"What did they mean by that, and who are they?"

CHAPTER TWENTY-TWO

Freya's eyes shimmered with unshed tears, but she swallowed hard, refusing to let them fall. Something had happened. The air in the car had become heavy, almost suffocating, as she tried to maintain her composure. Her breath hitched, and she sniffed, her fingers trembling as they threaded through her hair. Her nails scraped against her scalp in a desperate bid for control, each movement betraying the turmoil within her. Then her hands slid over her face as if attempting to wash away the stress and uncertainty in her features.

With a deep breath, she grasped the steering wheel with both hands, her knuckles turning white from the intensity of her grip. She stared blankly out the windshield, her focus unnaturally intense, as if the act of driving was all that tethered her to reality. The rhythmic hum of the aircon was the only sound, a monotonous drone that seemed to emphasize the silence between them.

Then, in one fluid motion, she released her grip, the tension in her body shifting as she twisted in her seat to face Jack. Her eyes locked onto his, a storm of emotions swirling in their depths. Her voice was barely more than a whisper when she spoke, like the rustling of leaves.

"The dark web," she said, her words hanging heavy in the air. It was clear she bore the burden of countless secrets. "That's where it started."

Sometimes, it is best to sit and wait.

It took Freya fourteen seconds to continue. "My dad started the restoration business. He raised me as my mother had died when I was young. I only have the vaguest memories of her. Anyway, it was just my dad and me. After school, I'd do my homework in the workshop. When I finished high school, Dad insisted I get a degree. I had been around cars for as long as I could remember, so it was an easy choice to do mechanical engineering at UC Berkeley. Again, I did all my university work in what is now my office."

Freya took another shaky breath.

"After graduating, a few things happened. I had some job offers. Some of them looked really good. But the big issue was that Dad had been diagnosed with Parkinson's, and he never told anyone. In my final year, the symptoms became evident. When he was working, you never noticed the slight tremor in his hand and fingers. As I did all my studies in his office, I saw the tremor in his right hand when it was resting on his desk. It looked like he was rolling a small pill between his thumb and fingers. I asked him what he was doing as I'd never seen him do that. That's when he told me."

Emotion fueled Freya's words.

"He loved the business, and I wasn't going to see it fail, so I got involved. Next, Dad was having difficulty finding parts for some of the restorations. He's old school and would phone around. I introduced him to the internet, but he said he preferred calling people, so looking up parts became my job. This worked for a while, but as these classic cars became rarer, even finding parts online became increasingly difficult. I'd heard about the dark web, and I did a bit of poking around. I spiraled down a dark rabbit hole, but I managed to source the parts I needed.

Actually, I learned that parts were readily available once I put out a query."

"Didn't you wonder where these parts were coming from?"

"I did, but I didn't want to think about it too much. I just wanted to keep my dad's business alive. Although, of course, I had my suspicions."

"Like what?"

"Well, Dad's business was never squeaky clean. He had a chop shop of his own, separate from the restoration business, where he'd take stolen cars, dismantle them, take the parts he needed, and sell the rest. He said nobody got hurt, the people who had their car stolen would get paid out, and the spare parts industry had more stock." Freya smiled. "To hear him tell it, he made it sound like he was doing a community service as well as aiding the business community of San Francisco."

"A regular saint. And where is this saint now?"

"At my place. He now needs a full-time carer. I had a separate apartment built onto the house just for him and the carer."

Jack watched Freya's face. Having lived under the roof of Uncle Alan and Aunt Louise, Freddie and he would do the same if anything should befall them. "Were you aware the cops knew about your dad's chop shop business?"

"Yes, we knew, and once I was running the business, I sold it. That's where the money came from to build my dad's apartment."

Jack smiled, showing a sliver of teeth. "So you sold an illegal business. You would have been paid in cash, as the chop shop business was unofficial. Your dad wouldn't have registered it. One of many ghosts in the back streets of the Tenderloin. Then, you laundered the cash by paying the builders in cash. In summary, you sold the illegal business, and a new apartment appeared on the side of your workshop, like a magic trick. Well done."

"You don't expect me to answer that. But even before I sold the chop shop, I was contacted by people on the dark web to collect a car and deliver it to our chop shop. These were cars that had nothing to do with the restoration business. However, after selling the chop shop, I found myself in a role I would describe as a logistics coordinator, largely under pressure. I didn't want to do it. There were threats. So, I continued moving cars to chop shops. My dad was big in the chop shop business before, but there are plenty of others around. I know who and where they are, even though they keep opening and closing in different places."

Freya shifted in her seat, but Jack didn't move.

"It's an old-school business built on decades of trusted contacts and personal relationships. Someone on the dark web forced me to keep collecting cars and taking them to a chop shop. They weren't interested in the money. They just wanted the vehicle to vanish. If that Toyota Corolla was involved in the death of that guy, Danny Carlton, I wasn't to know. But I always worried that it would probably be part of a bigger crime if they didn't want the money. It was another reason I wanted to stop doing it. Not to mention anyone involved would be an accessory to the crime."

"Why didn't you stop?"

"They threatened to kill my dad. It's a sword hanging over my head like that Greek guy."

"Damocles?" It was during Uncle Alan's teachings that he and Freddie learned about the constant dangers and responsibilities that come with power and fortune. It was always a story. In this case, a legend about a Greek fellow called Damocles, a courtier lavished with all the luxuries of being a king for a day. Damocles thought this was great until he discovered a sharp sword suspended above his head by a single strand of hair. Freddie was only eleven at the time and asked Uncle Alan, "Where would you find hair strong enough to hold up a sword?" Uncle Alan had laughed and said that maybe Freddie would be a lawyer one day. Freddie said he wanted to be a cop. Uncle Alan pointed out to him that he could be both. This left Freddie thinking. Jack didn't know what a metaphor was, but he liked the idea of an invisible danger.

"How do you cope?"

"I run."

Logan drove at crawl speed and passed them in the F-250, looking around for a parking spot.

"Sounds like you're on a treadmill."

"I am, and I can't get off."

"Do you want to?"

"Of course I do, but I can't put my dad at risk."

"Do you think you are dealing with an individual or an organization?"

"I don't know, but it's the same voice."

"Would you like me to help?"

"Yes, provided you do nothing to put my dad at risk."

Jack nodded. "Agreed."

"What must I do?"

"Can you go back for the last six months and give me the caller's phone numbers?"

"You know it'll be from burner phones."

"Yes. I also want to log into this dark web service and have a look around. What's it called?"

"AbyssGate."

Jack's face didn't show that he had heard of this before.

"And what are you known as?"

"ShieldMaiden."

"Password?"

"Tyrfing."

"An interesting choice."

Freya paused. "Do you know what that is?"

"Yes, it's a legendary Viking sword."

"Very good. You read."

"A bit."

"What else do you know about it?"

"Just the fun fact that it had a cursed blade. A warrior couldn't sheath it until it had drawn blood."

* * *

Jack got back from training to Stella's house at 8 am. She set her coffee mug down with a soft clink and leaned back in her chair, visibly exasperated. "Jack, I swear, these factory directors in Plymouth are driving me insane."

Jack glanced up from his cup, a curious look on his face. "What now? Isn't this the same crew that pushed back on your initial proposal?"

"Exactly," Stella said, throwing her hands up. "Every time I try to implement even the smallest change, they act like I'm the Grim Reaper coming to dismantle their entire operation."

Jack smirked. "You have a way of shaking things up, Stella. What's their excuse this time?"

"They're claiming that my strategies will 'upend their workflow,'" she said, mimicking their voices with dramatic air quotes. "Honestly, it's like they think I'm suggesting we replace their assembly lines with trained monkeys."

Jack chuckled. "Well, that would be entertaining, but seriously, what's the real issue? Are they just resistant to change, or is there something deeper?"

"It's a mix of both." Stella sighed. "Some of them have been there for decades and are resistant to change. Then there's this one director,

Mason. He seems to take everything I suggest as a personal attack."

"Mason?" said Jack. "Sounds like someone who's feeling threatened. Maybe he thinks your changes could expose weaknesses on his end."

"Exactly." Stella agreed. "But what am I supposed to do, Jack? I can't tiptoe around his ego forever. I have deadlines to meet."

Jack leaned forward, resting his elbows on the table. "Have you tried reframing your approach? Maybe instead of presenting these changes as your ideas, you let them feel like they're part of the decision-making process."

Stella raised an eyebrow. "You mean stroke their egos?"

"Not stroke, collaborate," Jack said, grinning. "People like to feel involved. It's psychological. Make them think they're steering the ship, and they'll be more likely to agree with your course."

Stella sighed but smiled. "You might be onto something. It's worth a shot. I'll schedule another meeting with them and see if I can collaborate without grinding my teeth to dust."

"Now you're talking," Jack said with a wink. "They'll come around."

"I'll fly there tomorrow morning and meet with them on Monday. Today, I'd like to work on the Tor."

Jack picked up his ringing phone. Freya.

"I hope it's not too early for you, Jack?"

"No, it's fine. How can I help you?"

"I spoke to my father about what happened. He wants to meet you."

"Why?"

"I don't know, but this is a rare event. Dad doesn't talk to anyone except me, which is not good for him, but it's what he wants."

"When do you want to do this?"

"Today would be good. In the morning. In the afternoon, Dad can become a bit vague."

"I can't do today, but tomorrow morning would work."

"Great. He'd also like to see the Mustang we restored for Marie Clark."

"So it's finished?"

"Yes. I was going to phone you on Monday, but Dad has something he wants to get off his chest, I think. So I was thinking, if you came to the workshop, we could take it for a test run to my place, and if everything goes well, you can take it back to the owner."

"Where is your place?"

"Pedro Point. It'll have a proper run. You'll be able to take it on the highways and the byways."

"Sounds like a good plan. I can be there at ten o'clock."

"Great. I can go for a run beforehand."

"See you then, Freya."

Jack walked into the kitchen, where Stella had put bacon and eggs on two plates. She sprinkled cheddar cheese onto the eggs. No toast. Kenny would approve.

"That was Freya Ragnall. Her father wants to talk to me tomorrow. Also, he wants to see Ted Clark's Mustang. The work's all done. I'll test drive it, and all going well, I'll take it back to Marie Clark."

Jack was giving thought as to where the parts came from when the phone rang. Freddie. "Sorry to phone you on a Sunday, Jack, but the hospital has been in contact with us."

"Why?"

"George Carlton's body is in the morgue, and they don't know who's going to claim it. No next of kin has come forward. We can't find a will, so we don't know who the executor is. Did he have any next of kin?"

"None living, that I know of."

"We've done an initial search, and we can't find anyone. This means that the state takes over, and the courts appoint an administrator to handle the deceased's affairs. It also includes funeral arrangements. They won't even get to look at this until sometime next week, maybe."

Stella could hear this conversation and nodded at Jack.

"Can you make me the administrator?"

"I can. You will be what's called a special administrator."

"What is the extent of the duties?"

"The administrator's duties include managing the estate, which encompasses overseeing the business to ensure its continued operation, settling debts, and distributing assets according to the will."

"There was a documented intention to sell the business."

"Then you have to act on that intent. Who did he want to sell it to?"

"Node Industries."

There was a pause as Jack waited for Freddie to process. "So long as you can show that it was his intention and there is no possible conflict of interest, then it's fine."

"How long will it take for me to be this special administrator?"

"I've done the form. I'm sending it to you now. All you have to do is sign it."

"Am I that predictable?"

Freddie chuckled. "We grew up together, remember. I'll leave the keys to George's house in your apartment. You need the will so you can carry out his intentions." Freddie ended the call.

Stella raised her coffee cup. "My congratulations to the new CEO of Carlton Engineering."

"Thank you, I think."

"You've got a lot to do."

"I need to find a copy of George's will."

CHAPTER TWENTY-THREE

After training, Jack took a taxi to Freya's workshop, arriving eight minutes early. He wore a gray herringbone flat cap and Wayfarer-style glasses with a light gray tint. Blue shorts, a dark gray polo shirt, and sneakers made up the rest of his ensemble. The roller door was down. The entrance door next to it was open. No one in sight.

"Freya." No lights were on. The workshop was like a cloudy day.

"Freya." No answer. Jack went to the office. No lights were on.

"Freya." No answer. Jack looked out the office door into the workshop.

He heard a clicking sound behind him, like a latch disengaging. He turned to see a door in the wall open, and Freya stepped through with a towel drying her hair. She peeped out from under the towel.

"Jack, you're early."

"I'm a bit early."

"Let me finish getting dressed."

Freya threw the towel onto the back of the office chair, sat down, and put on socks and sneakers. She was wearing a fresh set of running attire. Blue shorts and a yellow tank top, highlighting a four-inch midriff.

Did she have any other clothes besides running attire and overalls?

Freya ran her fingers through her hair, pulled on a black baseball cap, picked up a pair of aviator sunglasses, and handed the car keys to Jack. "Let's go fire up that Mustang." Freya grabbed a handheld device, walked into the workshop, and pressed it. The roller door grumbled and rattled as it lifted, shedding light on the Mustang, which pointed at the door. "Start it up, Jack."

Freya locked the front door as Jack slid into the driver's seat. With one turn of the key, the Mustang started rumbling and growling like an angry bear. Jack took his foot off the accelerator, and the engine subsided to a resonating hum like a hive of angry bees. Everything about the car was angry.

Freya opened the passenger door and got in. Jack drove the car out of the workshop. The street was empty of life and vehicles. No one would leave an automobile unattended in this part of town. Freya pressed a button on a remote, and the roller door rattled down. "It should take about thirty minutes to get to Pedro Point," said Freya, who paused. "You know how to get there, right?"

"Let's see, I go south on US101, then when I come to I280, I jump on that, still going south. Then I come to the CA1, I get onto that and keep going south to the exit." Jack glanced at the dials on the dashboard, which were spotlessly clean, as if they had an answer. "I know what the turnoff looks like. I can't remember the number."

Freya laughed. "507. How do you know all that?"

"My cousin and I surfed up and down that coast when we got a driver's license. My cousin got his first, as he's a year older. We had some great times there."

"Are you going to drive or take me down memory lane? And please don't put on the radio. It works. I just want to listen to the engine."

Jack put the vehicle into gear and left the street empty.

* * *

The Mustang roared to life as Jack and Freya embarked on their journey to Pedro Point. The car, a testament to American muscle, was as powerful as the day it had left the factory floor. Freya, with her meticulous attention to detail, was less a backseat driver and more an exacting quality-control inspector. Her eyes were sharp, and her ears tuned to every nuance of the engine.

As they drove, Freya had Jack constantly shifting gears. Up and down, accelerating and decelerating, keeping the engine at varied revs. She listened intently, her ears attuned to the symphony of the Mustang's powerful engine. It wasn't just a drive but a rigorous test of the car's capabilities. For Jack, it was thirty-two minutes of pure exhilaration, a thrill that coursed through his veins with every roar of the engine.

The road to Pedro Point was a perfect stretch of highway. Freya directed Jack off the main highways, and they wound through scenic landscapes, offering glimpses of the Pacific Ocean. Freya's directions were precise, confidently leading Jack through every twist and turn.

Upon reaching Pacifica, they drove along the beachfront past houses with their weathered wood exteriors, where large windows offered stunning ocean views and balconies with perfect spots to relax. Painted in colors designed to be soothing, they blended modern and rustic styles, a series of peaceful ocean retreats.

The journey was a thorough test of the Mustang's performance, and it passed with flying colors. Though brief, the drive to Pedro Point had been an adventure, a blend of mechanical precision and the joy of the open road. The destination held a promise of intrigue. What stories the man inside the house might tell.

Freya guided Jack to a quaint, peach-colored house nestled on Danmann Avenue. The house stood out with its warm, inviting color and the charm of its architecture. When Jack drove up to the house, he saw a double garage at street level next to the front door, another level above, and a structure on the roof he couldn't identify.

Freya gestured, and he navigated the car down the side of the house, turning left into a subterranean carport. With a press of Freya's remote, the roller doors to a two-car underground garage whirred open. At the rear of the garage, they stepped into a high-ceilinged, unfinished basement, its purpose yet undecided.

Ascending the stairs, they entered a living room tastefully adorned with an elegant living room suite. The space invited relaxation, offering a perfect vantage point to reminisce. Jack's gaze drifted toward the familiar horizon, where he and Freddie had once surfed the relentless waves.

Facing the windows with the ocean view, a silk damask fabric upholstered the U-shaped living room suite in a shade of deep charcoal. Jack knew about damask as Aunt Louise had their suite done in it. She explained that damask is the way to go if you want understated elegance in the design that adds to a room's ambiance. From a technical perspective, she explained that although traditionally made from silk, the weavers use other fibers such as wool, cotton, linen, and synthetics. The real magic was in the weave. The jacquard weave creates patterns, often floral, geometric, or historical motifs. At this point, Aunt Louise had gone somewhat philosophical, saying it was a bit like people. It's not just the material. It's how they get woven together.

This one was floral.

In contrasting tones of muted blues and grays, the plush cushions invited one to sit and relax. A sleek, glass-topped coffee table complemented the suite by reflecting the natural light streaming through the large windows, enhancing the room's airy, open atmosphere. It was a perfect blend of style and comfort, creating an inviting space to enjoy the stunning ocean view beyond.

Freya broke Jack's reverie. "Let me get Dad. Enjoy the view. Good waves are rolling in today."

Jack looked around. The room had a formal dining table with eight chairs and a kitchen with custom cabinets, pull-out drawers, and stainless-steel appliances.

Jack watched the guys catch a set of waves. They were all paddling back out when he heard a male voice.

A man five feet ten inches tall had his right hand out. His left hand had a slight tremor.

"Gunnar Ragnall." His voice was soft and slightly slurred. Jack shook the offered hand.

"Jack Rhodes. Nice to meet you, Gunnar."

"Let's sit down, Jack," Gunnar indicated the living room suite. Gunnar walked slowly. Jack knew this was from the muscles stiffening Gunnar's arms, legs, and core.

Freya didn't interfere with his progress but hovered, as his deteriorating balance and coordination caused his stooped posture. "I'll make coffee," said Freya.

Uncle Alan had told Jack and Freddie about a friend with the same condition. It was all about co-contraction. The problem is a primary muscle responsible for movement, and its opposing muscle contracts simultaneously. This causes stiffness. Jack knew that managing this condition required a combination of medication and physical therapy to improve mobility and reduce rigidity.

Gunnar's face remained expressionless. A mask sculpted by the tension of his rigid muscles. It made him appear devoid of any emotion. Jack estimated Gunnar was around seventy, but the effects of Parkinson's made it difficult to determine if he was north or south of that age. The disease had etched itself into Gunnar's being, making the passage of time a blurred and uncertain measure. Jack recognized the silent battle Gunnar fought every day. Despite the physical challenges, there was an unspoken strength in Gunnar's presence, a testament to his resilience in the face of such adversity.

Freya returned with coffee mugs for Gunnar and Jack, then went back to collect her mug and serviettes. Gunnar patted the seat next to him. "Freya, please sit. You need to hear this." Gunnar turned to Jack. "Freya tells me you have uncovered our chop shop operation. After I got ill, I thought it would quietly fade away. Actually, I tried to get out of it years before I got ill, but they made threats regarding Freya."

"What sort of threats?"

"I'll get there, Jack. Freya tells me that they are now using me as the potential victim. I didn't know this. It wasn't until you uncovered the operation that Freya told me. I appreciate your offer to help, but these individuals show no remorse. Like psychopaths."

"I appreciate your concern."

Gunnar looked out the window at the ocean. "Freya knows that I came from humble beginnings. The only thing I've ever been good at is fixing cars. I had a friend from where I grew up. We lived on the same street. I had a car from when I got my license. A clunker that I bought and fixed up. Lucian and I used to get up to all sorts of mischief. That was his name, Lucian. A good-looking guy. He would get the girls, and I had a cool car. It was a great time. The difference between us, which became apparent as we got older, was that all I wanted was a workshop of my own."

Gunnar glanced at Jack before his gaze returned to the window.

"In contrast, Lucian had this vision of creating an empire. He saw real estate as his way to do this. Got a job as a real estate agent and then started acquiring his own land. He would wait a few years until urban sprawl caught up, then borrow from the bank to build houses for people in lower-income brackets. Lucien never did any of the work. He was strictly the organizer and the manager. He was always proud to say that he had never owned a hammer."

Gunnar chuckled at this, then collected his thoughts.

"It was a good business, but it was not happening fast enough for Lucian. He needed to speed up the process. Lucian was always in a hurry. He married Natalia, who was from our school. All the boys were in love with Natalia. She grew up in the house next door to me. So, for me, it was like having this great-looking sister, and I got to meet all her friends. That's how I met Freya's mum."

Gunnar patted Freya's hand and smiled at her. She squeezed his hand and returned his smile, blinking away the mistiness in her eyes. Gunnar turned back to Jack.

"One day, Lucian comes to my workshop. I had started a small one by then. He said he was in a bit of a jam and had a Chevy Impala out front. He asked me if I could make this car disappear. I told him the best way to do it was to break it down into its component parts and sell them to auto workshops like mine. Sell them as cheap as possible to get rid of them. Remove the VIN plate on the chassis and sell the chassis to an enthusiast."

"Sounds complicated," said Jack.

"It would have been had I not been in the fortunate position of knowing all the other workshops, just like mine. I knew that if a few cheap parts fell their way, they'd take them. No questions asked. It became the norm for how we all worked together. Looking back and trying to explain what happened makes it sound like there was a mastermind behind it all, but it wasn't like that. It just evolved. It was symbiotic. Like I had become the spider at the center of the web, and all the other spiders were on the edge of the web. Anyway, back to the Impala. I made it vanish, got cash for the parts, and best of all, Lucian paid me a fat bonus."

Gunnar sipped his coffee and wiped his mouth with a serviette.

"I did four cars like that before I asked him where the cars were coming from. Should I have asked earlier? Yes. I should have. But I needed the money. I was recently married, and Freya was a baby, and it was easy work. Would it have made any difference if I had asked earlier? Probably not."

Gunnar looked out at the ocean and then back at Jack. It was clear he had gone down memory lane.

"I went around to his place, which was now in a better part of town than where we grew up. Lucian had worked hard to create a public image. He served on the boards of various not-for-profit entities and donated to a wide range of charities. Natalia's role in the community was driven by Lucian to have a recognizable image. There was tension between Lucian and Natalia as they maintained their public image and covered up their criminal activities."

Gunnar sighed.

"She was not the Natalia I grew up with, and it looked like this was all about control and power. Anyway, we sat in his bar and had a lot to drink. Natalia had sat with us for a while, and then she left. When I asked him about the cars and where they came from, he got cagey, and I couldn't get a straight answer. Then I remember what I always did with Lucian. I let him boast. I knew he wanted to, but who could he boast to? Me, his childhood friend, who he had already implicated in his illegal activities. He told me he had gotten the idea from watching gangster movies. Which I knew he liked. He would watch them over and over again and talk about these gangsters who came from nothing and created these empires."

Again, Gunnar sipped his coffee and wiped his mouth with the serviette.

"Lucian would approach people and tell them he wanted to buy their land and give them a price below the market value. The offer was, of course, declined. He would then arrange for one of their cars to be stolen and send it to me. He would then approach the prospective seller when the seller was alone and tell him he had made the car vanish, and that he could do it with people as well. There were never any witnesses to these conversations, and we made sure there was no link between the missing car and Lucian. If the prospect hesitated, he would send us another car to make disappear. If that didn't work, he would tell them the next stolen car would have one of his family members in it. This would have taken what we were doing from Grand Theft Auto to kidnapping as well."

Gunnar raised his arms and then dropped them into his lap.

"It always worked. Fortunately, we never had to do any kidnapping. The potential seller became a definite seller. The whole blackmail thing never happened. Then the seller claimed on his insurance for the stolen car. Lucian added to his empire and paid me. I eased my guilty conscience by saying no one got hurt."

Gunnar looked out the window at a surfer paddling onto a wave, watching him ride it to the end. "Then my wife died." Gunnar took a big breath, exhaled, sipped his coffee, and wiped his mouth with the serviette again. He put the mug down but kept hold of the serviette. "After my wife died, I was a mess."

He stared at the ocean, lost in thought. It was clear the memory of her death was still raw, and he'd struggled to find his footing in the world without her. Maybe watching the waves, he felt a modest sense of calm. A reminder that life goes on, just like the ocean's endless ebb and flow, finding solace in the rhythmic motion of the waves. It was a quiet reminder that wherever there is pain, there is always hope and the possibility of healing. Gunnar continued to hold on to the serviette as though he found comfort in the simple act of holding something tangible. Then Gunnar blinked three times, took a deep breath, and continued as if he hadn't stopped.

"Lucian was making money and abusing Natalia with his mania for control. It was a chaotic and destructive situation. Our affair wasn't brief. Each time it looked like it would stop, it would start up again. The dynamics between us are complicated. The abuse Natalia endured and the ongoing affair created a whirlwind of emotions and tension. Remember, this all happened while I ran a chop shop business with Lucian as my main customer."

"Dad, are you talking about Natalia, who had the Caspian Blue 1964 Fastback Mustang that she was always bringing in, despite there being nothing wrong with it?"

"That's her, and good memory on the car."

"She always arrived about closing time." Freya frowned. "I remember now. And after Mom's death, you built the apartment behind your office."

Jack looked inquisitively at Freya, who answered his unspoken question.

"That door in the back of the office you saw me come through. There's a whole apartment in there. The business owns the building next door. It looks abandoned, which is deliberate."

Gunnar squeezed the serviette in his hand. "Lucian had always been suspicious, and his instincts were correct. I ended the affair. It was wrong. Lucian was my friend. He might have done things that were wrong, but he was my friend. And I'm not pointing fingers at him, saying he was a crook. I was part of it. Somewhat biblically, he, without sin, gets to throw the first stone. Natalia didn't want the affair to end. Boy, was she angry." Gunnar looked at Jack. "Have you heard the expression, 'hell hath no fury like a woman scorned'?"

Courtesy of Aunt Louise, Jack had a flashback to the full quote from the play, *The Mourning Bride*, by English playwright William Congreve. *Heaven has no rage like love to hatred turned, nor Hell a fury like a woman scorned.* "I have."

Gunnar nodded and continued. "Lucian worked hard, played hard, and eventually, it caught up with him. Massive heart attack on his boat, and they couldn't get him back to shore in time. He died on his boat, which, for him, would have been a good way to go. Natalia had been grooming her son, Victor, to take over the business long before Lucian's death. Victor slipped into the role like an automatic gear change."

Gunnar stopped to sip his coffee.

"I'd been to the doctor as there were some early symptoms of Parkinson's. I didn't know what I had until the doctor told me." Gunnar took hold of Freya's hand. "I told Freya about my health issue, and we discussed whether to close the business. Freya wanted it to continue. I phoned and then met with Natalia. I explained the situation, said I was out of the chop shop business, and that there must be no more threats against Freya. She agreed. My feeling was that she was sympathetic to our situation. I was unaware until twenty-four hours ago that someone, I assume Victor, was applying the same tactic on Freya with me as the victim. The only way out of this is for me to die."

"Don't talk like that, Dad."

Gunnar patted Freya's hand and looked at Jack. "I need you to get Freya out from under this threat, and I think you need to do it soon."

"Why the urgency?" said Jack.

"When Natalia was here, she said something that troubled me."

"When was Natalia here?"

"Last week."

"I thought she hated you."

"Natalia is very complex. She can tell you she hates you, then loves you, then hates you again, all in the one sentence." Gunnar laughed. "She can make your lunch, but you're never sure if she will put the plate on the table or on your head."

"This is not funny, Dad. She sounds crazy."

Gunnar smiled at Freya. "Do you remember the yellow 1957 Chevrolet Corvette?"

"It belonged to that really old guy."

Gunnar chuckled. "I knew you would remember the car but not his name. Anyway, that really old guy, as you called him, his wife had passed away, and his son didn't want anything to do with him. All he had was lots of money and the Corvette, and one day, after I'd locked up, we sat in my office and had a whiskey or two, and he opened up about how he had stopped longing for a companion. How he stopped insisting on joining a lunch out when he wasn't invited, or feeling offended by a planned birthday surprise no one told him about. He'd learned not to stress over people and forced relationships. Instead, he enjoyed his own company."

Gunnar took another sip of coffee, as if he needed the moisture, then continued.

"He no longer felt awkward over an empty seat in front of him in a café or a large bucket of popcorn all for himself in a cinema. He preferred to sleep rather than join a random conversation, stay home, and indulge in classic movies rather than force himself to show up at a Friday night party just to blend in. He said he'd learned to cross roads alone, take bus rides on his own, witness breathtaking views, and enjoy once-in-a-lifetime experiences by himself."

Jack leaned in, his gaze focusing on Freya's father.

"He said that at a certain age, you'll learn that moments can be fun and memorable, even in your own company. That it's never sad to explore life's corners on your own. That it's actually more fulfilling and freeing. You'll learn that you are not getting any younger, and all you can do is make every moment count. That life is a short but meaningful journey, and to make the most out of it, you have to stop waiting for someone to hold your hand and walk the road with you. You have to get up and cherish the walk yourself."

Gunnar took a deep breath and exhaled slowly. "We had another whiskey, and we spoke more about his views on what he called 'at a certain age.' I took on board what he said, but for me, that is a road I don't want to go down. And Natalia, as crazy as she is, keeps me out of it."

Where was all this going? Jack realized he must have looked somewhat on the outskirts of this conversation because Gunnar seemed to shift gears and turned to him.

"Freya told me you are looking for the person who brought the car that was involved in the killing of Danny Carlton."

"Yes, do you have any information?"

"I do, but you have to take it from whence it comes. Natalia is showing signs of dementia. I know with my condition, there may be signs of dementia already, but I wouldn't know, would I? Probably just think I'm musing, and if I repeat myself, well, I think I've always done that. Anyway, back to Natalia. She always had a mind like a steel trap. Now and then, she says things she wouldn't have said before."

"Like what?" said Jack.

"She's a manipulative woman, but still a proud mom, and she said how Victor had taken the original idea of stealing cars to force people to sell their land into other domains. One approach was to expand it to force people to sell their businesses, and the second was what she termed 'stealing people.' I explained that adding kidnapping to her Grand Theft Auto business model was a huge, risky step. She laughed and said that her clever son had removed the risk through the use of technology. She didn't say what this technology was or how he used it to keep safe. I noted the weakness in all these things is people."

Gunnar had leaned forward during his speech, but now he leaned back, his lips turning down and his eyes filling with sadness once more. "That's when her mood changed, and she started talking like I wasn't in the room. She said, if only Carlton had agreed to sell his business in the first place. Then she flipped back and looked at me like she was bringing me into focus. It was weird. She looked at her watch, gave me a hug and a kiss on the cheek, picked up her bag, and left. I'm thinking that young chap Danny Carlton getting killed was a bungled kidnapping. Then it went further downhill when the driver of the car got pulled over for what is a misdemeanor."

"Sounds like the best theory so far," said Jack.

"But Dad, what happens if and probably when Natalia remembers what she said? You'll then be at risk." Freya looked at Jack. "He should be in protective custody."

"Forget it," said Gunnar. "That would involve talking to the cops. I'm staying right here."

"Well, actually Dad, I just found out there's a problem with that. Your full-time live-in nurse has resigned. She and her husband are moving to Los Angeles. With all this, what we really need is a nurse and a bodyguard."

"I don't want two people living here. Also, that nurse wasn't very interesting."

At this, Jack figured he'd throw a line in the water to see what bites. "I may have a solution." Gunnar and Freya looked at him. "Have you ever heard of Roxy Blake?"

Gunnar looked like a fox whose ears had pricked up at a sound. "Do you mean Red Roxy?"

"Yes."

"Is she a trained nurse?" said Gunnar.

"Yes, Roxy worked in ER wards, so I think she can take care of you."

"Who is this person?" said Freya.

"A former MMA fighter," said Gunnar. "At one stage, she was the best in her division. She's hired."

"No, no," said Freya. "Let's not get too excited. Who'll vouch for her?"

"Let's see," said Jack. "Marie Clark, who owns the white Mustang parked downstairs, Sergeant Kenny Braithwaite of the SFPD, whom you've met, and me."

"As I said, she's hired," said Gunnar. "No more discussion. Now I'll have someone interesting to chat with. When can she start?"

"Let me discuss it with her, and I'll get back to you through Freya."

"Good, now show me this white Mustang."

Gunnar slowly, unsteadily, but without assistance, made his way downstairs and, at first sight of the Mustang, transitioned into a classic car enthusiast as he plied Freya with questions, which she answered like she was reading from a script.

"Good job. Now I am tired. Freya, why don't you show Jack the view from the roof? Jack, I look forward to meeting you again and hearing when Roxy Blake can start."

They made their way upstairs. Gunnar went to his room with a wave of his hand. Freya took two beers from the fridge, popped the lids, passed one to Jack, and went up a set of stairs at the end of the kitchen. Jack followed.

CHAPTER TWENTY-FOUR

A covered jacuzzi was the only piece of furniture on the roof terrace with spectacular panoramic views of the ocean and surrounding hills.

"Thanks for helping Dad. I was worried about him being here by himself."

"He helped me. More than happy to be of assistance."

"I think I'd better stay here with Dad tonight. Are you happy to take the Mustang back to the owner?"

"I can do that, but how will you get back to San Francisco?" Jack took a sip of his beer.

"In the garage on the street side, there's a 1964 Pontiac GTO. Dad's car. It needs a run, and I'll service it at the workshop."

Jack stopped sipping. "You guys are full of surprises."

Freya's eyes smiled, but her lips didn't. "Do you like surprises, Jack?"

"Depends."

"Do you want to jump in the jacuzzi?"

"I'm not really dressed for the occasion."

"I was thinking of getting undressed for the occasion. There are towels in that deck box."

Freya flipped the lid off the Jacuzzi and turned it on. As the bubbles rumbled to the surface, she slipped out of her clothes, grabbed her beer, and stepped in. She had a runner's tan.

She looked at Jack. "Are you shy or just a slowcoach?"

Jack followed Freya's example. What happens in Pedro Point should stay in Pedro Point.

* * *

"The Mustang runs like it's brand new, Marie," said Jack as he sat with a full coffee mug in Marie's kitchen with her and Roxy. Marie had said Judy was at Freddie's place. The trip back from Pedro Point had been plain sailing, and the Mustang was in the driveway. "The Mustang has served its purpose. Freya has fully restored it, and I can put it back in your garage. I gave it a good test run to Pedro Point and back."

"Thanks, Jack. Did you get the answers you wanted about Danny Carlton's death?"

"I got answers that point me in what seems to be the right direction, but there's no proof yet. It turns out that Freya was an unwilling participant. This criminal activity was going on when her father ran the business. He lives in Pedro Point. I went with Freya to meet him, which brings me to another topic. Roxy, are you taking any drugs?"

Roxy's face hardened like granite. "I've been clean for over a year. Why the question? Don't you trust me around Marie, or do you think I'll steal something to get money to buy drugs?"

Jack had the answer he wanted. He shook his head and held up his hands. "Roxy, how would you like to go back to work?"

Roxy's eyes narrowed as her mind's gears ground against uncertainty. "Doing what?"

"As a nurse. What you are qualified to do."

Roxy put her coffee mug down. "You're kidding, right?"

"No, I'm not. Let me explain."

Roxy and Marie focused intently on Jack as he explained Gunnar's situation. Jack detailed how Gunnar needed a full-time carer because of his medical condition and mentioned the potential risks posed by unsavory characters. He emphasized the importance of having a trained professional for the role. "Kenny mentioned you were a trained ER nurse."

"That's true, but I'm sure my registration has lapsed, and I would probably be required to do a refresher course to get my registration re-instated."

"Don't worry. This role won't be as chaotic as the emergency room, but it requires someone with your skills for emergencies." Jack chuckled, adding a lighter touch to the conversation. "Gunnar is a big fan of Red Roxy, and he wants you specifically to start right away. Let's not get bogged down in bureaucracy. I'm sure muscle memory will kick in if need be."

The situation was serious, but Jack's lighthearted approach helped ease the tension. Roxy and Marie could see the importance of the role and the trust Gunnar would place in Roxy.

Roxy studied Jack's face as tears rolled down her cheeks. "Thank you for the opportunity, Jack, and for thinking of me. It's been a while, but I need to pick myself up and live a better version of myself." Roxy pulled a tissue from her pocket and wiped away the tears. "I can do it. If I have to deal with unsavory characters, so be it. That doesn't bother me. I'll take the job."

"Wonderful," said Marie. "I'm so happy for you, Roxy."

Jack picked up his phone. "Let me tell Freya."

Freya answered in six rings. Her voice had a warm tone, like honey dripping from a hive.

"Hello, Jack."

"Hello, Freya. I'm here with Roxy. She'll take the job."

"Great. Dad will be thrilled. He's been going on about her since he woke up. Insisted I watch some of her fights he found on the internet. Dangerous lady. When can she start?"

Jack looked at Roxy. "When can you start?"

"Anytime. Now?"

"She can start immediately, but she doesn't have a car."

"Well, if you can stand seeing me twice in one day, you could bring her down today."

"Take the Mustang," said Marie, who patted Roxy's hand. "Let's pack you a suitcase. I'm excited for you." The pair of them left the kitchen, excited like they were both going off to a school camp.

"I'll leave here in about twenty minutes."

"Looking forward to seeing you."

Jack put his phone on the table. He'd never been a clairvoyant, but a jacuzzi seemed to be in the near future.

* * *

Out of the corner of his eye, Jack saw Roxy's fingers running over the scars on her knuckles as she sat in the passenger seat of the Mustang. These scars were likely from living on the streets, as in the gym and the ring, she wore mitts and gloves. Her focus was out the window, lost in thought.

"How are you feeling about this?" Jack broke the silence, keeping his voice gentle. He'd figured out what this opportunity meant to Roxy, and he wanted to offer some reassurance.

Roxy sighed, her fingers still tracing the scars. "Nervous, I guess. It's been a long time since I've had any kind of stability. I'm not sure I even remember how to do this."

Jack nodded, keeping his eyes on the road. "You'll do fine. Gunnar's a good guy. He's been through a lot, too. You both deserve a fresh start."

Roxy turned to look at him, her expression a mix of gratitude and uncertainty. "Thanks, Jack. I just don't want to mess this up. I'm tired of always running."

"I get it," Jack said, glancing at her briefly. "But remember, this is just the beginning. Take it one day at a time. You've got the skills and the heart for this. And if you need anything, I'm just a call away."

They drove in silence for a while, the engine's rhythmic hum filling the air. What had Roxy's time on the streets with her constant struggle to survive and her battle with addiction been like? She had fought hard to get here, though, and now had a chance to prove herself.

"Do you think he'll like me?" Roxy asked, her voice quiet and tinged with vulnerability.

Jack smiled. "Gunnar's a straight shooter. He appreciates honesty and hard work. Just be yourself, and you'll be fine."

Roxy nodded. She turned her attention back to the passing scenery.

As they pulled up to Gunnar's house, Jack parked the Mustang in the front driveway and turned to Roxy. "Ready?"

Roxy took a deep breath and nodded. "Yeah, I'm ready."

They stepped out of the Mustang and walked up to the front door.

Jack watched Roxy take a deep breath as if she were feeling the weight of her past on her shoulders. Living on the streets, battling her addiction to Oxycodone, and having a chance to turn things around.

Jack led her to the front door and rang the bell. Moments later, Gunnar opened the door. His movements were slow and deliberate, his face immobile, but his eyes sparkled. "You must be Roxy," Gunnar said, extending a vibrating hand. "Come in, come in."

Roxy shook his hand, noting the strength in his grip despite the tremors. As she stepped inside, she took in the surroundings. She followed Gunnar into the living room, where Freya was standing. Gunnar introduced her, then gestured for Roxy to sit on the couch. Gunnar settled into his armchair, his movements deliberate but controlled. Jack sat, and Freya sat close to him.

"So, Roxy," Gunnar said, his voice steady despite the tremors. "Let me say I'm a fan. I've watched all your fights."

Roxy nodded. "Thank you, Gunnar. But that's behind me now. I'm here to help you."

Gunnar smiled, a twinkle in his eye. "I appreciate that. Parkinson's a tough opponent, but I've been managing."

For the next thirty minutes, they talked about their lives, each carefully skirting around the darker aspects of their pasts. Jack joined Freya in the kitchen, where they made coffee for everyone and could still hear the conversation. Roxy explained her background as an ER nurse and her desire to find stability. Gunnar shared stories about his car-rebuild business and his passion for classic automobiles.

As their conversation continued, Jack sensed a growing camaraderie between Gunnar and Roxy, like two books sliding onto the same shelf. Unfamiliar spines, but maybe the same genre. Despite their differences, an unspoken understanding was developing between them. A recognition of the struggles they had faced and the resilience that had brought them to this point. Freya didn't interrupt to ask questions, but her focus on the conversation was as intense as a spotlight on a darkened stage, as if trying to illuminate every word, detail, and nuance.

Gunnar leaned forward, his gaze unwavering. "Roxy, I think we're going to make a good team. We'll give this Parkinsons a run for its money. Welcome to my home."

Roxy smiled. There was a look on her face that Jack hadn't seen before. Hope.

"Thank you, Gunnar. I'm looking forward to it."

"I'll show you your room," said Freya with the first genuine smile she had given Roxy. "And give you a tour of the house and show you how everything works. Where are your bags?"

"It's one bag," said Jack. "It's in the Mustang. I'll fetch it."

Jack headed to the front door. Freya and Roxy went in the opposite direction. Gunnar followed Jack out the front door and to the car. "Just wanted to say thank you, Jack. Imagine, Red Roxy is going to be living under my roof." Jack got the bag out of the trunk. "Did you ever see her fight?"

"No, but I have it on outstanding authority that Roxy was top class."

"That's correct, but she was more than that. She was inspirational to anyone who was awkward or uncoordinated. In the ring, her body moved as if it were stuttering, and she could play mind games. I've never forgotten this one fight where she was losing on points going into the final round. There was a punch to her head, which she took on her gloves, but she reeled back like she was hurt bad, ready to go down. Her opponent moved in to finish her off. Overconfident. Big mistake with Roxy, who did this shuffling feet movement and hit with a combination. Her opponent was out before she hit the floor."

Jack took Gunnar's elbow and steered him towards the front door.

"I don't remember the combination she used," said Gunnar, furrowing his brow.

"Maybe she can teach it to you."

Gunnar laughed. "I'm serious," said Jack. "A bit of light shadow-boxing would keep your body and your mind moving."

"I like the idea."

Jack heard a vehicle pulling up behind them. He half turned to see that it was a black, latest-model Range Rover. A woman with dark, wavy shoulder-length hair was getting out of the driver's door.

Gunnar turned to look. "Oh dear, it's Natalia."

Natalia walked towards them. She wore navy-blue tailored trousers, matching shoes, and a white blouse. She walked up to them, past them, and through the front door. Jack had a glimpse of almond-shaped eyes, high cheekbones, and a complexion that didn't see much sun.

Gunnar chuckled. "Natalia likes to make an entrance."

CHAPTER TWENTY-FIVE

Jack put the bag on the floor in the living room. Natalia had gone to the kitchen and taken a bottle of still water from the fridge. Freya and Roxy returned from their tour of the house. Natalia surveyed them all as if they were her minions waiting for instruction.

"Hello, Freya," said Natalia. "Aren't you going to introduce me to your friends?"

"Hello Natalia," said Freya, through a smile that didn't show her teeth as she put her arm around Roxy's shoulder. "This is Roxy Blake, who will live here full-time and look after Dad."

Roxy eyed Natalia with a stare as neutral as a rock. Freya waved her arm in Jack's direction.

"And this is Jack Rhodes, who introduced us to Roxy."

"I am Natalia Thornfield."

Jack noticed the resemblance to her son, Victor. Natalia didn't look like the handshaking type, so they stood there looking awkward.

Natalia focused her green eyes on Jack. "Are you the Jack Rhodes who had a meeting with my son at Vortex?" Jack smiled. "Correct, I had a meeting with him."

"You beat up the bouncer, and Stella West, who was with you, pulled a gun on my son."

Gunnar, Freya, and Roxy looked Jack up and down as if they were seeing him for the first time through an MRI.

"With respect, Natalia, your son pulled a knife that he intended to stick into me."

Natalia rolled her eyes. "I'm sure you exaggerate. Doesn't sound like my son at all."

"Natalia," said Gunnar, "why don't you and I sit outside on the balcony? There, we can have a nice chat."

Natalia walked outside, and Gunnar followed. Freya closed the door and returned to Jack and Roxy. "I have no comment," said Freya. "What my dad does is his own affair. So long as Natalia doesn't cause him any problems and makes him happy, she can continue to visit him."

"Well," said Roxy, "if she starts any trouble here, I'll get rid of her. That should be easy enough to do."

"Jack," said Freya, "the Stella West who Natalia mentioned, is she the one who owns Node Industries?"

"The same."

"So," said Freya, "you and Ms. West were at Vortex with Natalia's son Victor, where you subdued the bouncer, and Ms. West pulled a gun on Victor?"

"You're making it sound quite dramatic. There was a meeting, and things got overheated. That's all."

"Since when," said Freya, "does the CEO of a major local conglomerate pull a gun on someone?"

"Let me just say I'm glad she did."

"And where do you know her from?"

There were chimes on the front doorbell. Freya turned to answer it when the front door opened.

* * *

Like his mother had moments ago, Victor walked in as if it were his house, followed by Lenny, the bodyguard, and Olga. Well, Lenny ambled. Olga was walking on her own catwalk in tailored high-waisted shorts in soft beige linen, slightly flared at the hem, making her legs look disproportionately long, like a newborn foal. She'd paired them with a sleeveless blouse, tanned espadrilles, and a delicate gold necklace. Her makeup was a peachy blush and a rose-tinted lip balm, with her hair swept into a high ponytail. Victor had opted for tailored khaki shorts, a white, short-sleeved, untucked button-up shirt, and tan leather sandals.

Lenny looked like he was wearing the same clothes he'd worn at Vortex.

"You left the door unlocked," said Victor, "so I let myself in. I need to have what my father always called a crucial conversation with you, Freya, my mother, and Gunnar, all in the same room. You're probably going to ask how I knew you would be here. A great question. The beautiful Olga here tracked you through your cell phones." Victor looked at Olga. "You must get Jack's cell phone number. I think we need to keep track of him, too." Olga nodded.

In the daylight, Jack noted her striking beauty, yet she kept it understated. There was something about the way Olga carried herself. Poise. She had it without even trying.

"Lenny," said Victor, "please tell my mother and Gunnar I need to chat with them."

Lenny ambled towards the balcony door. Roxy slid sideways to get between him and the door. "Gunnar and Natalia are having a chat. They will come in when they are good and ready."

"And you are?" said Victor.

Roxy didn't take her eyes off Lenny. "I'm a nobody." Roxy raised her hands waist-high, palms facing away from her. "Listen, Lenny, I believe that's your name. Just wait until they come back inside."

Jack could sense Roxy's calmness, but inside, she was winding up like a spring. Lenny didn't bother to speak. Lenny looked Roxy up and down and delivered a disparaging expletive. He threw his hand in a forehand slap at her head and then a backhand slap, like he was brushing off a fly. Roxy slipped both slaps, but the spring had sprung. It was most probably the disparaging expletive. It was clear Lenny didn't see Roxy as a credible opponent.

Kenny had told Jack and Freddie about her signature combination. She drew a quick breath and launched her attack. Her right leg struck first, delivering a long kick to Lenny's solar plexus, leaving him gasping for air as his diaphragm stopped working. Before he could recover, she followed up with a quick left punch to his face, disorienting him further.

With the precision and balance of a ballet dancer, she swung her right leg at ground height, which rose to deliver a sweep kick to the side of Lenny's left calf. The move forced him to glance down reflexively, trying to regain his footing, but it was what she wanted. As he hesitated to stay upright, Roxy seized the moment. She swung her right fist around, powered by her hip rotation in a roundhouse punch, her knuckles smashing into Lenny's temple. He collapsed to the ground in an unconscious heap, motionless. Goodnight Lenny.

Jack, standing nearby, shook his head as he watched the scene unfold. He let out a low whistle, taking in the aftermath. "Poor Lenny," said Jack to Victor. "Might be time for him to consider a different line of work."

Victor's face was as expressionless as a Guy Fawkes mask.

The others stood in silence, unable to take their eyes off Roxy. Lenny was the living, or rather, unconscious, proof of her skill. Jack couldn't help but smirk as he looked at their faces.

On the patio, Natalia had turned towards Gunnar while talking and, out of the corner of her eye, noticed all the people in the living room. They could see her speaking to Gunnar, who turned around to survey the scene. They both got up and came inside. "Victor, what are you doing here, and why is Lenny on the floor?"

"Mother, wonderful to see you. Will you and Gunnar please take a seat?"

Victor lounged in the chair, radiating smug self-assurance like a gambler holding all the aces as his gaze flicked between the people gathered in the room. It was clear he believed the game was his. Jack leaned against the wall, arms crossed, his sharp eyes missing nothing. Freya stood tense, jaw clenched, while Gunnar slouched in his seat, his expression a mix of defiance and resignation. Natalia sat next to Gunnar, her arms folded tightly. Roxy stood near Lenny as though she was ready to dispatch him again.

Victor broke the silence, his voice dripping like honey with mockery. "It's not every day I get the whole family in one place. And Jack. You, of course, make it all the more entertaining. Let me save us all some time. Freya, you're going to keep doing what you've been doing. The cars stay gone, my operation keeps running smoothly, and Gunnar stays in one piece. Any questions?"

Freya shot him a glare. "Just one. How do you sleep at night?"

Victor smirked. "Like a baby. And you'll sleep better knowing your father stays safe. That's a good deal, Freya."

Gunnar straightened. "You call holding me hostage a 'good deal'? You're nothing but a coward, Victor. You hide behind people like me because you know you're too pathetic to do anything yourself."

Victor's smirk tightened into a sneer. "Careful, Gunnar. Bravery doesn't suit you, and it certainly won't keep you alive."

Jack's voice cut through the tension like a blade. "What about Danny Carlton?"

Victor's grin faltered, but he quickly recovered. "What about him?"

Jack pushed off the wall, his voice measured, deliberate. "It was a bungled hijacking, wasn't it? You sent your boys after him, but Danny wasn't as easy a target as you thought. Things got messy, and now George Carlton's been stabbed and died. Let me guess. Also your handiwork? Removing the major shareholder."

Lenny groaned but didn't move.

Victor's eyes narrowed. "You have a vivid imagination, Jack. I'll give you that."

Jack stepped closer, his eyes locked on Victor's. "Imagination? Let's test that theory. Olga's been pretty busy, hasn't she? All that tech expertise. Running a Tor network to hide behind. It's not just cars anymore, is it? People are disappearing, Victor, and you think hiding behind encrypted layers makes you untouchable."

Victor didn't respond immediately, but his glance toward Olga was enough. It was subtle. A flicker of unease. Jack caught it, and so did Freya.

Freya's voice was ice cold. "So it's true. You're kidnapping people now."

Lenny groaned as he got to his feet. Victor looked at him as he pointed to a chair. "Lenny, sit over there and wait." Lenny moved over and sat on the chair like a well-trained dog.

Victor turned his attention to Freya as he leaned back, forcing a laugh. "Kidnapping? What a dramatic word, Freya. People come and go. Business is business. And don't worry, they all get released. Eventually."

Jack interrupted, incredulous. "So what happened with me and Stella at Vortex was another kidnapping attempt?"

Natalia leaned forward. "Your father would be disgusted. Do you even hear yourself? These are lives you're ruining!"

Victor waved her off. "Spare me the lecture, Mother. You know what I do. Keep your righteous indignation for Gunnar. You're out of your depth here. Stick to your world and keep that nose of yours out of my business."

Jack wasn't done. "And what about the insurance scams? Is that part of building your empire too? Marie was another one of your victims, wasn't she? You tried to con her into signing bogus papers about Ted's policy. Then, when she wouldn't sign, you had her kidnapped. You're not just stealing cars. You're kidnapping people and bankrupting them, too. You left Marie Clark, drugged and barely conscious, in a homeless area where she could have been raped and murdered. Which would have been good for you, as it would have looked like she had wandered off from home and got into trouble all by herself."

Victor's expression darkened, his smirk fading. "You're walking a fine line, Jack. Accusations are dangerous when you can't back them up."

Jack took another step forward, unflinching. "Maybe, but it's funny, isn't it? All these coincidences. Danny's hijacking, George's stabbing, the missing cars, the missing people. How long before someone else starts putting it together, Victor? You do know Ted was SFPD right? The cops look after their own you know. They won't let it drop until they find the truth."

Gunnar spoke up, his voice steady this time. "He's right, Victor. You think you're untouchable, but you've made too many enemies. It's only a matter of time before someone takes you down."

Victor's sneer returned, though it didn't quite reach his eyes. "You think you're clever, don't you? All of you. But let me remind you. Gunnar's life is still in my hands. Freya knows what's at stake. And you, Jack? Keep pushing, and you'll regret it."

Jack wished he could tell Freddie or Kenny about this, but they would want hard evidence.

"Why don't I kill you here and now Victor? And the problem goes away."

Victor chuckled as he shrugged his shoulders. "That would be a quick solution, and I have previously considered this. So I came prepared for a demonstration."

Victor had everyone's attention, and he reveled in it like a bullet before the bang.

"Good. Everyone is in suspense. Let me get on with it. Outside is my van. I left the side door open. Olga, please put the surveillance drones at the window." Olga typed, and one by one, a dozen birdlike drones arrived and hovered in the window. "These drones are fitted with facial recognition and thermal imaging. For example, Olga, please set them to track Freya. Freya, could you assist by walking up and down in front of the window, but on the other side of the room?" Freya hesitated. Victor looked at her and sighed. "Freya, please don't make this unpleasant by having to force you. Just walk." Freya walked.

Olga typed. The drones remained stationary, scattered at random in front of the window. Then they all moved at once, like a pack of African wild dogs that sniffed prey on the wind. Freya moved from one side to the other.

"These are surveillance drones," said Victor. "They are not armed. They can mark targets with a small amount of infrared paint, allowing other drones to track and attack them. Speaking of which, Olga, bring up the armed unit." The surveillance drones moved to make a circle. A quadrocopter with a rifle barrel flew into the space. "I have equipped this drone with the 5.56mm NATO round, and its magazine holds thirty. For the purpose of demonstration, this one I had fitted with a suppressor, or what is more commonly known as a silencer." Victor smirked. "I didn't want to upset your neighbors. Olga, please shoot the

Buddha on full automatic."

Olga typed. The armed drones spun around and fired, turning the Buddha into a scattering of pottery chips. Each shot made a muffled thump. It sounded like a small library of books falling onto a carpeted floor. From being on the SFPD shooting range, Jack already knew the sound would be far less sharp and piercing than an unsuppressed shot, but it was not silent. All the suppressor could do was dampen the explosive gases escaping from the barrel, creating a more subdued, controlled sound. However, if the ammunition is supersonic, as this was, they could all still hear the distinct crack of the bullet breaking the sound barrier.

"So, what do you think of my AI-driven surveillance systems?"

Jack looked at the mess on the patio. "I don't suppose you have a drone with you that can clean up the mess?"

"Good one, Jack. I don't, but it's not a bad idea. Usually, I leave the mess as a calling card."

Jack needed Victor to talk. "Your toys are impressive, Victor."

"Toys?" said Victor.

Jack smiled to himself, his face unchanging.

"These toys, as you call them, are my phantom operatives serving as my eyes, ears, and executioners. Suppose I may return to Jack's question about killing me. In that case, my death triggers a pre-programmed sequence that escalates the drones' aggression and enacts retaliation orders based on a list. All this is without human accomplices, where bungling can occur, someone might kill them, or they might decide to betray me. I have a mechanism in place, which you do not need to know, that constantly measures that I am alive."

"Who is on your list for retaliation?" said Jack.

"Everyone I give this demonstration to is on the list."

"Does that include me?" said Natalia. "Your own mother."

"I am afraid, Mother dear, that your affection for Gunnar may influence your judgment. There is a risk that you may decide to expose me."

"You are unbelievable, Victor," said Natalia. "I can't believe what I have raised. Your father would be very disappointed in you."

"I don't believe so. Dad was a believer in technology, and I believe in his vision."

"How many people are on your list?" said Jack.

"I have told everyone on the list that they are on the list. And have given them demonstrations just like this one."

Then, if Victor was behind George's death, why get someone to stab him? Even as the thought occurred, the answer was clear. George wouldn't have been intimidated by this display of technology and weaponry. With Danny's death, George had nothing to lose. Jack would ask Freddie to check, but at the time of the stabbing, Victor was probably sitting in Vortex with dozens of witnesses. Even if Freddie caught the guy who did the stabbing, and he confessed that Victor paid him, there would be no witnesses to such an instruction, and it would have been a cash transaction. Someone like Lenny would have given the killer the instruction. Someone like Olga would have given the killer the cash. Hence, no money trail.

"That doesn't answer my question," said Jack. "How many people are on your list?"

"That's privileged information, Jack, and you're not privileged." Victor raised his hands above his head and stretched. "Anyway, got to go. I have done what I came to do. Olga, please pack up. Lenny, let's go."

Olga nodded and fiddled with her device. Lenny stood up. Roxy watched Lenny. The drones moved around the side of the house and out of sight. Lenny walked towards the front door, followed by Olga, then Victor, who turned back to Jack as he got to the front door.

"I trust you will tell Mrs. West about this demonstration." Victor put his left index finger on his chin. "Or maybe I'll give her a demonstration of her own. She still lives on Vallejo Street in Pacific Heights, doesn't she?"

The room fell silent. Jack's fists wanted to clench, but he kept them open as his mind was already racing, and it was time to be calm. Victor had shown more than he realized.

CHAPTER TWENTY-SIX

Jack phoned Stella on the hands-free as soon as he drove away from Gunnar's house. No answer. He was halfway back to Marie Clark's house when the phone rang. Stella.

"Sorry it took so long to return your call, Jack."

"I need to give you an update on what just happened at Gunnar Ragnall's house."

Jack spent the next eight minutes talking without Stella interrupting. "Any questions?"

"Lots, like where he keeps his drones, how many drones he has, where the server is that controls them, and what data about a person makes the drone find that person."

"I've got the same questions."

"Any thoughts on how to find the answers?"

"Nothing at this stage."

Sometimes, it's better to keep thoughts that sound vague and tenuous to yourself, because saying them out loud can make them vanish in the face of cold logic.

"Anyway, I have George's funeral tomorrow. Are you coming?"

"I really should, but I'm stuck here in Plymouth. Infighting among the board members. It has come to the attention of our biggest customer. He has asked me to be in his office tomorrow at nine. By the end of today, I will be two directors less. So I will have something positive to say, but I feel bad about George's funeral. I hadn't known him for long, but still."

"I'm sure George would understand and agree with your decision. Besides, I'm sure there'll be plenty of people there."

* * *

Jack stood alone at the edge of the small, sun-drenched crematorium garden, the only attendee besides the preacher. The sky was a vibrant blue, and the warm sun cast defined shadows on the ground. The preacher, dressed in simple black-and-white robes, stood by the crematorium, his voice laden with solemnity as he recited prayers to honor the departed.

Jack fixed his gaze on the urn. The weight of the moment bore down on him, filling his mind with thoughts and memories of the departed. The preacher's solemn words resonated in the stillness. Jack's focus remained unwavering, locked on the simple, elegant vessel that now held all that remained of a once-living soul.

He hadn't known George long enough to say he knew him well, but there was something about the solitude of the moment that compelled him to stay longer than he needed to. It was a sense of duty to be there, so at least someone was there to bear witness to a life that had now come to an end. The sun's rays felt almost too bright for the occasion, starkly contrasting with the quiet somberness that filled Jack's heart.

As he stood there, Jack couldn't help but reflect on the fact that no one else had turned up for the funeral. It struck him as profoundly sad that a life could end with no one to mourn its passing. What other circumstances led to this solitude? Had George lived a lonely life? He had outlived his wife and son, and there was no other family. Perhaps he'd just spent too much time at work. But he was popular with the board and his employees. Jack wondered why they hadn't come to the funeral. Had he slipped through the cracks of a bustling world? Were people too busy to notice him, or was he too busy to notice them? Maybe Frank Lund had an answer for why he or any of the board members didn't appear. Apart from a lone motorcyclist at the entrance to the long tree-covered drive into the crematorium, no one else was there. Slim shape, gray helmet, gray leathers, gray bike built for speed, not for noisy cruising.

Jack's thoughts drifted to his own life. He considered the people who might attend his funeral one day. To mourn him. Would there be someone to hold a white rose and remember the times they had shared? The thought brought a lump to his throat. The isolation of the moment was a harsh reminder of the fragility of human connection.

The preacher concluded with a gentle prayer, blessing the departed's soul and offering comfort to those left behind. There was only Jack, who stepped forward, holding a single white rose. He kneeled by the urn and placed the flower gently beside it, a final gesture of farewell. The simplicity of the act felt almost too small, too insignificant in the face of a life now gone. Yet, it was all he could offer.

As the ceremony ended, the preacher placed a comforting hand on Jack's shoulder and offered a few words of solace before departing, leaving Jack alone in the garden's quiet. He stood there for a while, lost in his thoughts, contemplating the fleeting nature of life and the importance of human connections. The preacher's words echoed in his mind, blending with the rustling leaves and distant bird calls.

Jack took a deep breath, feeling a mix of emotions. Sorrow for the departed, gratitude for his own connections, and a renewed resolve to cherish the people in his life. He thought about the small moments, the phone calls, the shared meals, the unspoken bonds that tied him to those he cared about. He realized these connections gave life meaning, which made the journey worthwhile.

The sun continued to shine brightly, casting a warm glow over the solemn scene. Jack's shadow stretched long across the ground, a silent testament to his presence. As he stood there, he made a quiet promise to himself: to reach out more, to be present in the lives of those he loved, to ensure that no one he cared about would ever face the end alone.

Finally, he turned to leave. The bike was gone, the echoes of the preacher's words lingering in the air, a quiet tribute to a life that had touched Jack, albeit briefly. The walk back to his truck seemed long. Each step was a reminder of the vow he had made. The world outside the garden seemed almost too bright, too busy, too unaware of the quiet introspection that had taken place within its bounds.

As Jack drove away to the wake he had organized for George, he glanced at the empty seat beside him, imagining for a moment that George was there, sharing the silence.

* * *

Palo Alto was not a familiar haunt for Jack. For George's wake, he had selected a place that would reflect George: sophisticated, with an extensive wine and whiskey selection and small plates. It was a tapas bar with more whiskey on offer than usual. He had circulated the time to the board members for the ceremony at the crematorium and the wake afterward. Jack parked his truck and went inside the restaurant. There was a separate room in the back for private functions, which he had booked. As he was the only one who turned up at the crematorium, he figured he would have a few drinks there by himself and donate the food to the staff, probably students. In all likelihood, the owner paid them the minimum wage plus tips. He'd been there, done that.

The tapas bar's exterior was classic Mexican hacienda charm, with white stucco walls, red clay roof tiles, and ornate wrought-iron detailing. Arched doorways and vibrant bougainvillea vines framed the grand wooden entrance. Lantern-style lights on the exterior of the building added a rustic elegance. Lush cacti in terracotta pots arranged between the lights, blended with hanging plants and climbing vines.

Inside, the floors were intricate, colorful ceramic tiles that formed geometric patterns. Ambient lighting came from string lights.

In the seating area, exposed wooden beams, rustic wooden chairs with carved details, and colorful cushions featuring traditional Mexican patterns were on display. Tables were polished, dark wood with their tops of hand-painted ceramic tiles that mirrored the vibrant designs on the floor. Seating arrangements varied, with smaller tables for intimate gatherings and larger communal ones for group celebrations. Cozy benches with high backs lined the walls, often draped in woven blankets or serapes for added comfort and a splash of color. Dimly lit lanterns hung from wrought-iron fixtures, casting a warm light on each table.

Sam, the owner, guided Jack to a private function room with a similar aesthetic. Sam couldn't linger as he had to get back to the kitchen. A beige wooden table against the wall had a white cloth on which sat a range of glasses and an ice bucket. The wall had racks of spirits, wines, and liqueurs. In the middle of the room was a wooden table covered in an orange tablecloth, with chairs for twelve people. Frank Lund was pouring himself a drink at the bar, dressed in a walking outfit consisting of gray shorts, a white long-sleeve shirt, and white walking shoes. A sand-colored bucket hat and a pair of sunglasses sat at the bar.

"Frank, you weren't at the crematorium, yet you show up here. Care to explain why?"

"Keep it down, Jack. You don't know who might be listening."

Jack took off his jacket and tie and threw them over a chair. "Listening? What are you talking about? You missed the service, Frank. You weren't there for him. And your clothes. Doesn't exactly show respect. What's your excuse?"

A man and woman walked into the room, glanced at Jack and Frank, and entered the private room's toilets. They both wore shorts, T-shirts, and sandals. The man was Jack's height but about forty pounds heavier. The woman was two inches shorter and about one hundred and thirty pounds. "Who are they, Frank? More freeloaders?"

"I don't know them, Jack."

* * *

Just the thought of more people showing disrespect towards George was almost letting out the genie that kept his PTSD in the cave at the base of his spine. Jack went to the toilets. It was unisex, with two doors to get through. There were three cubicles on the left in dark mahogany and a marble counter on the right with two basins. Jack estimated there were four feet between the cubicle and the marble counter. The woman was chopping up cocaine and making lines with a credit card. The man was behind her, trying to undo her shorts. She slapped him with the hand that was not making lines.

"Stop it, Tiny. We said we'd do some lines, nothing else."

"C'mon, Stretch, did you think lines was all I wanted to do with you?" Tiny slapped her backside with his right hand hard enough to cause her to gasp.

"That hurt, Tiny. I said, No."

Jack had some triggers, and hitting women was one of them. Tiny was so focused on slapping Stretch again that he looked surprised when

Jack grabbed his right wrist.

"You two," said Jack, "take your stash and leave now, right now. And you, Tiny, don't hit her again. I heard her say, stop it, and no."

Tiny attempted to wrench his wrist away. "When we've finished, we'll be out of here."

Jack increased the pressure on Tiny's wrist. "I said you leave now. This is a private function room where we're honoring the passing of a friend."

"Sorry for your loss, buddy, but we always use this toilet."

"You leave now."

Jack let go of Tiny's wrist, who used the opportunity and the position of his arm to throw a backhand punch at Jack's head. It would have hurt if it had connected, but Jack moved his head back, and Tiny's fist snapped past Jack's face. Tiny's face was now open. Jack threw a straight left to Tiny's nose and a roundhouse to the temple.

Stretch shouted. "Don't hurt him."

Tiny staggered but was recovering and raising his fists. Jack grabbed Tiny behind the head with both hands and pulled Tiny's head down as he brought his knee up into Tiny's face. Jack half-turned Tiny and pushed him into a cubicle, where he bounced as he hit the toilet and collapsed to the floor between the toilet and the cubicle wall.

Stretch rushed past Jack to Tiny, making cooing noises and saying she was sorry. Jack looked at Stretch. Once again, human relationships surprised him.

"Do you need help with Tiny?"

"No, I'm good."

Stretch pocketed the remainder of the stash and struggled to get Tiny. Jack held the doors, and they departed as one comrade helping another. "Stretch," said Jack, "on your way out, ask Sam to come here."

"Yeah, sure, will do."

Jack walked over to Frank, who was holding a glass and watching Tiny and Stretch.

"So why weren't you or any of the board at the funeral?"

Jack looked at Frank, waiting for an answer.

Sam arrived as flustered as a cat at a dog show. "What's going on here? I've just had one of my best customers leave all beaten up."

"I'm helping you here, Sam. Those customers use these toilets as their private snorting room, and Tiny slapped Stretch. So what do you want to do? The cops and the press would love this story, though they probably already know. They just don't have evidence, but now I can give it to them."

"How do you know their names?"

"They introduced themselves."

"Understood, I'll clean up the toilets. There is nothing I can do about Tiny and Stretch. They have a complicated arrangement, and the cost of this function is on the house."

"Half right. You clean up the toilets, and I pay for what we consume. Any leftover food goes to your staff."

Sam left. Jack turned back to Frank as the dark thing shrunk down his spine and into its cave. Frank was staring into his glass as if the amber liquid held some kind of answer. The dark rings beneath his eyes spoke of sleepless nights wrestling with thoughts that refused to let him sleep. Frank scratched absentmindedly at the rough stubble along his jawline.

Shaving had been an afterthought, something he couldn't bring himself to care about. His shirt clung awkwardly to him, as if he had no memory of pulling it from the laundry heap. Its creases and wrinkles were a reminder that he'd stopped fussing over appearances. The uneven roll of his cuffs caught his eye, but he didn't bother fixing them. He had a look that suggested everything felt like too much effort. Even standing upright required a kind of energy he didn't seem to have. His shoulders sagged forward, as if there was a weight he couldn't see, but he felt it all the same, pressing down on him.

"Why weren't you there, Frank?"

Frank hesitated, sighed, hesitated, and then spoke. "It was Victor Thornfield. He made it clear. We'd be next if any of us showed up at the crematorium. He doesn't bluff, Jack. I had to sneak here like I was going for a walk, and then I slipped in."

"Victor threatened you? All of you? The whole board?"

Frank nodded, his hands gripping his glass almost to the point of it cracking. "You don't understand, Jack. He's not someone you cross. The board members have families to consider, and I have two boys. Victor has these drones that can find you and kill you. You don't know about these drones."

"I know about the drones. Victor recently gave me a demonstration."

"Really. When was that?"

"Recently."

"Then you understand the reach Victor has."

"I got a demonstration of the surveillance drones, followed up by the armed drone."

"That's what he showed each of us." Frank looked away, his voice barely above a whisper. "I failed George by not going to his funeral, but I'm here now, aren't I? I'm trying to make it right."

Jack looked at Frank. "All right, sorry I came down on you so hard."

"I feel like I'm aging in front of myself."

"How old are you, Frank?"

Frank gave a glimmer of a smile. "I like to say my age is somewhere between too late to start over and too early to give up."

"That sounds pessimistic."

"Sorry, I am finding it difficult to be anything else at the moment, and I am very sad about not being there for George's funeral."

Jack thought that even if it were just the two of them, George would have his wake. "Do you remember what whiskey George liked?"

"Lagavulin. How could I forget? Some of my best memories of George are of drinking Lagavulin with him."

"Let's raise a glass of Lagavulin to him."

"Well, I'm two ahead, but let's do it."

Frank's phone rang. Frank looked at it. "Odd, no caller ID." Frank pressed the Accept button. "Hello, hello." Frank looked at Jack as he waited for a response. There was none. Frank ended the call, shrugged his shoulders, and looked at Jack. "Probably one of those automated marketing calls."

Jack was thinking it could be Victor testing their tracking. "Yeah, we all get those."

Jack opened the whiskey bottle, topped up Frank's glass, poured a double dose for himself, and then, in unison, "To George."

Jack heard a familiar noise but couldn't recall what it was. Then, he did. A drone. One of Victor's surveillance drones came through the door, followed by its big brother, the armed quadrocopter. Jack threw the bottle of Lagavulin at the armed quadrocopter. "Frank, throw whatever you can at them."

The manufacturers of Lagavulin didn't make it to smash quadrocopters in mid-air. It wobbled, but then the quadcopter resettled. Frank was throwing whiskey bottles at the drones. The drones were nimble, more nimble than Jack had ever seen drones in action. Jack threw all the ice at the surveillance drone, followed by the ice bucket. The armed drone seemed to be waiting for instructions. Jack swung a chair at them, hitting the surveillance drone and breaking a rotor, sending it spinning in an elliptical pattern to the floor. Jack flipped it over with his foot, making it look like a turtle on its back. Frank threw a two-thousand-dollar bottle of Glenfiddich at the armed drone that was lining him up. The rotors broke the bottle as it opened up on Frank.

The rounds shredded Frank's white shirt into exploding red blotches. Frank jerked and twitched as he went to the floor, his face a grimace of pain, then nothing. The armed drone spun around as if it were looking for its friend. It stopped, looking Jack in the face from three feet. Jack heard the hammer of the armed drone click as it hit an empty chamber. It flew out the door, and all was quiet, with the sulfurous smell that gunpowder leaves, reminiscent of burned chemicals. Jack threw his jacket over the surveillance drone and kicked it aside. He put an unopened bottle of Lagavulin on top of it. Not every day does one get to look death in the face.

Sam arrived, his breath catching as he took in the scene. His face twisted through a range of emotions. Shock, anger, disbelief. "What happened?"

"A drone flew in and shot Frank."

"I don't believe you. I'm calling the cops."

"That's a good idea. I'm just going to drop my jacket in my truck and get my phone. I must have left it there, and I need to make a call."

Sam left, talking on his phone. Jack picked up his jacket and the drone, walked to his truck, and put the drone in the front passenger-side footwell, upside down. He looked at the base for compartments. He saw a place for batteries. There was an unnamed one. He flicked it open. It was what he was looking for. The GPS. He started walking back, holding the GPS. There was a twenty-year-old F-250 that had seen better days with Nevada plates, and underneath the number, the words 'Golden Knights'. Clearly a supporter of the Las Vegas hockey team. It had an open cargo area with a weather-worn tarpaulin pulled over it. Jack slid his hand under the tarp and dropped the GPS. He had barely broken stride and kept going until he was back in the private room. Sam left, closing the doors on his way out. It was just him and Frank.

Their original bottle of Lagavulin was still on the bar. Jack grabbed it and drank like it was water, and he had run a marathon. George's wake would always be memorable.

CHAPTER TWENTY-SEVEN

Four uniformed officers quickly cordoned off the private room, their movements precise as they marked evidence and secured the perimeter. The yellow tape created an unsettling boundary between the chaos inside and the curious murmurs from diners and staff outside. Sergeant Atlee stepped into the room, his eyes sharp and focused like a predator entering its hunting ground. He could have been a diner in his jeans and white long-sleeved shirt except for the badge clipped onto his belt, which said he was from the local police department.

Jack stood by the far wall, trying to blend in with the shadows with his hands stuffed deep into his pockets. His face betrayed no emotion, but his mind was busy. The surveillance drone was tucked away safely in his truck outside. Saying anything now would only invite more trouble.

As Atlee approached, his boots crunching against shards of broken glass, Jack estimated him to be about fifty years old, five feet ten inches tall, and one hundred and sixty pounds. He stopped short, surveying the room, the overturned chairs, the smear of blood on the floor, and Frank's lifeless body riddled with thirty bullet holes. Atlee asked Jack for identification. Jack gave him his driver's license. Atlee studied it like it was a recently unearthed archeological artifact, then looked up at Jack. "Tell me something, Jack," Atlee said, his tone calm and measured like the soft click of chess pieces moving, "does this look like the work of an armed drone to you?"

"It's what I saw."

Atlee smirked, a smile that carried no warmth. "Right. A killer drone flies in, turns the victim into Swiss cheese, then vanishes into thin air. Sounds a little convenient, don't you think?"

Jack met his gaze, forcing his voice to stay steady. "Believe what you want. That's the truth."

Atlee stepped closer, his eyes narrowing. "Truth? You want to talk about truth? Truth is, thirty rounds in a man's chest usually means someone wanted him very, very dead. And I don't see any sign of your magic drone or the gun that fired the shots."

Jack knew from Freddie that this technique of coming in hard and fast meant someone might slip up.

"What aren't you telling me?"

Jack exhaled, keeping his expression neutral. "I barely knew the guy."

"Barely knew him, huh?" Atlee echoed him, his skepticism evident. He pulled out a notepad and began jotting down notes. "Funny thing about cases like this. They scream gangland. A lot of firepower for one guy, don't you think?"

Jack hesitated for a moment, then nodded. It was clear Atlee had a theory he was intent on proving. "Yeah. Makes sense, I guess."

Atlee studied him carefully. "Makes sense? You don't strike me as the type to dabble in guessing games. Did Frank have any enemies? Connections we should know about?"

Jack shook his head. "As far as I know, he was clean. Just a guy I occasionally worked with. Consulting gig at Carlton Engineering. That's all."

Atlee frowned, pacing the room as he processed Jack's words. "Clean doesn't usually get you thirty holes in the chest, Jack. Either you don't know him as well as you think you do, or you're lying. Which is it?"

Jack's jaw tightened. He'd rehearsed this answer in his head a dozen times. "I didn't know him well," he repeated. "And I didn't lie."

"Convenient," Atlee said, the word little more than a mutter. He stopped near Frank's body, crouching down to examine the blood-soaked carpet. "You know what I think? You're keeping quiet because you don't want anyone else dragged into this, because you don't want to be a rat, or you're scared of the consequences, or you're involved. I mean, look at you. You don't have a scratch on you."

Jack stood still, as no response could lead Atlee to explore his theories further.

Atlee stood, his expression shifting to something more calculated, like a fisherman deciding to change the lure at the end of his line. "Sometimes, letting others draw their own conclusions can make you look guilty."

Jack kept his tone even. "I've told you everything I know. Take it or leave it."

Atlee walked over, stopping within inches of Jack. "Here's the thing, Jack. You don't strike me as the type to get caught up in something you didn't plan for. You're calm and collected, but people slip up eventually. Maybe not today, maybe not tomorrow, but soon." He lowered his voice for dramatic effect, as if he were on the stage. "And when you do, I'll be there."

Jack didn't respond. He doubted the dramatic effect ever worked. He made a point of not glancing toward the parking lot, where his truck sat with the surveillance drone safely hidden. Jack had no intention of revealing it. Then he would have some explaining to do. Best to let Atlee keep guessing. Thornfield would also be wondering as to the whereabouts of his drone.

The detective sighed, turning toward the forensic team that had arrived. "Bag it and tag it," he said. "This isn't your average homicide. Too clean, too calculated."

As the forensic team moved in to collect evidence and take photographs, Atlee turned back to Jack, his voice edged with suspicion. "We'll be in touch, Jack. Don't go far."

Jack nodded, keeping his expression neutral even as his mind raced. He stepped out of the room with a last look at Frank. Letting people draw their own conclusions might be risky, but it was the least worst option for now.

Who was going to tell his sons? Even though they didn't speak to their father for whatever reason, they shouldn't read about it or hear about it on social media. The air seemed heavy, as if the scene had lent it weight.

Jack got in his truck, closed the door, and checked that his jacket covered the drone.

* * *

Jack sat at the boardroom table at Arcane Studios. The brothers, Matthew and Nicholas, sat on opposite sides, their postures stiff, their expressions unreadable.

Matthew leaned forward. "What's so important, Jack, that you pushed your way into our offices and insisted on seeing us?"

"I need to tell you something."

Nicholas slid his coffee mug from one hand to the other. "If it's not about Stella West being an investor, I'm not interested."

"I don't have an update for you from Ms. West. It's about your father."

Matthew's jaw tightened, his arms crossing defensively. Nicholas stopped sliding his mug and held it between his hands, his brows knitting together. Neither spoke. Their silence urged Jack to continue. "It's about Frank. He's gone. Shot. A few hours ago."

Nicholas inhaled sharply through his nose, his eyes widening. "Shot. What do you mean, shot?"

"He's dead."

Matthew leaned back, his gaze fixed on the ceiling as if searching for answers in the plaster. "Who would shoot him?"

Jack hesitated, his hands clenching into fists at his sides. "The police are investigating. They're still piecing it together."

Nicholas shook his head, his hands gripping the edge of the couch. "I don't understand. Why would anyone?"

Matthew cut him off with a laugh. "Why not? Maybe his gambling activities finally caught up with him."

Nicholas turned to his brother. "That's not fair, Matthew. He wasn't perfect, but shot?"

"I know," said Matthew. "I cut him off over something, which now that he's gone, it seems so tiny."

Nicholas nodded, his eyes glistening with unshed tears. "I agree, Matthew. It all feels so small now."

"He cared about you both," said Jack. "That I can tell you, and I didn't know him for very long."

The brothers sat in silence.

Sometimes, words can settle like a lead blanket.

Nicholas broke the silence as he slid the mug between his hands. "Do they know who did it?"

Jack hesitated again, his eyes meeting theirs. "It wasn't a person," he said, dragging out his words. "A drone shot Frank."

"What do the police have to say?" said Matthew.

"They've come up with a theory that it was a gangland shooting."

"And," said Nicholas, "what do you think?"

"Well, there's a bit more to what happened. Before the armed drone arrived, a smaller surveillance drone arrived, found Frank, and then the armed drone killed him. What's been bothering me is how fast the surveillance drone found Frank. I recently had the pleasure of seeing these two drones in action, albeit at a fairly static event, as it involved a group of people in a room. This time, the surveillance drone probably picked up Frank's location from his cell phone. The restaurant was crowded, with people coming and going. The surveillance drone looked at all those faces before it zeroed in on Frank. It must have done this fast because no one in the restaurant remembered seeing a drone. I only saw it when it was in front of Frank. So here's my question. Do you know anybody who has facial recognition software that is that quick?"

Jack sat and waited. He who blinks first loses. The brothers looked at each other, and Matthew responded. "I believe our facial recognition software is far faster than anything else at the moment."

"You said you sold it to the military. Now, listen carefully and answer me truthfully. Have you sold this technology to anyone else?"

Matthew and Nicholas adjusted their seating positions and exchanged a glance.

"Yes," said Matthew.

"Who to?"

"I'd prefer not to say," said Matthew. "It's a complicated arrangement."

"Complicated? I can show you the result of complicated. The attack drone emptied the whole magazine into your dad's chest. That's thirty 5.56mm by 45mm bullets. And they are going to ask you, as next of kin, to identify the body. Now tell me, who have you sold the technology to?"

"Can I just explain?" said Nicholas. "If you recall, I told you there was a woman we know who is an excellent software developer. We needed her help, but she had to get permission from her employer, who is also her boyfriend. The employer agreed, provided he had access to the software. He had us over a barrel."

"Who's the employer, and who is the developer?"

"Victor Thornfield and Olga Volkov," said Nicholas

"Do you think Olga could have modified your software and installed her version in a drone?"

"She's more than capable of doing that," said Matthew.

"If we had one of those surveillance drones, we could tell you," said Nicholas.

"I happen to have one in my truck. I'll go get it."

"Where did you get that?" said Matthew.

"When the drones attacked, I hit it with a whiskey bottle. It crashed. I flipped it onto its back and threw my coat onto it."

"Isn't it evidence?" said Nicholas. "Shouldn't the police have it?"

"I'm confused," Jack said, his voice low as he studied their faces. "Aren't you two interested in finding out who killed your father?"

Matthew and Nicholas exchanged a glance. It was fleeting yet heavy, like the passing shadow of a storm cloud. Nicholas broke first, his voice soft. "We are."

Matthew frowned, his jaw flexing. "Yeah, I guess we are," he said, though his tone lacked conviction.

Jack's brow furrowed. "You don't sound so sure."

Matthew exhaled sharply, leaning back in his chair, his eyes fixed on the ceiling. "We cut him off, Jack. We did it because we were angry. Because we felt slighted. At the time, I justified it to myself. Now it feels, I don't know." Matthew looked at Nicholas and then back at Jack. "Hollow."

Nicholas rubbed his temples, his voice trembling. "I thought he didn't care. I thought he wasn't there for us in the way he should've been, but maybe we were wrong. Maybe we didn't see everything he was trying to do for us."

Jack hesitated, as one who had lost his parents when he was five, his knuckles white as he gripped the edge of the table. "Frank never stopped caring about you both. He was trying, even when you felt he wasn't. And now—"

Matthew cut in, his voice bitter. "Now he's gone, and we can't undo the years we wasted."

Nicholas nodded, his eyes glistening. "We let anger burn bridges we didn't think we'd need or care about. And on top of that, we now discover our work could have contributed to our own father's death."

The words lingered in the room, curling like smoke from a candle just snuffed out, refusing to dissipate. Jack watched them. With his arms crossed tightly, Matthew, a fortress built to guard against the trespass of emotion, and Nicholas, hunched over as though carrying the weight of their shared history on his shoulders. They didn't speak, but Jack could feel the turmoil beneath the stillness as if their silence roared louder than any words could.

Matthew, his expression as sharp and impenetrable as a cliff face, yet his eyes betrayed him, a flicker of something. Was it regret? Resentment? Jack couldn't tell. All those years Matthew had spent cataloging slights, assembling them into a shield against reconciliation, only to realize now that his shield had cracked. Nicholas, though, his face, pale and drawn, seemed carved from grief itself. Had he possibly felt too deeply and tried to bury it under a mask of indifference? But Jack saw it now, the glisten in his eyes that refused to fall as tears.

What were they thinking? The same question had surfaced the first time he'd met them. Was the guilt gnawing at them as unrelenting as a tide that eroded their justifications over the years? Did they finally see how slight, how laughably minute their reasons for cutting off Frank had been? Jack could almost sense their thoughts, disjointed and colliding: Matthew's bitter self-recrimination, Nicholas's quiet pleading with a past he could no longer rewrite. And yet, as their father's death settled over them like an iron shroud, it offered no solace, only the unyielding ache of the irreparable.

Jack shifted his weight. The creak of the chair punctuated the silence, and still, neither of them moved. The room itself seemed to hold its breath. He thought of Frank then, the man who had tried, in his flawed and fumbling way, to reach his sons. Jack imagined Frank's words rehearsed but never spoken. And now here they sat, the two of them, bathed in the aftermath of loss, too consumed by the wreckage of their guilt to recognize they were, however, frayed by the fragile threads of family, still tethered.

The truth hung in the air like an unanswered question. Jack held it alone. Would either of them ever honestly confront it, or if they merely let it linger, unresolved and haunting, like the echo of a half-forgotten song?

"Can you please get the drone?" said Matthew. "And keep the camera covered."

CHAPTER TWENTY-EIGHT

The drone sat on the desk upside down with the camera, its eyes, staring at a coffee cup. A thin black cable ran from an even thinner port in its underbelly. The other end connected to Nicholas's laptop, which, via a projector, displayed the image on the wall. It displayed a sequence of computer code.

"How familiar are you with Python code, Jack?" said Nicholas.

Sometimes, it's better to keep your abilities to yourself.

"I get by. Go slow for me and explain as you go."

"Alright," said Matthew. "I don't know what you know about facial recognition."

"Assume I know nothing."

"Nicholas, you take Jack through the phases as you go through the code, and let's see where Olga has made changes."

"Sounds good to me," said Jack. "Let's go."

"First, we must identify the face via an image or video frame. You can use algorithms to do this, but we use deep learning models called convolutional neural networks. It pinpoints key facial features like the eyes, nose, and mouth to define a face. Once the face is detected, the system extracts unique features. These are the distances between facial landmarks, such as the space between the eyes, the shape of the jawline, or skin texture. From this, we create a numerical representation of the face, often called a faceprint. It's like a fingerprint, but for the face. The detected face is aligned and standardized to ensure consistent analysis. This involves adjusting the face's angle, size, and orientation to match the templates used for comparison."

Nicholas looked at Jack to check he understood. Jack inclined his head. "The software compares the faceprint to a database of stored faceprints. Machine learning algorithms assess similarities to find matches or verify identities. Databases can also store faceprints of individuals. Depending on the application, the system verifies the face against a specific identity or identifies the person from a pool of candidates. The software provides probabilities or confidence scores. Based on the results, the system performs a specific task, such as unlocking a device, granting access, or flagging a mismatch."

"Or," said Matthew, standing up to point to a specific piece of code on the screen, "sending a message to another device which has its own task to perform. Like an armed drone."

"These facial recognition systems," said Nicholas, "rely on vast amounts of data for training and continual learning to improve accuracy and adaptability. As you know, people use them for security, personalization, and analytics purposes, but they raise ethical and privacy concerns."

"Which you ignore, I imagine," said Jack.

Matthew smiled. "Let's just move on, shall we?"

"Right," said Nicholas. "Now we have to deal with processing the data. We developed two ways of doing this. Look at the code. This process is server-based. The drone captures the data and sends it to a remote server for processing. The server performs facial recognition by comparing the captured data against a database of known faces."

"This approach," said Matthew, "is common when the drone lacks the computational power for onboard processing or when access to a large database is required. It requires the drone to have connectivity to the server."

"The other option," said Nicholas, "is onboard processing. A prerequisite is to equip these drones with powerful processors and AI algorithms that allow them to perform facial recognition directly on the device. This means that reading and analyzing facial features occurs on the drone without sending data to an external server. This setup is faster and more secure, reducing the risk of data interception during transmission."

"Nicholas and I built both because it gave the military more options depending on the task and the drones at their disposal, the complexity of the facial recognition task, and whether there is a need for real-time results."

"In summary," said Nicholas, "server-based processing is better suited for more extensive or resource-intensive operations, whereas onboard processing is ideal for quick, localized tasks, which is what Olga has done here."

An image of Frank's face appeared on the screen with the associated data points. "What she has done," Nicholas swallowed, "is load up one image, our father's, and process facial features until it got a match."

"How would it process a whole restaurant so fast?" said Jack.

"Look at the code," said Matthew. "Remember, we told you earlier that probabilities determine the match. The code gets data for the macro elements of a face. The distance between the eyes is often considered the most significant macro element in facial recognition. It serves as a stable, defining feature that helps anchor the spatial relationships of other facial landmarks, making it crucial for accurately identifying or verifying a person. See the code. If there is no match on that characteristic, it moves on."

"How close does it have to be to be effective?"

"With 95% probability," said Nicholas, "it is accurate up to fifty feet, but you should also ask the opposite question."

"Which is?"

"At what distance can we rule out someone? The answer is that the software can rule someone out at one hundred and twenty feet with 99% probability."

"So a surveillance drone could sneak into the restaurant, which is not a quiet place, and no one would hear it because of the noise. It would position itself near the ceiling and survey the faces. Getting rejects, it went to the private room."

Nicholas changed the screen. "Correct. And look at the hardware. This thing is a flying supercomputer."

"Understood," said Jack.

"Now," said Nicholas, "this is where I think we'll see some of Olga's magic." Nicholas typed for three minutes. He stopped, panicked, and went to the drone. "Where's the GPS? I should have thought of it earlier. They can track us here."

"Relax," said Jack. "I removed it before I put it in my truck at the restaurant."

"Where is it now?" said Matthew.

"With any luck, it's on its way to Las Vegas."

"I don't need to know how that happened," said Nicholas. "Can we get back to the clever stuff that Olga did?" Nicholas didn't wait for an answer but returned to his keyboard and continued scrolling through the code for the next four minutes. "Olga has integrated the cell phone into the facial recognition software."

Matthew leaned forward, running a hand through his hair. "Olga's software has taken things to a whole new level. It's not just facial recognition anymore. Cell phones are now a key part of the process."

Jack exhaled sharply, shaking his head. "It's crazy. Phones are always within reach. People carry them everywhere, and half the time, they don't even realize what's happening in the background. All those apps they've installed? Most of them have permission to track the location set when they install the app, and no one even thinks twice about it."

Nicholas nodded. "That's the scary part. The location tracking gives them a starting point. A rough idea of where you are. Then, the facial recognition software steps in to confirm it's you. It's two steps, and there's no escaping it if you're unprepared."

Jack leaned back in his chair, folding his arms. "People don't have control over their cell phones. Personally, I've gone through every app on my phone and disabled location tracking one by one. Then, I turned off Wi-Fi and started using a VPN. It's a bit of a hassle, but it's worth it. What do you guys do?"

Nicholas shrugged. "Same here. We've been working through a VPN for a while now. It's not perfect, but it's better than nothing."

Jack tilted his head. "People must wake up to how much they're giving away without even realizing it, but they won't. They'll just carry on assuming there's no harm in letting an app know where you are all the time. If this kind of integration becomes widespread, privacy is going to be a thing of the past."

Matthew leaned back, a thoughtful expression crossing his face. "You're right. It's not just technology anymore. It's about control. And if we don't start taking it seriously, we'll regret it."

"You're right, Matthew," said Jack, "and Victor understands that. But I have a question for you guys," Jack paused. "Does this drone have the ability to find its way back home?"

"You mean like a homing pigeon," said Matthew.

"Exactly."

Nicholas hunched over the keyboard, typing rapidly. "Without

GPS, it can't navigate automatically, but don't worry. Olga has built functionality to log everything. The flight path, altitude, and speed. It's all in the internal memory, and there is also an SD card on this drone where she logs, including video."

Matthew straightened up and went to the drone. "Let me get the card. We'll need those logs as well."

Matthew grabbed a fine-pointed pen and inspected the drone's side. "Here it is," he said, pressing the pen into the slot. The microSD card popped out with a soft click, barely noticeable in his hand. He held it up between his fingers. "These tiny things are amazing, aren't they? Smaller than a fingernail, and they can hold up to a terabyte."

Nicholas nodded and handed him a card reader. "Let's load it up."

Matthew carefully inserted the card, and data appeared on the workstation screen two seconds later. "Alright, here's the flight log," Nicholas said, pulling it up alongside the stored video feed. "Let's scroll back to where it all started."

The room grew quiet as the video played in reverse, syncing perfectly with the log data. Jack leaned in closer, his curiosity evident. "Slow it down right there," he said, pointing at the screen. Nicholas froze the playback, and they all leaned in together.

Matthew furrowed his brow. "It's coming out of an air shaft," he said, his tone tinged with surprise. "That building behind the Vortex Club."

"Yeah," Matthew said, nodding at Nicholas. "The area is familiar. Everything on that block has been boarded up except for Vortex. It's like it's the last survivor on the block."

Nicholas leaned back in his chair, rubbing the back of his neck as the screen displayed the flight data. He let out a heavy sigh. "If the drone tracked to that air shaft, then there's something there."

Jack fixed his eyes on the monitor, his voice quiet but sharp.

"Something Victor and Olga don't want us to see."

Matthew broke the silence, his voice careful but insistent. "Jack, let us help you with this. We owe it to our father."

Jack didn't move.

Nicholas leaned forward, his tone heavy with regret. "I know how we treated Dad, but we can't fix that now. What we can do is be here now. Let us do this, Jack."

Jack glanced over at him, his face hard. "Is this your way of looking for absolution?"

Matthew stepped in, his tone softer but no less determined. "No, we're not looking for a free pass, Jack. We can't undo how distant we were or how we shut him out, but we're here now. And if this leads to answers about what happened to him, then we have to be part of that. He deserves that."

Jack turned to face them, his jaw tight. "This isn't just a puzzle to solve. Victor is dangerous. Your father's murder proves that. And it's not going to bring him back."

Nicholas nodded solemnly. "We know, but we don't want to keep running from the guilt. This is about doing something for him."

Matthew put a hand on Jack's shoulder. "We let our father down when he was alive, Jack. Don't ask us to sit back and do nothing now."

Jack studied them for a long moment, his expression unreadable. Then he exhaled, the tension easing just slightly.

"Boys," he said, his voice quieter. "I was orphaned when I was young. It's like neither of you understands that a family is like a ship going through calm and stormy waters. There are times when you don't agree with the captain or argue with the crew. Regardless, you stay on the ship until the waters are calmer. You got off the ship. That ship has now sailed."

CHAPTER TWENTY-NINE

It was after 7 pm when Jack got to his apartment. He phoned Stella. It rang out, and then a text came through. *Give me 10.*

Jack opened the bottle of Lagavulin he had taken from the restaurant, poured two solid fingers, and looked in the cupboards for something to eat. There were protein shakes, as he expected. Whiskey and protein shakes. The breakfast of champions for training with Kenny tomorrow.

One protein shake promised all the ingredients were organic and had a custard-filled cinnamon donut flavor. He spooned the recommended quantity into the blender with the required volume of water. The blender did its magic. Jack hit stop and drank from the container. They had lied about the taste, so he rinsed his mouth with whiskey and swallowed as the phone rang. Stella.

"Hello Jack, how did the funeral go?"

"Eventful, I need to give you an update. And your day? How many directors do you need to hire?"

"Well, I got rid of the two I spoke about, but I'll go slowly with rehiring. Anyway, moving on. The Tor project, we had a crack at. Can you go to your screen so I can share?"

"Sure, give me a moment."

Jack fired up his laptop and shared his screen. Stella and Jack sat in their own spaces over two thousand miles apart. Their screens glowed like tiny portals into a hidden world.

"Every packet of data has to move through a relay," said Stella. "I tried out a method called Timing Attacks," said Stella, "using tiny delays in the network traffic to trace its source. I've set up the timing analysis. Those delays will betray them."

"I understand, but it's risky. They're probably monitoring for anomalies."

"But if this works, we can pinpoint the original server hiding behind the layers."

"Let's cross our fingers they haven't set up decoys."

"If they had, we'd already be chasing our tails. Look at this, Jack. Node twelve. It consistently shows a slight lag during heavy data transfers. It's not random. That could be our first clue."

"You're onto something. We should see a correlation if you measure that lag against traffic patterns at the exit nodes. Let me pull up the log from thirty minutes ago and overlay the timing data."

Stella waited, watching him work. Her confidence masked a flicker of nervous energy. Timing Attacks were like tracking shadows in a dark maze. It was all about precision.

"Got it!" said Jack, pointing with his cursor. "The same lag pattern shows up. It's subtle, but it's there. The source is starting to give itself away."

"Let me refine this further," said Stella. "Timing differences amplify when they send smaller packets of data. If we can isolate those."

She typed swiftly, the data stream on her screen transforming into a series of colorful graphs. Her pointer indicated one. "See this spike? It's unique to one path. If my math is right, this is our lead."

"You're brilliant. That spike matches up with one of the suspected exit points. Let's drill down further. If it's the source, it'll have a more consistent lag profile across multiple streams."

The clock ticked in the background as they worked. Each second bringing them closer to their goal or to a new discovery. Jack's screen lit up with a notification.

"There it is," said Stella. "That's the node. We've isolated the origin. Someone thought they could stay hidden by bouncing through relays, but Timing Attacks don't lie. Never underestimate the power of data and patience."

"But do you see the address, Stella?"

"I do, but it's not really an address. It's pointing to a building behind where we met with Victor Thornfield. My recollection is that apart from his club, no businesses were operating on that whole block. That's weird."

Jack sipped his protein shake and then his whiskey. "Maybe not. Let me tell you about my day."

Including interjections with questions from Stella, it took Jack twenty-two minutes to tell Stella what had happened. "If I tell Freddie about this, he'll want more evidence before doing anything. That's the process he has to follow."

"You want to have a look inside that building, don't you, Jack?"

"Don't you?"

"Who can resist a building full of secrets?"

"Speaking of secrets, did George's will have any?"

"I don't have it yet. Frank Lund told me he knew George had a private lawyer, but George never said who it was. I'm going to his house tomorrow to scratch around."

Stella chuckled. "Like a chicken?"

"Exactly."

* * *

Jack was surprised at how well he performed at Kenny's morning training session. Last night's food and drink intake might just be a winning formula. After a shower at his apartment and a quick breakfast of scrambled eggs with cheese and black coffee, he drove to George's house. Renovations were happening at the house across the street, and a truck had blocked George's driveway. Jack parked two houses down the street, walked back, and let himself in.

Jack pushed open the oak door of George Carlton's study, the hinges not making a sound. Despite the activity in the street and across the road, the silence enveloped him like a blanket, broken only by the distant ticking of the grandfather clock down the hall. The dim glow from the hallway illuminated the room, casting shadows across the desk and a bookcase. He pulled open the navy-blue floor-to-ceiling curtains behind the desk. Danny's cottage was in the garden, a sad reminder as he stood in George's house that son and now father were dead.

Jack let out a quiet sigh, running a hand through his hair. His role as estate administrator could bring its burden of legal complexities, but nothing could happen until he found George's will.

The study exuded meticulousness, with nothing on the mahogany desk but a large screen and a keyboard. There was a small printer in the corner of the room. Old leather and faint cigar smoke lingered as if the man himself were still there. Jack's gaze swept over the room. He sat in the leather chair at the desk and went through the drawers. The papers were in disarray, indicating the cops had already rummaged through them. Jack walked across the oak floor to the mahogany bookcase. His eyes trailed along the spines of the neatly arranged titles. There were literary classics, philosophy, and engineering manuals.

Among the engineering manuals was a hard-cover copy of *Zen and the Art of Motorcycle Maintenance* by Robert M. Pirsig. Not strictly an engineering book. It was more of a philosophical journey connecting engineering and life. It did this by exploring the art of quality and balance. Jack had not read it in many years, and his hand reached out without realizing it, pulling it from the shelves. He opened it to see which edition it was, only to find someone had cut away the inside, and nestling in there was a notebook roughly four by five inches. Jack took it out and rifled through the pages with his thumb. It was just over halfway full.

Something caught his eye outside the notebook. He switched on his cell phone's torch and pointed it at the floor. The floor near the bookcase bore faint wear marks. Jack went to the other end of the bookcase and leaned on it. The bookcase slid across with minimal effort or noise, revealing a steel door with a keypad. Jack stared at it for a moment. He pulled out George's notebook, flipping through the pages, looking for a code. Cryptic notes and codes filled the pages, scrawled in the late man's familiar, precise handwriting. He considered pairing his phone with the keypad and trying a blunt-force attack. That is, the app on his phone starts at 0001 and keeps trying and incrementing until it opens. Who knew how long it would take? Jack took another look at the keypad. It was not a new model. Possibly over ten years old. It looked like the kind you get in your hotel room. He decided on a more straightforward way.

Jack walked to the kitchen and through the door to the garage. There was the latest-model Range Rover. It was black. In the corner was the fuse box. Jack flipped up the lid and cut the power to the house. He returned the way he had come to the library to find the steel door hanging open. He opened the door and used his cell phone's torch to look inside. A Maglite was hanging from a hook. It was almost eighteen inches long, probably the one with five batteries. It was a roughly twenty-foot-square room with shelving and what looked like books. Jack needed the lights back on. He turned and saw that the steel door had a manual handle on the inside so that you couldn't get locked inside.

Jack turned on the lights and returned to the library. The steel door's keypad was asking for a new four-digit code. He entered the last two digits of Stella's birth year, followed by the last two digits of his birth year, closed the door, and tested it. The door opened.

The shelves inside held about twenty-five tall books. He pulled one down and opened it on the table. It was what Jack referred to as an old-style manual ledger. He frowned. As he flipped through the pages, his frown deepened. The ledger was over a year old. He scanned the shelves and took the last one on the right-hand side. There were entries in about one-third of the ledger. Carlton Engineering had been sending money to offshore accounts and cryptically named projects. The terms "Helios" and "Vortex" were featured the most often. Jack was familiar with Vortex. Thanks to Aunt Louise, he knew Helios as the Greek god who personified the sun. Jack recalled pictures of Helios driving his chariot across the sky. George didn't want these transactions sitting on a computer. Someone could hack it. This was old-school security. How had he reconciled these entries with what was in the computerized Carlton Engineering ledger? Jack pulled more ledgers from the shelves and reviewed them.

Jack shook his head. "What were you involved in, George?"

As the administrator of George's estate, his mission was clear. Find the will and execute it. Yet these ledgers hinted at secrets. Did they fit into his role as an administrator? Just as Jack was getting down another ledger, he heard voices. *No one else should be here.*

* * *

"I told you I knew how to pick a lock. Was I right?" said an older, gruff voice.

"You were right," said a younger voice, sounding exasperated.

"When I'm right, I'm right. Remember that."

"I will."

Jack closed the steel door, slid the bookcase back in place, slipped behind the curtains, and then realized he still had the Maglite in his right hand.

"Victor said to check the study first for the ledgers," said Gruff.

Jack frowned. Victor's men. He heard them walk into the study as they trod on the wooden floor. He could hear them rummaging around in George's desk. Then, they started pulling books off the shelves and rifling through the pages.

After four minutes, Younger said, "Here's a book with the inside removed."

"Gimme that," said Gruff.

"Alright, don't grab," said Younger.

Jack heard him walk to the window, almost within touching distance of Jack. "Open the curtains some more," said Gruff.

Younger pulled the curtain back to reveal Jack, who was already swinging the Maglite in an upward backhand. They were reaching for their guns.

To take a knife to a gunfight is deemed stupid, but to take a torch to a gunfight takes the level of stupidity to a new low. Jack had a half-second of surprise on them. The upward swing caught Younger under the chin. Jack shoulder-charged him into Gruff. Gruff fired, but it went wide. Jack swung the torch into Gruff's temple. Jack grabbed the hand with the gun and pointed it at the floor. He rained blows on Gruff's head until he went limp. Jack let him fall to the floor as he twisted the pistol out of Gruff's grip. He picked up Younger's pistol and put them both on the desk. 9mm Glocks. He noted which gun had belonged to whom.

Jack unplugged the keyboard from the computer on the desk and used it to tie Younger's hands to his feet, with the keyboard on his feet. He used the printer cable to do the same to Gruff. Jack took photos of both villains and sent them to Freddie and Kenny simultaneously. He sat in George's chair with the torch and waited. He hit the 'on' switch. It worked. He flicked it off and examined it. No broken glass or dents in the bodywork. As he grew bored waiting, he considered sending the manufacturer a glowing report on the product's resilience. Maybe they would prefer not to hear under what field conditions Jack had tested it. He placed the torch on the desk. The phone rang. Freddie.

"Why are you sending me photos of two known criminals who look like they're unconscious?"

"You're not special. I also sent them to Kenny."

"What's this all about?" Freddie sounded exasperated.

Jack kept it short. "Remember the administrator role I am fulfilling for George Carlton's estate? Well, I ran into a bit of a hiccup."

"Is that what's in the photos?"

"Yes."

"Where are you?"

"George's house, Palo Alto."

"It's outside my jurisdiction. The locals must handle it."

"I didn't think you had a jurisdiction."

"No comment. Someone will be there soon. Update me later." Freddie ended the call.

* * *

By the time there was a knock at the front door, Jack had caught up with all the emails on his phone and was bored with the string of obscenities and threats from the two on the floor. He opened the door to see Sergeant Atlee, who blinked with surprise, accompanied by two uniformed cops.

"You again," said Atlee. "What are you doing here?"

Jack smiled. "And a pleasure to see you again, too, Sergeant."

"I got a call about a disturbance at this address. What are you doing here?"

"I am the administrator of George Carlton's estate. I came here to catalog his papers when two intruders attacked me. Follow me, please."

Jack didn't wait for further comment from Sergeant Atlee but walked back to the study. Atlee and the two uniforms stood in a semicircle around the trussed-up intruders. Jack explained which pistol belonged to whom and where the fired bullet had gone. Atlee looked Jack up and down. "Two armed intruders arrive, and you subdue them without a weapon."

"I had a torch."

"A torch?"

"Yes, that one on the desk."

Atlee looked at the two uniformed cops. "Bag the pistols and the torch. Untie and handcuff these two and take them to the station."

Atlee and Jack watched as the cops did their job, escorting their charges down the hall. Atlee looked at Jack. "I don't know what to make of you."

"Some days, Sergeant, neither do I."

CHAPTER THIRTY

Jack sat in Stella's workroom. The twenty-three ledgers he'd taken from George's place were on top of the work surface. The dim light of the workroom created shadows that seemed to mirror the weight of his thoughts. Stella was at her laptop, her face illuminated by its faint glow, her hands moving deftly over the keyboard. The quiet hum of their laptops punctuated the silence between them.

"The ledgers," said Jack, "tell a story that George was involved with Vortex and something else called Helios. I haven't found a will yet, so whatever his interest was, at this stage, we don't know who or what he planned to bequeath it to."

"Strange about the will," said Stella.

"Yes, but I'll keep looking. The ledgers do not have any documentation on Helios, just payments. What is odd is that George invested in Vortex. It seems contrary to the man I met."

"I agree. I also think it's odd that George created a whole story around Victor and then pretended he didn't know him. He must have been trying to 'get out' of any involvement with him and that's why Victor wanted to buy the company. I'm guessing Danny had no idea."

Jack paused. "Helios could be an organization, a product, or a service. Maybe it's what he calls his drones. I wonder how many drones he has. I wonder what's in the Vortex building where Victor keeps his drones. A lot of unknowns."

"We only saw the ground floor of the club. We don't have the floor plans to see what spaces there are in the rest of the building." Stella smiled. "To sneak in and have a look, what must we do? Wear disguises. Paste a mustache on you, add glasses, and a dark-haired wig."

"I know you're joking, but we have to assume he has our faces in his database, and facial recognition software will see past such things."

Stella finally looked up, her expression serious. "Yes, I know. In addition, Victor has integrated his monitoring systems into every layer of his network. I have to be so careful with the hacking I'm doing right now. If he catches even a hint of tampering, he'll know exactly what we're up to."

"Tread softly because you tread on my dreams."

"Who said that?"

"William Butler Yeats."

"No doubt taught to you by your Aunt Louise."

"Correct."

"On a more pragmatic note, I may have found a weakness in his system. There could be our backdoor. If we use it right, it could give us the edge we need."

Jack hesitated. "And if we use it wrong?"

"It alerts him to our presence," Stella said. Her voice softened slightly as though sensing his hesitation.

Jack nodded slowly. He glanced at the ledgers spread across the table. The financial records painted a picture of George's involvement in Vortex and Helios. Nothing else. No mention of what Vortex and Helios were doing.

"You've been quiet about George," said Stella. "What's going on in that head of yours?"

"George wasn't what he appeared to be."

"You're right. It seems he had two faces. Or maybe he was lying to himself about whatever he was involved in."

Jack went back to trawling through the ledgers and trying to make sense of the small notebook. Stella continued hacking. Jack finished going through the notebook.

"I'm not an engineer, and I don't know the full product range at Carlton Engineering, but these cryptic scribblings and the sketches have version numbers attached, making me think these are George's thoughts on enhancements to the existing product range. The sketches don't look like a complete product. They look like part of a product. Like a component."

"Jack," Stella called out, her voice sharp. He turned to see her staring at her laptop screen, her brow furrowed. "Something's happening."

"What do you mean?" Jack asked, walking over to her.

She gestured to the screen, where lines of code flickered erratically. "The backdoor. It's showing activity, but it's not coming from us."

Jack's pulse quickened. "Victor?"

"Maybe," Stella muttered something, her fingers flying over the keyboard. "It's like someone's probing the system, trying to see what we're doing."

"Can you stop it?"

"I don't know. I'm trying to cut the connection."

Her words trailed off as the screen suddenly went blank.

"What happened?" said Jack.

Stella swallowed. "Somebody just shut Numbers out."

Jack's cell phone pinged. He picked it up, read it, and showed it to Stella.

Vortex. Tonight. 8 pm. Don't be late. I thought you might like to see the empire George helped build. Come alone. It'll be entertaining.

* * *

Jack paced the length of the workroom. Stella pulled up the Vortex website. A private gathering at Vortex, exclusive and elite, was scheduled for tonight.

"It's a trap," said Jack. "But we know it's a trap."

"Victor doesn't do anything unless it serves his agenda, but you can't ignore this. It's our chance to get inside."

"He knows we're onto him. He likes to play games. He wants us on his turf and vulnerable."

Stella held his gaze. "Which is why we need to play smart. If you don't go, we lose the opportunity to gather intel on Helios. But if you go, we must be prepared for anything."

Jack exhaled deeply and sat beside her, his hands resting on his knees. He couldn't deny the truth of her words. This was their only shot at getting closer.

Stella looked at her laptop screen, pulling up the event's details. "The event is formal and exclusive. You'll need to look the part." She smirked, her eyes glinting with amusement.

Jack raised an eyebrow. "Look the part?"

"Yes," Stella said, the glow in her eyes suggesting she was already making a mental checklist. "You'll need to look like you belong. Like you're part of Victor's crowd."

Jack ran his hand through his hair. "Clothes-wise, I'm not exactly comfortable in that kind of crowd."

Stella grinned. "Don't worry. I'll make sure you wear the right outfit."

"Thank you."

"Remember, this isn't just a party. Every move you make will be under scrutiny."

Jack nodded slowly, his mind already working through the implications. He didn't trust Victor, but he trusted Stella's instincts. He had to stay sharp if they were going to pull this off.

As Stella jotted notes on a notepad, Jack's phone buzzed. He frowned, pulling it from his pocket. The screen displayed a new message from Victor. Jack's jaw tightened as he read the words aloud.

You must come alone. No relatives or friends, or she'll regret it.

Stella's pen hovered above the notepad. "What does he mean? Alone?"

Jack leaned back, his expression dark as chocolate. "I'm guessing he's made the connection between me and Freddie and Kenny." Stella looked at him, her lips pressed into a thin line. "And am I the 'she' he's referring to?"

"I can't think of anyone else."

Stella nodded her head as she took that on board. "Nothing like a threat. Anyway, Jack, if you're going to face Victor in his club, you must expect the unexpected. He'll have eyes on you from the moment you walk in."

Stella stood, her movements quick and decisive, like a chipmunk. "Your tuxedo is still here from the charity event we attended. Let's dust it off. Get the pants and the shirt pressed. You'll be the belle of the ball."

As the hours ticked by, Stella transformed Jack's clothes into something sleek and sophisticated. Jack's tuxedo still fit him perfectly. Stella had made sure he purchased this garment correctly. At the time, she had told the tailor to make it project confidence and authority.

She stood before him, holding a small skin-colored earpiece. "This one acts as a microphone as well." Jack inserted his earpiece into his left ear. "Now, put on your special bowtie." In the middle of the bowtie was a fisheye camera the size of a fingernail. It was matte-black and unde-tectable unless you looked closely. Bluetooth connected the earpiece and the camera to Jack's cell phone, and Stella had eyes on his phone. She sat in front of her screen.

"Let's test for sound and visuals." Jack walked from the workroom into the living room.

"Can you hear me?"

"Load and clear."

"Remember, when talking, to keep your lips parted, but still like the ventriloquists do, otherwise, you'll look demented like you're talking to yourself, and Victor's security may figure out that you have an earpiece."

"Very funny but thank you for pointing it out. Now, let's test the camera. What am I facing?"

"You're facing the window, looking at Alcatraz."

Jack walked back into the workroom. "This may be just a fishing exercise."

"What do you mean?"

"Victor, by now, is assuming I have the ledgers. I'm guessing he doesn't know what's in them. Which is why he wants them so badly. I'm thinking he thinks we know more about Vortex and Helios than we do, which, apart from some financial transactions, is nothing. I think Victor wants to know how much I know."

"What are you suggesting?"

"I'm suggesting I let Victor believe that the ledgers have revealed everything about Vortex and Helios and that we found an electronic copy as well."

Stella smiled. "I love it. It'll be like being in a play."

"I hadn't quite thought of it like that, but yes." Jack looked at his watch. "The taxi should be outside." Jack frowned. "Are you happy being here by yourself? You don't want to go to a hotel until I get back?"

Stella stood on her toes and kissed Jack on the lips. "Thank you for your concern, Sir Galahad, but this is my home. The likes of Thornfield will not chase me away."

Jack started to speak when Stella held up her left hand for silence. "If it makes you feel any better, I'll strap my Glock to my hip."

Jack knew her mind was set yet couldn't shake the unease gnawing at him as they left the workroom. Victor's text haunted him: *You must come alone. No relatives or friends, or she'll regret it*. He didn't react well to threats, particularly when they involved people close to him.

The crisp night air hit Jack like a wave when he stepped outside. His jaw clenched as he scanned the shadows for signs of danger.

CHAPTER THIRTY-ONE

The taxi pulled up to the curb with a soft hum, and Jack stepped out into the pulsating night of the city. The air's sharp chill did little to dampen the electricity that radiated from Vortex. Before him, the club loomed like a temple of excess, its glass-and-steel façade glinting with the reflections of shifting neon lights. Each flicker cast vibrant magenta and electric blue strokes across the pavement, creating a kaleidoscope of restless energy.

The air buzzed with the crowd's din. Laughter, muffled voices, and the ever-present thrum of bass vibrating from within the building. Jack scanned the scene, taking in every detail. The revelers had clothed themselves in the trappings of wealth. Silk gowns, tailored tuxedos, and glittering accessories. There was a practiced polish to their smiles. A hollowness beneath the surface mirrored the sleek emptiness of the club's design.

"Quite the spectacle," said Jack. "Can you see and hear it?"

"Loud and clear, and I've got a good visual."

Jack scanned the crowd, waiting to get in. There was an air of anticipation among them, like children arriving at a birthday party. Jack adjusted the cuffs of his shirt as they approached the velvet ropes. Two towering bouncers stood on either side of the entrance, their suits intentionally not concealing their hulking frames. Their earpieces were obvious. Their gazes swept over the crowd, searching for even the slightest hint of trouble.

"Name?" one of them asked. His name tag said Max, and his tone was clipped and businesslike.

"Jack Rhodes," said Jack, offering a polite but disinterested smile.

The bouncer consulted a sleek tablet, his thumb scrolling across the glowing screen. After a moment, he gave the faintest nod and stepped aside. The ropes parted, and the heavy glass doors of Vortex hissed open, releasing a flood of sound and light.

"Thank you, Max."

Max looked at Jack before attending to the next guest. "You're welcome."

Jack guessed this crowd didn't say thank you to the likes of Max too often. The first sensation was the music. It didn't just fill the space. It consumed it. The bass reverberated through the walls, the floors, even the air, a relentless rhythm that commanded attention. Strobe lights sliced through the darkness rapidly, creating a disorienting illusion of frozen, fragmented moments. Bodies moved in hypnotic sync on the expansive dance floor, the crowd surging and swaying like a living entity.

"You getting this?" said Jack.

"Very loud and very clear. Talk about sensory overload."

Jack's gaze swept over the room, taking in every detail with the practiced vigilance of someone who assumed danger would be nearby. Yellow light radiated over the bar, contrasting with the sleek curve of polished black marble. Bartenders moved with mechanical precision, their hands a blur as they poured and mixed drinks with theatrical flair. They passed tall, slender glasses brimming with vibrant cocktails to patrons who laughed too loudly, wore jewel-bright smiles, and leaned too close.

Above the dance floor, private balconies jutted out like dark sentinels. Glass walls ensured their occupants could watch and from below people could gaze up at their opulence. Jack's gaze lingered on one balcony in particular, where a single figure stood at the edge. Even in silhouette, there was no mistaking the man. Victor. He held a glass of amber liquid, and his smirk was visible even from this distance.

"Victor's on a private balcony, and he's watching me," said Jack.

"The fisheye camera can't pick that up," said Stella.

Jack looked at the ceiling.

"Now I can see him."

Jack moved deeper into the crowd, weaving between clusters of well-dressed patrons. He kept his pace slow and deliberate, his movements blending seamlessly with the casual arrogance of the club's elite. He moved so the camera could capture the location of every exit and staircase, the guards stationed at the room's edges, and the sharp glint of surveillance cameras hidden in plain sight. "This place is locked down tighter than I expected," said Jack

"It's not just a club. It's a fortress," said Stella.

Lenny, the bouncer, pushed through the crowd, his imposing frame impossible to ignore. Jack stayed relaxed, but he was ready. He stopped in front of Jack with an expression that betrayed nothing. No malice, no amusement, just the blank professionalism of someone used to carrying out orders. "Victor wants to see you. Now."

The club's pounding music and chaotic energy faded into the background. Jack smiled at Lenny. An invitation and a summons rolled into one.

* * *

Jack stepped into Victor's private lounge. The transition from the chaotic energy of Vortex's main floor to this serene, intimidating space was almost disorienting. Victor had created an atmosphere of calculated luxury, designed less for comfort than for command. Golden light from twisted-metal sconces spilled across the room, casting intricate patterns onto the matte-black, gold-trimmed walls. Plush crimson sofas framed a low glass table on which a crystal decanter gleamed, its amber liquid reflecting the light like molten fire.

The centerpiece, however, was the view. Floor-to-ceiling windows stretched across one side of the room, offering a panorama of the city's sprawling skyline. Victor stood near the windows, his reflection fractured and multiplied by the glass, creating an almost spectral image of himself.

Victor turned as Jack entered, his movements measured and precise. He wore his smirk like armor, every inch of his posture radiating control. He was both host and predator, and Jack could feel Victor's invisible leash around the situation.

"Jack," said Victor, his voice smooth, almost cordial. "What a pleasure it is to welcome you to an event at Vortex."

Jack stopped just short of the center of the room, his expression as unreadable as the Mona Lisa.

Victor chuckled softly, his smirk deepening. "Please, don't stand on ceremony, Jack. Sit. Relax. Enjoy the view." Victor's hand waved toward the skyline as if he owned it. "You'll find it's quite inspiring."

"I'm not here to admire the view, Victor," said Jack. "If you have something to say, say it."

"Ah, straight to the point," Victor said, a note of mock admiration in his tone. "You're very much like George in that regard. Though I imagine he had a little bit more patience than you." He paused, his gaze lingering on Jack's reaction. "But perhaps I'm wrong."

Jack didn't rise to the bait. Victor tilted his head as though considering his words like a wise owl. "Very well. Since you insist."

He moved toward the glass table, pouring himself a drink from the decanter. The liquid filling the glass was loud in the silence. He took a deliberate sip, giving himself a pause before speaking.

"You're here because you've been meddling in my affairs," he said, his tone light but edged with menace.

"Victor," said Jack. "You probably know I am the administrator of George Carlton's estate. Anything I do in that regard is not meddling. If what I am doing overlaps with what you're doing, so be it." Jack felt it was time to wing it like a method actor. "I have been doing my job despite your two henchmen breaking into George's house to steal the ledgers. I have the ledgers, and I've made electronic copies of them. So now they are floating around in the Cloud."

Victor smiled, showing a thin line of teeth. "How did you disarm two armed men with a torch, and where did you find the ledgers?"

"Both questions are irrelevant. What is relevant is what is in the ledgers. If you read the ledgers in sequence, you can see how Vortex and Helios came into existence, how they grew, and the funding they received."

Sometimes, it was best to sit back and watch how a lie could spin its web as others bought into it.

With the lights, it was impossible to tell if Victor's face had gone paler. But if it did, it was the only reaction he exhibited.

"Helios," said Victor, his voice sounding like someone was squeezing his throat, but the tone and volume didn't change, "is the culmination of years of work, investment, and vision. It is not something I take kindly to being tampered with." Victor laughed, the sound cold and sharp. "Do you even understand what Helios is? What it represents?"

Jack thought there could only be one thing Victor would want. "It represents control."

Victor's expression hardened, the smirk fading for the first time. "No, Jack. It represents order. Stability. Power. The kind of power George Carlton understood. He helped build Helios. Without him, it wouldn't exist."

Jack knew Stella was listening, and neither knew what Victor was talking about, so Jack continued with his method acting. "George trusted you, Victor. You used him. He never wanted this."

Victor took a step closer, his gaze boring into Jack's. "Didn't he? George wasn't the man you thought he was. He knew exactly what Helios was. He embraced it. He shaped it."

"You're lying," said Jack, still trying to get a reaction from Victor that would make him say what Helios and Vortex were.

Victor turned, his smirk returning. "Oh, Jack, you underestimate George. He wasn't just a supporter of Helios. He was an early architect. Every system, every connection, every decision. It was all him. When he realized he couldn't control it, he turned against it. Against me. But by then, it was too late."

"You're twisting the truth."

"Am I?" Victor said, his smirk widening. "Or are you just too afraid to face it?"

"Jack," said Stella, "step away so I can talk to you."

"I need to think, but I must say, Victor, the service here is not great. You haven't even offered me a drink."

Victor appeared horrified. "Deplorable on my part. I got so wrapped up in talking about Helios. What will you have?"

Jack needed a moment with Stella, so he thought of something that would take longer than splashing bourbon in a glass. "I would like a Bloody Mary. A proper one. Not just some tomato juice from a can with vodka, but with Worcestershire sauce, hot sauce, horseradish, and some spices with no greenery hanging on the lip. Is that possible?"

"Of course. I'll make sure they get it right," said Victor, who left for the bar.

Jack knew that the Bloody Mary order would keep Victor occupied for long enough while he spoke with Stella as he turned, walked to the window and murmured. "What's up?"

"Can you move around a bit more so I can get more visuals of the room? It's important. You're standing still. That's not helpful."

Jack maintained a look of casual ease as he moved around. The pounding bass from the main floor below reverberated up into Victor's lounge, a reminder of the revelry below. Vortex was a stronghold masquerading as a playground for the elite.

The sofas were a carefully curated stage. Their gold-edged velvet cushions, along with the abstract art, spoke of decadence. The symmetry was unnerving, as though Victor had arranged it for surveillance rather than comfort. Victor returned and began another pitch about Helios, his voice polished like a shiny dress shoe, yet dripping with condescension like melting ice cream in a cone flowing over the edges and running down and puddling in your hand as you tried to contain it.

It was difficult to pretend you knew something the other person thinks you do while trying to get them to explain it using words of no more than two syllables.

Stella, meanwhile, would play her part with eyes that missed nothing. Jack knew the staircases would get her attention. They curved up from the edges of the sofa, elegant but utilitarian beneath the glow of muted up-lighting. Stella noted the patterns of use. Faint scuff marks at the edges of the polished wood spoke of frequent use.

A waiter handed Jack a highball glass with its red contents. Jack sipped it. "Thank you. It's perfect."

"Good. Back to business, Jack." His tone had become mollifying, as if he were making peanut butter and jelly sandwiches for a grumpy child. "Helios isn't just a tool. It's the future. If you stop clinging to the past, you could be part of that future."

Jack kept his posture relaxed, his hands in his pockets as he replied, "The past has a way of catching up with the present, doesn't it?"

Jack didn't have a clue what he was talking about. His words seemed to resonate with Victor, eliciting a response, but they didn't reveal any information.

Victor's smirk widened, but Jack didn't look at him. His eyes shifted subtly toward a set of air ducts discreetly tucked into the far wall. Sleek black panels partially obscured the ducts, their minimalism blending seamlessly with the room's aesthetic. Stella noticed movement, and she zoomed the camera in. A small drone, barely larger than her palm, glided smoothly into the vent. Its reflective surface caught the light briefly before disappearing into the dark.

Jack's attention returned to Victor, who was swirling the amber liquid in his glass with casual arrogance. "Carlton Engineering was always about the use of technology," said Victor as his tone turned to that of a patient mentor. "You, Jack, could be part of something extraordinary."

"Victor, if you really wanted to impress me, you'd have shown me Helios by now." Jack gestured to the room. "All of this is a distraction, not a demonstration."

Victor's smirk faltered briefly, a flicker of annoyance crossing his face. "Patience, Jack. All in due time."

Jack shrugged his shoulders and walked to the balcony's edge over-looking the main floor. Victor was not being as forthcoming as he had hoped. The sea of partygoers below was a mesmerizing chaos of neon lights and shifting bodies, their movements synchronized to the relent-less rhythm of the music. But it wasn't the revelers Jack was watching. He scanned for exits, for blind spots in the security net Victor had draped over his domain. And then he saw her.

Amid the crowd, she stood apart, her dark silhouette cutting against the pulsating lights. She wasn't dancing or drinking like the others. She was watching. Watching them. The shadows partially obscured her face, but her posture was unmistakably alert. Jack noted the tilt of her head, the sharpness of her gaze as it met his, and then she was gone.

Jack walked back to Victor with no plan. The door to the lounge opened with a faint hiss. Jack turned, and the woman from the crowd entered, her movements precise and controlled. Up close, she was as striking as a raw gem shimmering in the light. She strode through the entrance, a vision of effortless sophistication. Her floor-length black silk gown draped her like a liquid shadow, hugging her figure with a slit from ankle to thigh. Her heels clicked against the marble floor.

A delicate bracelet glinted against her wrist, understated yet unmistakably Cartier. Her sleek chignon revealed the elegant curve of her neck, adorned with a single South Sea pearl, luminous under the golden glow of chandeliers. The club's ambient lighting cast playful shadows across her features, highlighting her high cheekbones, crimson lips, and eyes like tempered steel beneath the flutter of mink-lined lashes.

Victor's smirk returned, but it was tighter this time. "Ah, Olga," he said, his voice betraying a note of irritation. Olga made eye contact with Jack and nodded, a mere tilt of her head. Jack nodded back. *What was that about?*

"Always appearing uninvited. Let's pause for a moment and consider everything over a drink. Olga, what will you have?"

Olga looked at Jack's glass. "What are you having?"

"A Bloody Mary."

"A Bloody Mary sounds good."

Victor went to the bar. Olga moved closer to Jack until she was within whispering distance. "I believe you found George's ledgers. Is that correct?"

Jack sipped his Bloody Mary. How much information had Victor shared with Olga?

It was time to continue the spread of disinformation.

"I have them, and what interesting reading they made."

Olga pouted as if she was sipping through a straw. The impact of what Jack had said seemed to sink in. "I'm sure they did."

CHAPTER THIRTY-TWO

The baseline of Vortex's pulsating soundtrack thrummed in Jack's chest, matching the rhythm of his steady heartbeat. He let Victor talk as the three of them stood with their drinks. Jack positioned himself so that his bowtie camera faced the air ducts, allowing Stella to get a clear view of any activity.

"Helios isn't just a project, Jack," said Victor. "You could be part of something revolutionary."

Jack chuckled, the sound almost lost in the bass-heavy backdrop. He slipped his hands into his pockets, his posture relaxed but deliberate. "Revolutionary, huh? Quite a word to use in a sales pitch."

Victor gave the ghost of a smile. A shadow of amusement. "It's not a sales pitch. It's an opportunity."

Jack's voice softened, pitched lower as he leaned slightly toward Victor. "You know, I've been in many rooms like this. Rooms where men like you flaunt their wealth and power, thinking it means anything beyond the surface. But the thing is, Victor, opulence hides cracks. Every monument to control has a weakness."

Maybe this incoherent and inconsistent rambling would yield some results.

Victor's smile faltered for the briefest moment, but he quickly recovered. "You're so cynical, Jack. Imagine where you'd be if you spent half as much energy embracing innovation as you do resisting it."

"I'm right where I need to be," Jack said. "Question is, where are you now that George is not around?" Jack noted the slight tightening of Victor's jaw and the flicker of annoyance in his eyes. Victor wasn't as much in control as he wanted to seem. "I'm wondering if Helios is even real. You talk a lot, but I've seen nothing."

Victor's laugh was sharp, almost theatrical, as he raised his glass in mock celebration.

"Follow me, Jack."

* * *

Jack ascended the brightly lit staircase, the air growing colder and more sterile. The chaotic energy of the main floor faded into a low, distant hum, giving way to a stillness that made each step feel heavier. The walls were black and matte, devoid of any decorative flair, their surfaces smooth and unwelcoming.

There was a camera, its lens gleaming as it panned across the hallway in a slow, methodical sweep. Jack looked around to ensure Stella had a good view. Victor hurried, followed by Jack, then Olga, their footsteps muffled by the industrial-grade carpet beneath them. The corridor stretched out like a maze with sharp turns and bright lights. They arrived at two steel doors, each with a keypad. Jack looked at it so that Stella could get the code. Victor tapped on the keypad, entering a seven-digit code, and the door clicked open.

Jack pointed at the other door. "What's in there? Stationery supplies and cleaning equipment?"

Victor laughed. "Good one, Jack. That's my apartment." Victor tapped away at the keypad, and the door clicked and opened to reveal a room identical to the one they had just left, except this one had a better view. "You can see, Jack, I really do eat, sleep, and breathe Helios."

Victor closed the apartment door and pushed open the other door. They walked into a room the size of Stella's workroom, similar, except for one wall that was glass, looking into a server room. The server room seemed to stretch endlessly into the dimly lit area. It was a labyrinth of blinking lights and humming machines. Rows upon rows of sleek, black server racks stood like monolithic sentinels, their red, green, and blue LED indicators flickering in a hypnotic rhythm. Cables snaked neatly along the racks and trailed into overhead cable trays, forming a network as intricate as the veins of a living organism.

Jack knew the air inside would be cool and crisp, maintaining a low temperature to offset the servers' heat. The constant hum of cooling fans filled the space, and the polished floor reflected the glow of the equipment, creating an almost otherworldly atmosphere. A central console dominated one side of the room, its multiple monitors displaying data streams, network maps, and error logs. Backup batteries and cooling units lined one wall.

Two guys were working on their keyboards. They took their eyes off their screens and stood. One was about four inches taller than Jack and fifty pounds heavier. The other matched in weight but resembled a squished version of the tall one, compacted into a physique two inches shorter than Jack's. They both had the build of power lifters with big legs, backs, and chests built for heavy lifts.

Sometimes, one couldn't help giving people names to remember them by. These were now Grizzly and Tank.

They said hello and explained what they were doing. In Russian. Olga cut them off mid-sentence. Jack's Russian was less than mediocre, but he followed her enough as she told them not to speak in front of him and to get back to work. They raised their right hands from their sides as if they were going to salute. Olga made a noise that sounded like a bark. Jack didn't recognize it as a Russian word. The guys lowered their hands to their sides, nodded, and sat down, heads pointed at their screens.

Jack feigned ignorance. "What just happened?"

Olga smiled. "They were being polite, but they have a deadline to meet."

"What you are looking at is Helios's infrastructure," said Victor.

Jack nodded and walked over to the glass wall, passing the two guys at their screens, making sure Stella got a good visual of what they were doing. Jack knew Stella wouldn't waste a second. Lines of code would fill her screen as she worked to get through a backdoor, her fingers moving with precision.

"Can you take another walk past those two guys' screens?" said Stella into his ear.

Jack dawdled halfway back, stopped behind the two guys like he was thinking, turned back to the glass wall, and slowly turned to face Victor and Olga. "Got what I need," said Stella.

"You look like you have a question, Jack," said Victor.

"Yes, I do. Where's the bathroom?"

Victor pointed to a door to the side of the glass wall.

Inside the bathroom, Jack went into a stall and put his hand over his mouth. "I have to assume Victor has this bathroom monitored. What do you want me to do?"

"You still haven't got him to explain what Helios is?"

"I'm trying. You've heard. Victor keeps saying how great it is but avoids saying what it is."

"You'd better go."

Jack made a show of washing his hands, left the bathroom, and joined Victor and Olga, standing next to Grizzly and Tank. Olga was watching what they were doing. Victor looked like he'd been watching the bathroom door.

"I'm still waiting for an explanation about Helios," said Jack.

"Quite so. Olga will give you the technical explanation followed by a demonstration."

"I am assuming," said Olga, "you have some knowledge of Artificial Intelligence, AI."

"You can assume that."

"Then, I will explain what components in AI we used and our approaches. Does that suit you?"

"Perfect."

"As you know, AI improves over time through learning from data and refining its models. Helios scales to handle massive amounts of structured and unstructured data and identify patterns, relationships, and insights. We use machine learning models based on labeled and unlabeled examples. What we call supervised and unsupervised learning. Are you with me so far?"

Sometimes it was better to let someone take the lead and see where they went, leaving them to guess how much one knew. Not just the quantity of knowledge but the quality.

"Hanging in there. Keep going."

"What we have also developed are reinforcement learning models. That is, they improve through trial and error, much like we learn from experience. Helios is in continuous refinement mode. Adjusting and improving as it receives more feedback. For example, if it makes a mistake, it fine-tunes its algorithms to minimize future errors."

"What about interactions with users?"

"Same again. The more it interacts with users, the better Helios understands human language and preferences. To do this, our models use deep learning, which, I'm guessing you know, mimics how neurons in the brain work."

"Which means," said Victor, who was becoming as animated as a sports commentator, "Helios can now recognize images and speech with greater accuracy, generate more meaningful responses in conversation, and is better at predicting future trends."

"And," said Jack, "where is the human guidance to ensure ethical decision-making?"

Victor laughed. "I'm in charge of that."

"Why am I not surprised?" said Jack.

"There is more to Helios," said Olga. "What I have explained so far is what is called narrow AI. This is what is available today. It can do things like beat you at chess. What it doesn't truly do is mimic human thinking, as it can't reason, learn, or adapt across different situations, as the human brain does. This is known as Artificial General Intelligence, or AGI."

"Many companies," said Jack, "are throwing big money at this. At this stage, it's a theoretical AI as no one has developed a working model."

Olga gave a good impression of the Cheshire Cat in Alice in Wonderland. "We have developed small prototypes but are on the cusp of upgrading Helios into a fully functional AGI."

Jack knew Stella probably rocked back in her chair at the enormity of this. The thought of a fully functional AGI in Victor's hands was unsettling. However, it being in the hands of those who were also working on developing an AGI was equally concerning.

"What's holding you back?" said Jack.

"Money," said Victor. "It needs lots of money. You pointed out that companies are spending a lot of money on this. I don't have unlimited financial resources, so we must resort to measures like getting Marie Clark to sign over her husband's insurance policy. That's one of the demonstrations I wanted to show you. Olga, over to you."

Olga spoke to Grizzly and Tank. The central console came alive. "This is the data of all the hospitals in the San Francisco area."

"Have you downloaded the data?" said Jack, "or are you hacking in on an ad hoc basis?"

"I'm hacking in. I have a Tor in place so that no one can find me. Although recently, someone has been trying, but without success."

Jack kept his smile to himself as he knew Stella would be gritting her teeth.

"But I don't need all the data. What I want is a notification if a hospital has recorded a death." Olga spoke to Tank, and different data appeared. "Then I take that person's details and search across all the insurance companies in the country to see what policies they have in place. I download a copy or copies. People often have different policies with different insurers."

"Here," said Victor, "is where we had to do a bit of trial and error to get an effective way to get the policy signed over to a shell company. First, we tried emailing out the document for the person to sign. At the same time, someone would call the person and tell them they were from the insurance company, which was a process to expedite funds in their time of need. My assumption was that, as they were in a state of grief, they would simply sign, as they had other matters to attend to, such as a funeral. This process wasn't that effective, so we had to resort to sending people to the person's home. This face-to-face approach works much better, but in the case of Marie Clark, I believe you knocked your coffee over the guy's tablet."

"What can I say?" said Jack. "I'm clumsy. Why didn't that guy make a second attempt?"

"Great question. There was always a delay in returning for the second attempt, as they had usually held the funeral, and they weren't in such a vulnerable state. The people had time to read the document and notice the discrepancy in the bank account details. This led them to call the cops. I am hopeful," said Victor, "that our AGI will carry out a conversation so compelling that the person would sign the document. The AGI could try out different male and female voices of various ages."

"You kidnapped Marie to get her to sign. Wasn't there a risk in doing this?"

"You ask a good question, but let me back up a bit," said Victor. "I needed more streams of revenue. I created a lucrative hijack, kidnap, and ransom business. That's when I got involved with Gunnar and Freya Ragnall to get rid of the vehicles for me, but I used this approach sometimes to get people to sign." Victor shrugged. "So we kidnapped Marie."

"What happened with Danny Carlton?"

Victor slapped his hand onto his forehead. "What a mess. All I wanted to do was kidnap Danny for a while, just long enough for George to agree to sell his company to me."

"What do you mean, all you wanted to do? You planned a kidnapping."

"Danny was not to be hurt. My people were supposed to carjack him at his car. But no, they arrive late. Danny gets the impression there's a carjacking going on. The rest, you know. The trouble with the kidnapping business, Jack, is that too many people are involved. Not to mention the complication I have with my mother's infatuation with Gunnar Ragnall. I'm telling you, as soon as we have an operational AGI, I'll be out of the kidnapping business."

"The world will be pleased to hear that, Victor. But why did you want George's business in the first place?"

"Well, it's got some technology that I would use."

"And, I imagine, a convenient place to launder your ill-gotten money, with Carlton Engineering making loans to Vortex, which funds

Helios's development."

"Money laundering? You make it sound tacky."

"What do you call it?"

"Reallocation of funds."

"But why bother with all this? The first versions of AI sold for tens of billions of dollars. If you are so close to having a proper AGI, you could sell it now for billions or get billions in investment." Jack thought he knew Victor's answer but wanted to hear him say it.

"This is not about money. Sure, there will be money. Billions. It's about power and control. Governments will pass laws and policies on controlling AGI, but," Victor pointed at Grizzly and Tank, "how do you police what these two gentlemen are doing right now? Will they get a search warrant and audit the code? How many people have the skills to do that? As I mentioned earlier, we can establish order and stability since we will have the power. With this, you can control governments. Doesn't that excite you? It excites Olga. Right, Olga?"

"You know I like control, Victor."

Jack had a sudden mental picture of Olga in a leather catsuit with a whip. Not the time for such images.

Victor threw his hands in the air. "Well, Jack, what do you say? Are you on board?"

"I haven't decided yet. I would like to know where your drones fit into your plan. Where do you keep them? In the back here somewhere, like homing pigeons? Or someplace else?"

Victor's face lit up. "Follow me, Jack." Olga looked at Victor as if she was questioning what he was doing.

"You're giving me a lot of information here Victor. What if I say no?" said Jack.

"Well that's easy to answer Jack," said Victor. "You say no and all of this information will die with you, tonight."

CHAPTER THIRTY-THREE

Victor had punched a six-digit code into the keypad next to the center console. Jack had stood close enough for the camera to see the characters, but not close enough that it would look like he was trying to memorize the code. Victor pulled the door open.

"I call this the henhouse. The drones are my chickens, and like chickens, they come in all sizes."

"You forget, Victor, I saw them at Gunnar Ragnall's place."

"I didn't forget." Victor looked back into the room. "Olga, are you joining us?"

"I have seen the henhouse and have some work to do here."

Victor turned on the lights, and they were in a warehouse that took up the rest of the block. Jack walked down the aisle with Victor. There were racks of drones. Some were as small as a hand, up to some that looked about six feet long and five feet wide. Victor pointed at them.

"As you can see, Jack, some are bigger, and some are smaller than what you saw at Gunnar's house. And down there are the weapons. These we fit, depending on the drone's size and what we want them to do."

"Like the drone that attacked us at George's wake."

"Sorry about that. It seemed one of our drones went rogue. It was gone for a while but eventually returned. Quite strange."

"Maybe it was tired and stopped for a rest."

"Good one, Jack. Very amusing."

"How do you direct them? I saw Olga use a handheld controller at Gunnar's house. But how do you control them to work remotely?"

"There is another aspect of Helios we have built. Each drone has a camera linked to the workstation where Olga and our two colleagues are. They can direct it to a target. There's nothing new there. We can give a drone a target, and it will execute its task on that target. Now, a target can be many things, such as a GPS location, a photograph of someone or a building, or a vehicle's registration plate. The list goes on. The task can be anything from firing bullets to a rocket to doing a kamikaze run with a payload of explosives."

"And all of this is managed through Helios?"

"Correct."

"Impressive."

"There is always room for improvement, Jack. That's one reason I want Carlton Engineering."

"What improvements?"

"The business has unexploited technology. Like recoil. It's one challenge of firing a weapon from a drone. Recoil affects a drone's stability and shooting accuracy, especially when firing on full automatic. I know Carlton Engineering has developed technology that has made big improvements in this regard but has only released it to the military."

Jack was thinking about George's notebook as he walked deeper into the henhouse. There were automatic rifles in holders against the wall.

Victor pointed to an open box on the floor. "Do you recognize them? You can look, but don't touch."

Jack looked in the box and pulled back the wrapping paper. "Yes. Surface-to-air missile. How did you get them? These are American-made and are supposed to be sold only to the military."

Victor smiled. "Friends of friends. You see, Jack, I'm not the only person interested in the success of Helios."

"These were developed to be fired by a single operator standing on the ground. The recoil's considerable. Have you fitted one of these into a drone and tested it?"

"Fitted and tested. I need Carlton technology to reduce the recoil, which will improve the accuracy."

Jack looked around the warehouse. "How do you get them out of here and into the air?"

"I had to modify the building. Follow me." Victor walked to the end of the henhouse and up a flight of stairs to a platform with a roller door and a keypad. Jack kept his bowtie camera pointed at the keypad as Victor entered the code. The door went up, and they walked onto the rooftop, which was flat except for air ducts and an air conditioning unit. Victor pulled out his mobile phone, scrolled, and dialed. "Olga, I'm on the roof with Jack. Can you come here so you can show off our drones?"

Olga arrived holding a tablet, followed by a collection of large drones, like a general followed by foot soldiers. Two midsize drones hovered by the doors. Sentries. Palm-sized drones were emerging from the air ducts like bees from a hive. Olga sent them straight up into the night sky. Eventually, they looked like stars twinkling. She looked at Jack. "I can keep them up high so the target wouldn't know they were there and then drop them almost as fast as gravity down to the target."

"So long as they don't run out of power?" said Jack.

"Great question," said Olga. "But that applies to any piece of military equipment. In this case, the large drones run on gasoline and can fly for three hours. The small drones run on lithium batteries and are good for thirty minutes. It's horses for courses. Like, what do I need for a particular task? A nuclear sub or a tank. And as you saw at Gunnar Ragnall's house, we can control them individually or collectively."

"Impressive," said Jack. "But may I point out that the broader vision of AI was to help people in ways that were previously unimaginable. Education, healthcare, climate action, disaster response, and economic development were all opportunities for its use. What you have done is weaponized it."

"With Helios, we will be able to do all of those things, but without the interference and pettiness of governments, because Helios will have the power. You see, Jack, Helios is what power looks like. It's control over every government, every company, every system, every network, every decision. Helios won't just predict the future; it will shape it."

"And you, Victor, will be at the head of Helios. One person in total control. Sounds like a dictatorship. Why don't I simply expose you to the authorities?"

"That's where you are wrong. There is a board that governs Helios. George was originally on the board and a founder. As we developed Helios, George had the vision, yes, but he also had weaknesses. Doubt, sentimentality, and a crippling fear of his own creation once he saw its capabilities in action. George got cold feet and stopped funding the project. However, many other funders and people are candidates to take up positions on the board. Show him, Olga."

Olga tapped and scrolled on her tablet. Jack looked over her shoulder and watched her click on a file. *Project Helios – Active Sponsors and Board Members.*

Her fingers hesitated for a moment before she clicked on the file. The screen filled with lists of names, corporations, and financial records. Jack could hear Stella's breath catch as they scanned the information. Jack knew Stella would get all this. High-ranking government departments, corporate giants, and shadow organizations. Helios wasn't just Victor's creation. It was being bankrolled and supported by some of the most powerful figures in the world. The reach of Helios was far greater than Jack had imagined. The board members all had codenames, but it was the board chairperson who intrigued him. There was just a codename. The Architect.

"Do you see it now, Jack? The scope of what you're up against? You could expose me a thousand times over, and it wouldn't matter. These people don't fear consequences. They are the consequences."

"Who is The Architect?"

"Now that is a secret," said Victor. "So, Jack, now that I have shown you Helios and given a small demonstration, are you ready to join our merry band of visionaries and sell me Carlton Engineering?"

"As enticing as it sounds, Victor. I'm going to decline your offer."

Annoyance skipped across Victor's face like a flash of sheet lightning. "Olga, can you ask your two colleagues to join us here?"

Grizzly and Tank walked through the double doors and onto the rooftop. "Guys," said Victor, "will you please grab Jack here and hang him over the edge of the building by his ankles until I tell you to stop? If he resists, feel free to subdue him in any way necessary."

They looked at Olga, who translated. Grizzly and Tank smiled, as if this would be a nice break from working on a keyboard. Stella spoke into Jack's ear. "They're big. I'm getting close to getting into Helios. Can you keep them busy for a while? It will make it easier for me to get in."

Jack coughed into his hand and said a muffled, "Yes."

"Wait a moment, Victor," said Jack. "Let them have a go at subduing me."

"A contest. Great. But I'm warning you, they both have black belts in judo."

Jack wanted to thank Victor for giving him a heads-up about how they would fight. If they got him to the ground with a throw, they would use their powerlifting strength to apply locks and holds to finish him off. But probably not many punches or kicks.

"Olga," said Victor, "tell your colleagues that we have seen Jack fight, and he has martial arts skills."

Olga translated. Tank and Grizzly looked at Jack, then at each other. They snorted and chuckled.

Sometimes it is better if people underestimate you, but they're probably expecting standard combinations. If one is awkward, it may or may not help.

"Let me take off my jacket." Jack made a big show of taking off his jacket and looking for a place to put it. Victor and Olga didn't look like they would hold it, so he placed it over the mouth of the air duct. Could he fight them one at a time? Tank and Grizzly hunched over and started coming at him. Jack moved so that Tank, being shorter, was in front of Grizzly. This way, he could see both of them and move in case Grizzly made a move to the side to flank him.

Tank had his hands up and out like a wrestler. Tank went for a grab with his left hand. Jack used his forearm to deflect it across Tank's body as Jack slipped to the side and slapped Tank, full force, twisting his hips into the move, on his left ear with a cupped hand, hard enough to rupture his eardrum. Tank grunted, and his left hand went to his ear as he stumbled one step forward. That was one hand out of the way. Kenny had always stressed the importance of opportunity. Jack grabbed Tank's right wrist, spun, and pulled Tank's arm over his left shoulder with his bent elbow on Jack's shoulder. Jack kept the movement going as he pulled down on Tank's wrist, breaking the elbow joint. Tank screamed but remained standing. Jack gave a right-hand back fist to Tank's right temple, which staggered him like a wounded buffalo, but he could recover. Jack spun and delivered a roundhouse left punch to the same temple. Tank's lights were out before he hit the ground.

"I warned you," said Victor. "He has skills."

Olga translated, and Jack understood it to be about being careful. This was also good advice for him, as he watched Grizzly advance with his four-inch height advantage and longer reach, making shots to the head more difficult. Plus, Grizzly had already seen what Jack could do with his fists. Kenny would say, "go into a state of non-thinking." Which was the only advice available, but it sounded like non-advice.

Stella spoke into his ear. "Nearly there, keep stalling."

Jack moved in sync with Grizzly's small lunging movements as he circled Jack, testing Jack's reactions. It was a weird pas de deux. Jack kept him guessing by not reacting immediately as he had with Tank. How long did she need? "Never lose focus" was another one of Kenny's mantras. No feedback from Stella. Grizzly was quick with his hands and got hold of Jack's outstretched left hand. Jack spun away, twisting his hand inside Grizzly's arm like a snake. Grizzly swung Jack across the rooftop. Jack sensed his feet leave the ground as Grizzly threw him like a hammer-thrower. He hit the ground, rolling, to see Grizzly mid-air, about to do a body slam on top of him. Jack tumbled out before becoming the filling in a sandwich between Grizzly and the rooftop. Grizzly landed with a thump and a grunt.

Jack flipped from his back to a standing position. Grizzly got into a crouched position much slower than the speed with which he'd flown through the air. As he straightened to his full height, Jack did a reverse roundhouse kick, effective when delivered to the head. However, because of Grizzly's height, and he could be expecting it, Jack delivered it to the inside of his left knee. Jack saw the knee bend at a funny angle. Grizzly didn't think it was funny, as he screamed and bent over with both hands, grabbing his knee.

Jack punched him in the throat. Grizzly grabbed his throat with his right hand and kept his left on the bent knee, but he was still conscious. Being lower, it was now easier for Jack to deliver the reverse roundhouse kick, ensuring his heel connected with Grizzly's pterion. Kenny gave anatomy lessons, explaining that the temporal, sphenoid, frontal, and parietal bones intersected at this weak point, commonly known as the temple. The weakest part of the skull. This is why, when training, Kenny insisted on safety first.

Grizzly and Tank were on their sides, as if they were taking a nap. Victor turned to Olga. "Put Jack's photo up as the target and get the drones back here."

Jack thought it was time to get off the rooftop. He glanced at the doorway with the two hovering drones. Olga answered his unspoken question.

"They're armed."

* * *

The drones descended in perfect formation from where they had been quiet twinkles in the night sky. Jack could hear the high-pitched whine of the small ones above the deeper, louder hum of the larger ones.

Stella's voice burst through Jack's comm device, frantic and insistent. "Hold on! I've engaged a backdoor protocol. I can slow them down."

Jack winced, glancing upward. The drones faltered, their movements suddenly stuttering, like marionettes struggling against tangled strings. The hum shifted to a sporadic whine, disrupting their mechanical choreography. Victor's brow furrowed as he registered the disruption. Olga worked on her tablet.

"Olga. What's going on?" said Victor.

"Don't know."

"Just get them down and pointed at Jack."

The drones drifted down and surrounded Jack. He could hear Stella. "I'm loading some glitches."

"Alright, Jack," said Victor, "let's try another approach. These drones are armed. They have a photograph of you. You are now the target. As you know, Olga can control these individually. She can start with the small ones and shoot your toes right through your shoes. Very painful. Then she can move to your knees. Shoot them from the back, shattering your kneecap. Extremely painful. We can keep this up until you agree to sell me Carlton Engineering."

Stella's voice came through. "I changed your photo to Victor's photo. The glitches are spreading. I can't control them. It's like watching a virus."

The drones moved in unison, closing in on Victor, whose face registered alarm like any cornered animal, wide-eyed with that look of desperation. "Olga, what's going on?" Victor moved around the rooftop. The drones stayed with him.

Their sharp blades spun faster, their glowing sensors locking onto Victor. The drones didn't shoot. The drones didn't falter. They charged Victor. There was chaos as the large blades tore into his neck, spilling his blood from the ends of their blades. Victor's screams pierced the night air, desperate and guttural, as the drones tore into him like ravenous beasts. Then the screams stopped. The small drones hammered at his limbs like vultures ripping open a carcass, for that is what Victor had become. Had Victor ever anticipated the irony in meeting his demise by the very thing he created and championed?

Olga sprinted across the rooftop and through the doorway. Her sentries followed her. The roller door was coming down. Jack ran and had to dive and roll to get under it before it shut. His last view of the rooftop was of the drones on top of Victor, humming. Grizzly and Tank were still unconscious.

Jack stood and surveyed the weapons in the warehouse.

Stella's voice. "Jack, are you okay?"

Jack reached into a rack and pulled out an AK-47. He popped out the magazine, checked it was full, and then clicked it back into place. It had a strap, which he hooked over his head. "I'm okay. Victor's dead, and Olga's bolted. Have you downloaded all the files you need?" Jack took a second AK-47 and did the same procedure.

"I have downloaded everything that's on the infrastructure there, but there is undoubtedly a copy in the Cloud, and I haven't been able to find that."

Jack took a Glock 19 from a box, checked the magazine, and put it in his waistband. He took two full magazines and put one in each pocket. There was a Glock 42, the smallest of the range. The magazine only held six bullets, but they were .380 Auto. He put this in his right pocket. "The software to take a backup to the Cloud will be in what you've downloaded. We can find that later, but good, you have a copy. Can you shut down the facility here?"

"No, it'll need manual intervention."

"Got it."

"Don't forget, people are partying downstairs."

"Once it gets noisy, they'll start leaving, and someone will probably call 911."

"You'd better be gone before they get there."

Jack picked up an RPG from the box and hoisted it onto his shoulder. The RPG was a weapon for use against tanks. Jack had another use for it. He walked out of the henhouse, around the corner, and into the server room. Olga was at the console with her two drone bodyguards.

Jack shouted to Olga. "Duck."

Olga looked from the console to Jack, her face registering surprise. When she realized what Jack had on his shoulder, she threw up her hands and screamed. "Jack, wait."

CHAPTER THIRTY-FOUR

From her reaction, it was clear she knew what it could do. She was not ducking down. Jack had his finger on the trigger, already increasing pressure on his finger.

"Power off your two drone bodyguards."

Olga spoke in Russian, and the two drones went to the floor. Their rotors came to a standstill, but the hum of their motors was still there. "Thank you, Jack. You've saved me and my family, Jack."

Jack pointed the RPG at the floor. "What are you talking about?"

"Why do you think I was with Victor, sleeping in his bed, doing his bidding? My parents have been living in a constant state of fear, and so have I."

"And how long has this been going on?"

"The year before I graduated."

"Why did you run when the drones attacked Victor and leave me up there with the drones?"

"I didn't think Victor would make it. Helios was behaving strangely, so I needed to get down here to find out what was wrong. I'm sorry. I panicked."

"Not to mention, your two colleagues are still up there with some drones. Do you know the status of those drones?"

Olga looked at her screen. "I don't, but I would appreciate it if you could put that RPG down. It makes me nervous."

"Where do your parents live?"

"Palo Alto. Not too far from George Carlton's place."

"Can you give me an address?"

"Why would I do that?"

"Just trying to substantiate what you're saying. Do they have the same surname?"

"Yes."

Jack paused as if he were considering what Olga was telling him. Stella was in Jack's ear. "I can't find anyone with the name Volkov in Palo Alto. We watched a subtitled Russian movie once with the actress Olga Volkova."

"You're lying, Olga. I think you stole the name from the Russian actress Olga Volkova and chopped off the 'a' to make it into Volkov."

Olga chuckled. "Wow, Jack. That is quite a leap of logic. I must say I am impressed that you've even heard of Olga Volkova."

"Who are you?"

Olga brushed aside the question as if it were an annoying fly. "You told Victor that you didn't want to be part of Helios. I need a particular technology that's sitting in Carlton Engineering."

"Why do you need it? Victor's dead."

"Who do you think designed Helios? Who do you think did most of the coding? Victor? He was a silly, narcissistic boy. Just a means to an end."

"You're The Architect?"

"I thought you would've figured it out by now."

"Why all the subterfuge? Just use your real name, whatever that is."

Jack had a thought. "Matthew and Nicholas Lund knew you as Olga Volkov."

"Yes, I've been working on this for a long time. Helios developed into two things. It originally started as an AI product. That's when I met Victor. But he had limited vision. He was always going on about power and control, words he didn't really understand. It needed an organization. I created the Helios organization. The people on the board were a mixture of investors and important people who I blackmailed."

"Didn't they know who you were?"

"I created the persona of The Architect. All meetings were virtual. I used a voice synthesizer to sound like a mid-forties man from Idaho. Boards are still predominantly male, and the same is true for the chairperson. They always referred to me as the Chairman."

"Did Victor know you were The Architect?"

"No, he was a board member, and I let him be the face of Helios. Now you know everything."

"Why are you telling me all this?"

"Using Helios, I have researched every aspect of your life, including your relationship with Stella West. I want you to join the Helios board."

Jack knew that when he refused this offer, Olga would tell the drone bodyguards to shoot. Being on the floor, they would shoot his feet and ankles off his body. There was nowhere to hide. Distraction. Jack pointed at the racks of servers. "Why does that server have a blinking red light?"

Olga turned. Jack swung the AK-47 up and squeezed. On full automatic, eight bullets shredded one drone. He kept his finger on the trigger as he shifted his aim to the other drone, doing the same. Olga had put her hands to her ears.

Jack reached down, hoisted the RPG onto his shoulder, took two steps to the left to miss Olga, and pulled the trigger. It was loud enough that the manufacturers recommended ear protection. The RPG did its job, exploding on impact as it penetrated the server racks, generating a shock wave that would fracture the server components. More minor explosions and fires were starting. Jack figured this was from the lithium-ion batteries in the servers. The heat had caused an overload.

Olga ran out of the room, down the stairs, and into Victor's lounge, overlooking the people below. Jack followed to see her running down the stairs and joining the crowd stampeding to the door. She called out to a guard. Once she had his attention, she pointed at Jack. To slow Olga's progress, Jack emptied the rest of the magazine into the ceiling, increasing the stampede like maddened cattle. He dropped the AK and swung up the other one. The guard spoke into his lapel microphone. Four of them converged at the bottom of the stairs with pistols drawn. Jack shouted. "This AK is fully loaded. If you shoot, I will return fire."

They all raised their pistols. Jack got to the side of the staircase as they started firing. Jack peeped around the corner, squeezed the trigger, and sprayed them, emptying the magazine. All four went down. Jack dropped the AK and pulled the Glock from his waistband. Three of them were not moving. The fourth one raised his pistol. Jack shot him. Heat was coming through the door from the server room. Jack picked up both AKs and threw them through the server room door. Nothing like fire to get rid of fingerprints.

He could see Olga in the crowd. She was almost at the door. Jack ran down the stairs, avoiding stepping on the four bodies, although they would no longer care. Jack held the Glock behind his back as he hovered at the back of the crowd. He looked up at Victor's lounge. A red glow was emanating from the server room. He spoke to Stella. "This place is on fire and spreading. I need to get these people out of here. It's a stampede. They are jamming at the doorway, which is not helping."

"Two fire trucks, three ambulances, and lots of cops are on their way."

"Did you phone them?"

"No. Must have been someone at the club. You need to get out of there. The cops'll be processing people for hours. You don't want to be part of that."

"I agree."

The people at the back had looked back and up at Victor's lounge. Some shouted "Fire," which worsened the jam at the door. Jack was getting close to the door. He looked back to check that he would be the last one out. The doorman was pulling people through the door to break the logjam. As soon as he got one person through, another took his place, but he kept at it. The jamming eased until Jack was the last person at the door.

"Anyone else in there?" said the doorman. It was Max.

"I'm the last one. Good job, by the way, Max."

"Thanks. I gotta go. The cops can't interview me. I'm on parole. Not supposed to associate with known criminals. Half the people in the club are criminals. There was gunfire. I heard handguns and an automatic rifle."

"Understood. You didn't see where Victor's girlfriend, Olga, went."

"She ran down there." Max pointed to an alley that had no lights, which vanished into blackness.

"That goes to Sixth Street. Open-air drug trade goes on there. All gang-related."

"Exactly, that's why I can't risk being caught there either. I'm going in the other direction."

* * *

Jack jogged into the alley. It went for ninety feet, then into two more alleys, which would take him to Sixth Street. A woman screamed. Jack pulled the pistol from his waistband as he ran. He turned into an alley. At the end of the alley, a woman was on the ground, the slit in her long black dress open, displaying her from ankle to thigh, and a man was on top of her, tearing at her underclothes. The woman was Olga. The thing at the base of Jack's spine came out of its cave and rushed up his spine and across his body.

Jack shoved the gun into the back of the man's head. "Get off her."

The man turned and grinned. He was in his mid-twenties. He was looking behind Jack. Someone jabbed a gun into the back of Jack's head. "Give me the gun." It was a much older voice. Jack lifted his hand, and the older guy snatched the pistol. "Stand up and get against the wall." Jack complied, knowing they wouldn't be leaving witnesses. The young man on Olga got back to the job of tearing off her underclothes. Jack shuffled to the wall, turning his left side to his assailant, keeping his right hidden. He pulled the Glock 42 from his pocket and turned to see the older guy watching his younger accomplice. Jack fired all six rounds into the older guy. Center of mass. He was dead before he hit the ground. His pistol and Jack's fell out of his lifeless hands. Jack stepped forward and kicked the attempted rapist in the head. Olga pushed him off her, rolled, and grabbed the nearest pistol on the ground. The one that belonged to the dead guy. She fired at her assailant and kept firing until the gun was empty. Jack helped her to her feet. She was shaking. "Thank you, Jack."

She rearranged her clothing. Jack took the pistol from her hand. "I need to make this look like they shot each other." Jack pulled out his shirt, wiped the Glock 42 clean of prints, and put it in the hand of the attempted rapist. The other pistol was a CZ75, which he also wiped down with his shirttail, bent down, and put in the hand of the older guy.

"That should convince the cops."

There was no answer. Jack looked around. Olga was gone. He didn't know how many rounds he still had in his Glock magazine. Walking down to Sixth Street, he popped out the magazine, took a full one from his pocket, and clicked it in.

At Sixth Street, he looked each way. Homeless people lined the street. Gunshots must be a common occurrence, as no one looked like they had moved as they had hunkered down for the night. No sign of Olga. But then she could have sat down next to a homeless person, and he could have missed her. It would be like trying to find a particular tree in a forest. A police patrol car was coming. Jack sat down against the wall until it had passed. Taxis and ridesharing vehicles wouldn't be coming here. Walking to Stella's house in Pacific Heights would take less than an hour.

* * *

Nothing like a long walk through San Francisco with a nine-millimeter in your waistband to look at the stars and think. The city lights were becoming more visible as getting to Pacific Heights was mostly uphill. He needed a shower and some sleep, and for his clothes to go in the washing machine, as he needed to be at training tomorrow to avoid questions. He would appear unaware of what happened at the Vortex Club, but he needed to be there, fit and ready to go, no matter what Kenny had planned for that day.

Jack's mind was on the Glock. The bullets could go in with Stella's ammo, and she could shoot them off the next time she was at the range. The problem was the gun and its serial numbers on the frame, the slide, and the barrel. Even if he ground them off the hardened steel, forensic analysis could still recover them. He could throw it into a dumpster or a lake where a criminal, or worse still, a child, could get it. Walking produced an idea.

He would go to George's place tomorrow, phone Kenny, and say he found a Glock 17. Why was he there? His story would be that he was still looking for George's will. As the administrator of George's estate, Jack should do that. Jack had his conversation with Kenny planned out in his head. Jack looked at the stars. Work with me.

* * *

Jack had slept like he was dead, but not enough before he had to get up and be on time for training with Kenny. After training, the room was abuzz with news about the Vortex club. Jack wanted to find out how much they knew. He approached Kenny.

"What happened at this Vortex club the guys are talking about?"

"There was a fire. The fire brigade found one body on the roof."

If they only found one body, then Grizzly and Tank must have gotten away.

"Do they know how the fire started?"

"Not yet. But we're now involved."

"Why? Won't the local guys deal with it?"

"Normally, they would. But it's to do with what they found in the building."

"What did they find?"

"It's an ongoing investigation. You're a civilian. I can't discuss it with you. You know that."

"Sorry. You're right. It was just a reflex to ask the question."

"I've been put in charge of the investigation. I have a busy day ahead."

It was always good to set the stage for an upcoming event.

"I've got to drive down to Palo Alto, to George Carlton's house, to find his will."

"You haven't found it yet?"

"No. Remember, Freddie got me involved as the administrator. Without the will, I can't carry out his wishes."

"Good luck with that."

"Thanks."

Jack walked to his truck, thinking he needed more sleep.

CHAPTER THIRTY-FIVE

At Stella's house, he made breakfast for them both. Scrambled eggs cooked with cream and chives. Black coffee was already in mugs. Jack put the plates on the kitchen countertop. Stella sipped her coffee, then held the mug with two hands as she looked at Jack.

"Victor was interested in some recoil technology at Carlton Engineering. As we now know, Olga is The Architect. She would have been the one who wanted it. Victor was just the voice. I wonder what else she was after?"

"Not a clue. That's why I need to complete the sale to your company so you can take an inventory of what's there. You need to get trustworthy engineers and compare this to George's notebook. On the way to Palo Alto, I'll phone Carlton Engineering's lawyers to get them to draw up the paperwork. They need to bring in the auditors to conduct a valuation. Then I'll organize a board meeting, and we can get this signed off."

"Are you happy with doing this without the will?"

"Of course. George told us and the board that he wanted you to buy the company. I'm the administrator. Carlton Engineering is without a

CEO. You need to take charge of this as soon as possible."

"I have a fair idea what the deal is worth. So while we wait for the auditor's valuation, I'll ensure we have the funds available."

"Do you want to come for a drive to Palo Alto with me?"

"I'd love to, but I still have a company to run."

"I'll see you when I get back."

"Don't forget the Glock."

* * *

Jack parked at George's house and went inside, looking in the same places he had looked before. He'd wrapped the pistol in a tea towel, and he left it on George's desk while he searched. Last night's events, lack of sleep, and this morning's training were catching up. He remembered where George kept the coffee. Jack was sure George wouldn't mind him helping himself to a cup. He picked up the pistol and went to the kitchen. He made coffee and went to George's study. It was like a dull afternoon inside, with the curtains drawn. *Maybe the cops closed them?* Jack put the gun on the desk, went to the window, and opened the curtains. He was looking at Danny's cottage.

Jack remembered there was a collection of keys in the desk drawer. They were all labeled. Jack took the one that said, *Cottage*. He went back to the kitchen and out the back door. A paved pathway wound through the garden to the cottage. The grass needed cutting. He opened the door and stepped into one big room with a double bed, a giant screen on the wall in front of a three-seater couch, and a small dark wood coffee table. There was a door in the back, which Jack assumed was a bathroom. Surfing photos and posters adorned one wall. In the corner was a desk with a laptop. A pull-out drawer was under the desktop. Jack pulled it open. There were pens and highlighters scattered on top of a legal-sized beige envelope. Jack lifted it out. There was a document inside. Jack pulled it out and looked at the front page. It was George's will.

This made sense to Jack. At the time, Danny was George's only living relative. He would have told Danny he was leaving everything to him, so he ensured Danny didn't have to look far for the document, but things had changed. Jack sat on the couch to read the will, looking for the clause that said who the designated executor was and what would happen to the estate in the event of Danny's death preceding George's death.

Danny was to be the executor and the sole beneficiary. In the event of Danny's death preceding George's death, a state administrator was to be appointed. As Freddie had already appointed Jack, he had more work to do. He continued reading. The administrator was to sell all assets at market price. The proceeds were to be placed in a trust fund to support an annual scholarship to advance AI responsibly. Well, now he knew.

Jack phoned Kenny, who answered on the sixth ring. "What's up, Jack? I'm kinda busy."

"Remember, I told you this morning that I was going to Palo Alto to George Carlton's house to look for his will."

"Yes, hurry up."

"Well, I found it. It was in the son's cottage. In a drawer."

"Well done. What does this have to do with me?"

"There was a pistol in the drawer."

"Did you touch it?"

"Of course not, but I need the name of that local detective. I forgot it. And his contact details so that I can hand it in."

"You mean Sergeant Atlee?"

"That's the guy."

"I'll send you his details. Anything else?"

"Nope."

Kenny ended the call with, "See you tomorrow morning."

Jack phoned Sergeant Atlee, who was his usual pleasant self, and said he would be there in twenty minutes. Coffee was calling Jack, so he went to the study, took his untouched coffee to the kitchen, and put it in the microwave. He went to the living room and waited.

Atlee was true to his estimate of twenty minutes. Jack opened the door for him. A female uniformed cop with an evidence bag accompanied him. The name on her shirt said Reynolds. She was the same height and build as Jack, with honey-blond hair tied back in a short ponytail.

"Jack Rhodes. We meet again. How have you been?"

Jack went to answer when Atlee held up his hand. "You don't have to answer, but if you do, I have to look interested." Atlee smiled like a clown. "My superiors have told me to work on my people skills. There are specific things I have to say. For instance, this is Officer Reynolds. I have to introduce her, even though her name tag clearly reads 'Reynolds'. Now, where's this weapon you found?"

Jack nodded to Reynolds. "Nice to meet you, Officer Reynolds."

She smiled. "Nice to meet you."

"Follow me," said Jack.

Atlee had more to say. "People have been saying that I'm abrupt. What do you think?"

"Abrupt? Definitely not. One man's abrupt is another man's getting to the point."

Atlee looked at Reynolds and threw his hands in the air. "See. This is from the civilian I had to deal with at the crime scene."

Jack walked them through to Danny's cottage. Jack had left the drawer open. He held up the will. "This is the will. It was in the drawer. When I took it out, I saw the gun underneath."

Atlee looked at Reynolds. "Bag it." Then he turned his attention to the room. "We never searched this place. Can we do it now, or do I need a warrant?"

"I'm the administrator, so I'll authorize it. Go ahead."

It took them thirteen minutes to complete their search. All they found was a speargun and a dive knife. "Looks like he did spearfishing."

"Do you want to take those?"

"No, they're perfectly legal."

"Anything else?"

"Just one thing. We didn't find a gun-cleaning kit or any ammo."

Sometimes, when you realize your error, it is best to feign ignorance.

"Why is that important?"

"What do you know about guns?" said Atlee.

"Hardly anything. Why?"

Atlee looked at Reynolds and rolled his eyes. "Doesn't matter."

"Anything else?"

"Nope. Thank you for phoning this in and being most cooperative." Atlee looked at Reynolds. "How'm I doing?"

No comment from Reynolds, but she looked ready to swat him like a fly into the next-door property.

Jack walked them to the front door and watched them drive off with the Glock 17. Atlee would wonder why you would shoot a pistol and not clean it afterwards. Because you don't have a cleaning kit? Why not have one? They are not expensive. If you buy a gun, they sell you a cleaning kit at the same time. Those questions should take Atlee down the rabbit hole.

* * *

Jack arrived at Gunnar's house at Pedro Point. He parked on the street and knocked on the front door. Freya answered.

"Jack, it's wonderful to see you. Come on in."

She hugged Jack. Her hair was still wet. It smelled of flowers.

Jack walked in and looked around. "Where's Gunnar and Roxy?"

Freya chuckled. "I'll show you. Follow me."

They walked past the kitchen and down the stairs that led to the garage. Jack could hear Roxy's voice as they went down the stairs. "That's great, Gunnar. Left foot, slide up the right foot."

Jack followed Freya through the door. The garage was now an MMA-style gym. Gunnar and Roxy wore shorts, singlets, were barefoot, and wore lightweight gloves. Roxy had Gunnar doing the basic Muay Thai moves with feet and hands.

Roxy stopped when she saw Jack. "Jack; great to see you."

Jack hugged her. "How are you, Gunnar?"

Gunnar held up his gloved hands. "I'm doing great."

"That is enough for today, Gunnar," said Roxy. "I'm going down to the beach for a swim. You going to join me?"

"Absolutely," said Gunnar.

Freya and Jack went onto the patio and watched Gunnar and Roxy walk down to the beach with their towels. Jack looked at the remnants of the damage that Victor and Olga had caused. "I see you haven't replaced the Buddha statue."

"Not going to. I hated it. It was a gift from Natalia. It would have been inside the house if she had her way."

"How's it been going with Gunnar and Roxy? The MMA training wasn't something I expected to see."

"It's like she's breathed life into him. I've watched the training. She goes slow, and she is patient. Basically, it's an aerobic exercise where she gets him to move all limbs and keep his mind focused on what he's doing, which is what he was supposed to be doing but wasn't. He started doing Tai Chi but said it was boring. I battled to get him to go. Then he stopped, but he enjoys this training with Roxy. They often sit together and watch her fights on the TV, and he asks questions, and she explains."

"So there's been no problems?"

Freya laughed a nice, healthy laugh. "Just once at our local super-market here in Pedro Point."

Sometimes, things you set up don't work as expected.

Jack frowned. "What happened?"

"They were at the checkout at the supermarket when three surfer dudes pushed in front of them. Gunnar told them to get to the back of the queue. They laughed and pushed Gunnar, who was in front of her. Gunnar was falling when Roxy grabbed him and straightened him up. Then she lost it. She went to town on the three of them. Left them on the floor, semi-conscious. Someone filmed it and put it on the internet. Here, I'll show you."

Freya scrolled through her phone and passed it to Jack. The video was full of punches and kicks. Kenny had mentioned that Roxy was good with elbow strikes. Her opponents would testify to that.

"This is not great," said Jack.

"What do you mean? It's been great. I'll send you a copy of the video."

"How come?"

"Someone who watched the video recognized her as Red Roxy and posted some of her fights. Now, everyone knows who she is. My dad and Roxy go to the supermarket now, and everyone greets them. She created her own social media site and posted that people should have more empathy for people with Parkinson's. Because of this, complete strangers come up to my dad and chat with him." Freya laughed. "Under the watchful eye of Roxy, of course." Freya paused. "Switching topics, Jack. Did you hear about Victor?"

"I read there was a fire at the Vortex Club, and they found a body."

"That was Victor. The police notified Natalia."

"That's dreadful. How's Natalia taking it?"

"Reacting like any mother would, even though at their last meeting, Victor said he would kill her if she stood in his way. She's distraught and has been seeking comfort around here. It may sound harsh, but Roxy makes sure nobody does anything to make things difficult for my dad. That includes distraught mothers."

"How does this affect your chop shop activities?"

"We're done. We're out. I've discussed it with Dad. I can't tell you what a relief it is not to have to do that anymore. I'm just going to focus on restoring classic cars."

"And running."

Freya smiled. "Yes, and running."

"I'd better get going. Say goodbye for me to Gunnar and Roxy. I'll tell Marie how Roxy's doing. She'll be pleased. I'll call her from the car and see if she's home. Then I can tell her myself."

"And you? Shall we ever see you again?"

"I recall an expression, something about bad pennies keep turning up."

Freya jumped into a hug with Jack, and he reciprocated. Her hair was drier now, but still smelled of flowers.

"I don't think you're a bad penny."

* * *

Jack recognized Freddie's truck when he pulled into Marie's driveway. Marie greeted him with a big smile and a hug. The atmosphere between Freddie and Judy was as if a leaden canopy hung over them. Judy gave Jack a brief hug. Jack got a curt nod from Freddie.

"Jack," said Marie, "I want to show you something about the Mustang."

He followed Marie out the back door and into the garage. "There's nothing to show you on the Mustang. I just wanted to give Judy and

Freddie some space. Judy has to go back to New York. Apparently, there's a big case, and her firm insists she handle it."

"I could have come another time."

"Freddie arrived just before you did. He came over after her firm called her."

"Oh dear. That's not good, but Judy's firm must rate her highly."

"As a mother, I'm as proud as her father would have been. It's just that Freddie and her are so good together." Marie's eyes had become watery. She blinked it away. "Roxy. How's she doing?"

"Doing great." Jack told Marie what Freya had told him, and about the MMA-style gym where she trained Gunnar. Then he showed her the video.

"Goodness me. Roxy's an excellent fighter."

"You should go visit her and Gunnar. You'll like him. He's a good guy. I'll ask his daughter, Freya, to set it up."

"I'd like that."

"What are your thoughts on Judy and Freddie?

"I read a lot of historical fiction. One of Napoleon Bonaparte's quotes has arisen from the labyrinth I call my memory, which I read long ago. Nothing is more difficult, and therefore more precious, than to be able to decide."

* * *

Jack sat in Stella's workroom. He signed the last of the legal documents before him and pushed them over to Stella. "There you go, Stella. Carlton Engineering is yours."

"I'll look after it. The board seemed happy enough with the sale."

"Your reputation and that of Node Industries made them comfortable."

"What else do you have to do?"

"Sell off the remainder of his assets. Set up the trust for the student scholarships. Sign off that the money from the sale goes into the trust."

"Are you going to administer the trust, Jack?"

"For now, I'll have to."

"What about Olga? She's still out there." Stella threw her hands up in exasperation. "And she has all those people on her board. They can fund the building of another data center."

"Olga's not the only one chasing the AGI dream. They also have boards and funders."

"I've got a copy of Olga's software, Jack, but what am I going to do with it? Based on what she's done, she's probably a better software developer than both of us combined. She will take what she has in the Cloud and move beyond the AGI prototype stage."

"It's a mess, Stella. As I've mentioned, there was considerable controversy surrounding AI when it became available to consumers. Lots of positives and negatives. I don't believe the public is aware that AGI, Artificial General Intelligence, means what it says. They haven't grasped the impact of AGI being able to learn, understand, and apply knowledge in a way similar to humans."

"I wonder what they would think or do if they knew researchers are already working on something they're calling ASI, Artificial Superintelligence, where AI will surpass human intelligence in every aspect. They probably wouldn't believe it, Jack."

"This will happen whether people like it or not, or even understand what's happening around them. They will live in blissful ignorance that someone oversees all this and looks out for them. The UN has suggested a global AGI observatory and a certification system for secure AGI. That sounds good, but the likes of Olga will sign up for it and then do what they want, regardless of any UN resolution. We won't even know it's happening."

"I haven't forgotten, Jack, that we only stumbled on Olga by accident."

"We could do what Epictetus, the Stoic philosopher, taught."

"Yep. We should distinguish between what is within our control and what is not and focus our energies accordingly."

"In the end, Stella, these AI developments will wash over us like a giant wave, and all we can do is keep moving on with our lives, as there will be no walking away from it. For the Olgas of the world will always prevail."

www.ingramcontent.com/pod-product-compliance
Lightning Source LLC
Chambersburg PA
CBHW030936260626
47169CB00002B/504